"I'm on my way."

Jackson headed toward the door.

"Wait," Aimee said. "I'm not there. I got my stuff out. I just...don't have anywhere to go. I was hoping you'd know someone who could put me up for the night. I'd gladly pay..."

"You can stay here. I've got an entire upstairs, two bedrooms and a bathroom that I don't use. You're welcome to the entire floor."

"I can't put you—"

"At least for tonight. Something is going on here. No one has so many seemingly natural disasters or mistakes befall them in a single twenty-four-hour period..."

"I could be a klutz, for all you know."

"This isn't you doing things. These are things happening to you, and frankly, I'd feel better knowing you were under protection until we have time to figure out what's going on."

"Okay, then thank you. Like you, I've kind of come to the conclusion that someone doesn't want me here."

"Stay put," he told her, not liking the idea of her driving on dark mountain roads alone. "I'm coming in to get you and you can follow me home."

Dear Reader,

I'm a little envious you're just starting this book for the first time. I've been through it many times since I first experienced it, and I still love going back. It's just one of those books that takes me inside and makes me want to stay. I hope it brings you the same feeling, the same escape!

The story was born, and grew, solely in my imagination, but the town, the landscape, the world, while fictitious, is based on a real Arizona town in which I was spending time when the idea first occurred to me. All of the descriptions, the buildings, the landscapes—they are all real. And our hero's home—it's the place I was staying in. While I'm an Arizona girl, the world of small-town Northern Arizona was entirely new to me, and I absorbed every nuance I could.

Beyond that, I often wonder about biology versus environment, how much contributes to who we are born to be and who we actually become. This story doesn't answer that question. Rather, it made the question somewhat moot for me. Because ultimately we get to make choices every single day, and even one small one can bring happiness where there might not have been any. Happy reading! Happy escaping! And happy living and loving, too!

TTQ

COLD CASE
SHERIFF

Tara Taylor Quinn

HARLEQUIN®

ROMANTIC SUSPENSE™

Recycling programs for this product may not exist in your area.

ISBN-13: 978-1-335-73832-5

Cold Case Sheriff

Copyright © 2023 by TTQ Books LLC

For questions and comments about the quality of this book, please contact us at CustomerService@Harlequin.com.

Harlequin Enterprises ULC
22 Adelaide St. West, 41st Floor
Toronto, Ontario M5H 4E3, Canada
www.Harlequin.com

Printed in U.S.A.

A *USA TODAY* bestselling author of over 105 novels in twenty languages, **Tara Taylor Quinn** has sold more than seven million copies. Known for her intense emotional fiction, Ms. Quinn's novels have received critical acclaim in the UK and most recently from Harvard. She is the recipient of the Readers' Choice Award and has appeared often on local and national TV, including *CBS Sunday Morning*.

For TTQ offers, news and contests, visit www.tarataylorquinn.com!

Books by Tara Taylor Quinn

Harlequin Romantic Suspense

Sierra's Web

Tracking His Secret Child
Cold Case Sheriff

The Coltons of Colorado

Colton Countdown

Where Secrets are Safe

Her Detective's Secret Intent
Shielded in the Shadows
Falling for His Suspect

The Coltons of Grave Gulch

Colton's Killer Pursuit

The Coltons of New York

Protecting Colton's Baby

Visit the Author Profile page at Harlequin.com for more titles.

For Rachel. Because a mother's love never dies.

Chapter 1

The address was right. She'd checked the GPS four times. It insisted she'd arrived at her destination. She'd passed the number directly preceding the one she'd found in her aunt's things.

And the one after, too, before turning around.

She'd arrived at her destination.

There was no house.

How could there be no house?

No sign of a house ever having been there. Not even a dirt driveway leading off the road. Just rocky dirt and semidesert grassland. Nothing at all familiar. She'd swear on all of her possessions, even the heart of her heart—the fine, one-of-a-kind-work-of-art store she'd inherited from her aunt—that she'd never been on that plot of land before.

Why would her aunt have kept this address for Aimee's mother tucked away in her safe? Had the woman Aimee barely remembered, the woman who'd given birth to her in the small Arizona town, owned the land? Hoped to build on it someday?

Had she been robbed of the chance by the car accident that had taken both of her parents' lives?

Or…with horrifying clarity she glanced around…was this the spot where the drunk driver had hit her parents head-on? Was she standing on the ground where they'd been killed?

That would explain why she had no memories of the place.

And the explanation would allow her to keep alive the hope that the nightmarish dreams she'd been having recently could still find resolution in Evergreen. Just not at the address she'd expected to elicit them.

Still, she couldn't just leave. Not if that view was the last her parents had ever seen. No one knew where they'd been the day they'd been killed. Only that they'd said they'd had an appointment that Saturday afternoon they'd left her with a sitter. And that they'd be gone a couple of hours…

Hours that had turned into forever.

Had they kissed her goodbye before they'd departed for their mystery meeting? Or had she been too busy playing to notice their leaving for the last time?

Hugging her arms around herself as she glanced about, Aimee, shook her head. Ever since her aunt's shockingly unexpected accidental death the previous month, she'd been living in a mental and emotional space that was surreal. As though she'd been transported out of life as she'd known it to be, and into some paranormal zone where nothing was as it seemed.

It kind of made sense that Aunt Bonnie's tragic accident had brought forth buried memories from her past. The first section of her life had ended with a tragic accident. The time from birth to three when she'd been the adored daughter of two loving parents. Part of the stereotypical family dream.

Then had come section two. Growing up the adored niece of a loving perennially single artistic aunt. Which had also ended with tragedy.

Now came part three. In a travel-crumpled spandex midthigh-length black skirt, white T-shirt and glitzy flip-flops, she was standing on a Friday morning in early June beside a rental car on the side of a road in Evergreen, Arizona with no real plan of execution. Except some half-baked idea that her recent onslaught of nightmares could somehow be put to rest there.

Alongside another not quite rational notion that a part of her had been lost or left behind in the secluded little northern Arizona town and until she found it she'd never get to section four of her life. The part where she finally fell in love with an eligible bachelor—something she'd failed to do in the fourteen years she'd been dating—and got married. Had children of her own.

And became another statistic in the stereotypical family count.

Something that sounded a whole lot better than all alone in the world.

Something that had seemed like a far away magical dream even when she hadn't been all alone.

A vehicle whizzed past. Black. Big. Expensive looking. The first she'd seen since she'd been out on the deserted side road, alone with nature as far as she could see.

The trees weren't like the ones back home. She recognized some oak and aspen…but fewer of them than she was used to seeing. The leaves weren't as big and lush and…

That tree…

Off to the left of her. A good two hundred yards in from where she was standing…heart pumping, she stared…

Slowly, her gaze swept upward and…

Aimee held on as tightly as she could, 'cept her fingers didn't reach all around the ropes like he'd told her to do. He pushed from behind her and up she went, 'til she could see the branches way up in the sky. Curvy. Like…

"No!" A man's voice. In front of them. Coming closer. "What are you doing?" She knew the voice. Was scared at the way it sounded. And…whee…she came back down with a flip-flop in her belly and up she went again.

And then…he was crying.

Her head was shaking. Back and forth. No. No. No!

Becoming aware of the movement, Aimee stopped it. Immediately. Raised her hand up to smooth her short shock of wild and windblown-looking, textured dark hair, and noticed that the rest of her was shaky, too. Her hands. Her knees.

And her stomach…she was slightly nauseated. Which made no sense. She'd had her normal bagel for breakfast that morning in the Flagstaff airport before renting the car. She'd known she'd need to adjust to the new time zone and had purposely waited to sleep during the long flight and eat when she landed.

It wasn't lunchtime yet.

Standing alone beside her parked rental car just outside Evergreen, Arizona, on this balmy June day, Aimee tried to draw in a long, deep, healing breath. And shuddered, instead.

She couldn't possibly be remembering something real. She'd only been three when she'd left, she reminded herself. And the dreams…they'd had images, but hadn't included anything even vaguely familiar to the plot of land on which she stood. Or to the little drama that had just assaulted her.

But that tree…the way the branches formed an outward vee and then circled inward, back toward each other…

She could fall! You're going to hurt her!

I… I never…wouldn't…hurt her…

Aimee blinked and was standing alone at the edge of an unfamiliar vacant lot. Just as she'd been for the past several minutes. Alone and scared.

What was wrong with her? What was happening?

Was she…like…on some kind of psychotic break? Having visions now, to go along with the nightmares?

Yeah, Aunt Bonnie's death had been a shock. And the hardest thing she'd ever had to live through. But people lost loved ones. They didn't generally lose their minds over it.

She certainly wasn't going to do so. She was taking action. Taking control. That's why she was in Evergreen.

The little pep talk helped still the shaking inside her for a second or two.

Helped her clamp down on the doubts. She was not having an emotional breakdown because she was all alone in the world. Trying to rediscover all that she'd lost as a means of not feeling so alone.

There was something there. Something in Evergreen.

There had to be.

Determined to prove it to herself, she ignored the clearly-posted no trespassing signs, stepped off the road and onto the land. One step. Then two. And kept walking. Toward the tree. Since it was calling to her, she'd start there. There was no thought about whose property she could be on. No care given to the possibility of trespassing. She had to take action.

To confront the strange seemingly realistic images that, until those last few minutes, had only been present in her dreams. They weren't going to get the better of her. To rob her of the one thing she had left—herself. She'd made the decision to seek them out.

Walking more swiftly now, traversing the uneven ground as though it was blacktop and she was in tennis shoes, instead of bejeweled flip-flops, she dared herself to find something, anything, that would make sense of her presence in Evergreen.

Or of that particular address. After she checked into the little cabin-like summer home she'd rented for the month, she'd head to the courthouse. Find tax records for the property. She'd already tried to find them online, of course. Evergreen hadn't converted to online public access.

And if that didn't give her any answers she'd...

Crack! Crack!

Aimee dove for the ground, as something whizzed past her, close enough that she could see the trajectory. Lying flat on her belly, she sucked in to make herself as small as she could, praying that any more of the bullets she'd just heard would continue to miss her.

Lying there in the deafening silence that followed

the two booms, she slowed her breathing, keeping it as inobtrusive as she could, awaiting her fate.

Seconds seemed like days. And then turned into minutes.

Rocks dug into her, bruising a hip bone; dirt held her face, and a piece of straw-like grass was making her lip itch. Growing more and more aware of her immediate discomfort, she continued to wait. Until so much time passed that she realized she was going to have to come up with another plan.

Running for her car seemed like the best bet. It was harder to hit moving targets. And the car was her only hope of a package deal of cover and escape.

Assuming someone was after her for trespassing. She was doing that.

Maybe whoever shot the gun thought she was dead. If she got up and ran, he'd know she wasn't. But she'd have more of a chance of living if she was running, than if he came up to her, stood over her and found out she was alive...

Up and running like the wind on that last thought, Aimee darted back and forth, making a zigzagged line to her car, in case there were bullets to avoid.

None came.

On the road side of the car, she sank down for a second, on her haunches, trying to get her breath. To slow the shaking in her hands long enough to pull the rental key from the pocket of her skirt. To wait and see if there would be another shower of bullets.

When none were forthcoming, she climbed carefully into the car, keeping a low profile, started the engine and gunned it out of there, not stopping until she reached town.

With voice commands she gave GPS the address of the cabin she'd rented. Found the key in the magnet carrier stuck to the underside of a windowsill. Telling herself that maybe she needed to see a shrink. Maybe she really was imagining things that had no basis in reality.

Key in hand, she turned back to the silver sedan, intending to get her suitcase to wheel with her into the house so she didn't have to come back outside again until she had herself under control—had a shower—. and maybe slept a bit more—

And that's when she saw it.

The bullet stuck just above the wheel well in the passenger side metal of her car.

Jackson Redmond didn't usually make house calls. Not since he'd succeeded his father and taken over as Sheriff of Evergreen County, with jurisdiction over the town of Evergreen. But when Officer Lily Higley, the most junior of his sixteen law enforcement agents, had told him that a call had come in about a shooting on the Evergreen estate land, he'd thanked her for bringing it to him and grabbed his keys.

The last thing Boyd Evergreen needed was another hassle on his hands. The man had grown up serving the town and county named after his family. And had known more than his share of heartache. Lost his mother when he was still a kid, stood solid through his younger brother's tragedy then his father died far too early. Boyd had taken up the reins of the Evergreen fortune with grace. He was a man Jackson's father had respected. One Jackson had grown up respecting.

And most recently, the secluded mental institution Boyd's younger brother had been in for almost thirty-five years had burned in a brush fire. Grayson, who was in his late forties, had been happy in the facility—set as it was in the Arizona wilderness—where he'd been able to hike and fish, every day. He was having some problems in the Phoenix facility to which the patients had been moved.

Boyd, his twenty-five-year-old son Matthew, who'd left Evergreen with his mother after his parent's divorce, and Grayson, were the town's founding family's last living members.

So, yeah, he'd drop what he was doing to investigate the complaint himself.

In his usual dark blue uniform, short sleeved for the summer months, he rapped on the door of the rental cabin—one of six in the little cul-de-sac complex set off on a couple of acres of trees in front of one of the areas smaller lakes. Blooming Bridges was a newer such offering in a town whose population exploded during the summer months. So this newest visitor, Aimee Barker, was only one of the 25,000 tourists he and his deputies had to contend with that June morning.

Putting his Evergreen welcoming smile on his face as the door clicked open, he faltered a bit when he got a glimpse of the woman standing in front of him.

He'd been expecting someone much older. Blooming Bridges catered to the over fifty-five population giving the semblance of getting back to nature with none of the work that went along with really doing so. Each of the six cabins had wood-burning fireplaces, for Evergreen's cool evenings, but she'd never have to haul a log or clean a grate, either. At Blooming Bridges that was all done for her. Daily.

She thought she'd been shot at as she'd driven her

rental from the Flagstaff airport into town. More likely, there'd be some other explanation for the sound she'd heard. With her not being from around the area, a lot of things could seem strange at first.

She wasn't older. And he was standing there staring like someone who hadn't seen a woman from outside Evergreen in…he shook his head.

"I'm Sheriff Jackson Redmond," he said, regaining control of his senses, hoping his few-second lapse hadn't been noticed. "You want to tell me about the gunshot you heard?"

She nodded, opened the door, held it for him to enter and as he passed by her slim figure, he caught a whiff of something aromatic that ignited another part of him that had no business coming to life as he entered the small cabin's one main room.

So, yeah, she was pretty darn good-looking. Tall and slender frame visible in a tight black skirt, down to the bare, polished toes in sandals with glitzy junk on the straps.

"I was several yards in from the road," she started, standing just inside the door with him, and he felt another jolt. Her voice…it was a little deeper than the high pitch he'd imagined. And husky. Like she'd either just gotten out of bed, or had a cold, except that it was pretty clear it was just her normal voice. She wasn't sniffling or red-eyed or red-nosed either, for that matter. And no one got out of bed with their makeup looking that good.

And her words finally made it to his brain.

"You were out of your car?" he asked, his gaze homing in on her expression, rather than her beauty. Her frown made her concern obvious. And then his cop instincts finally booted up. "What were you doing several yards in from the road?" He'd been told the shot came from the Evergreen estate. He'd assumed she'd been driving by.

Lazy cop work, assuming things. Something he, like his father before him, didn't abide.

The way she immediately looked away put his cop senses further on alert. She was up to something she didn't want him knowing about.

So why call the police?

"I found the address written down among my aunt's things…wanted to know why she had it… I thought there'd be a house there or something. Who has an address just for a piece of land?" Pulling a piece of paper out of the back pocket of her skirt, she then handed it to him.

He knew the road. Didn't recognize the number. It fell right between two that designated Evergreen property. Which made it part of the Evergreen estate. There was no mistaking that. "This must be some mistake," he said.

Her shrug kind of left the question hanging there. Like she wasn't arguing his point, but needed a more definitive answer.

He'd get back to that.

"Tell me what you heard," he said. Get that out of the way, first.

"I heard two shots," she said. "One right after the other. I dove for the ground immediately, but one whizzed close enough by me that I was aware of it."

Frowning, he studied her. "You're saying an actual bullet came close enough to hitting you that you felt it?"

"Or heard it. It all happened so fast…"

She was telling him he'd almost had a dead body on his hands? He scrambled for other explanations.

"I wish I could tell you more, but I was…there was

this tree…it reminded me of something and I was kind of caught up with that…"

She met his gaze head-on. Held steady. And he still sensed hesitation about her.

Which made him doubt her story. That and the fact that bullets flying on Boyd's land made little sense. The man wasn't a hunter. Nor did he allow hunters on his property.

"And yet you drove here and checked in, before calling the police?" She'd said she'd been lost in a memory at an address that didn't exist. Could she be imagining the shots she'd heard?

"I drove away because I had to get out of there and I wanted to be inside where I felt safe. I made sure I wasn't followed. And the key was waiting for me here. I checked in online."

She made good sense.

"I figure someone didn't want me trespassing on their land," she offered. "I don't want to press charges, because… I didn't have permission to be there and should have thought about that instead of getting lost in my own needs. I just have to make a report because of the rental car."

"The rental car?"

"Sorry, other than a couple of uncomfortable hours on the plane, I haven't slept since I got up yesterday morning. A bullet is lodged just above the back wheel well of my rental car. I'll need an offical report from the sheriff's office for insurance purposes."

She had a bullet?

She had a bullet.

And that changed everything.

Chapter 2

She hadn't expected the sheriff to arrive in person. Was flattered. Flustered. And feeling a bit like she might have wasted his time, too. Most particularly when he started talking about hunters and the mountain lions that were legal game year-round in Arizona. If she'd been caught by a stray bullet on private land, that was on her.

And she told him so.

At which time he informed her that shooting toward a road or a person unless in immediate self-defense, was illegal in Evergreen County, even on private ground. He was outside by then, heading toward her car. He took pictures of the bullet with his phone. Grabbed an evidence kit out of his cruiser and bagged it. A nine millimeter.

And she stood back practically drooling. Like she'd

stepped on set of one of her favorite cop procedurals and he was the star. He wasn't her type. Standing six inches or more taller, than her, he was a bit overpowering. And the short shock of thick reddish hair, that looked like it would be permanently curly if he'd let it grow... She usually went for guys with short dark hair.

She needed to sleep. To find her wits and wrap them firmly about her.

She needed to find her answers and get the hell out of town. Back to Louisiana and the lucrative shop her aunt had so lovingly curated through all the years of single motherhood to Aimee. The one-of-a-kind art pieces they sold not only paid the bills, they brought joy to the world. And they were Aunt Bonnie's legacy.

"Can you tell me where I go to look up tax records and land parcels?" she asked as he finished up, back on track and needing to take charge of her life.

"The courthouse is just down from the sheriff department," he told her while taking more pictures of the car with the bullet removed. "But I can probably just as easily tell you whatever you want to know." He turned to glance at her. "You aren't from Arizona, are you?" His grin melted her knees a bit. She shook her head. Squinted at him in the sunlight.

"I'm from Louisiana," she told him. "New Orleans." And then stopped herself. "Although, actually, I am from here," she said, looking around. "Technically."

"From Arizona?" He seemed surprised. She didn't ask why. Maybe Arizonans had some secret code that distinguished them to each other. The fanciful thought wasn't all that far from some of the stuff she'd read about the rugged, mountainous state in the past month. The numbers of people in the state—Phoenix in the

winter and northern Arizona in the summer months—
were double and sometimes triple the state's registered,
full-time population. And apparently those who were
residents did seem to have some kind of bond with one
another.

"From Evergreen," she told him, still thinking more
about her reading than about her current surroundings.
The things she could see…they'd have changed greatly
in thirty years' time. And have looked vastly different
from a three-year-old perspective.

Sheriff Redmond straightened. Was staring at her.
"You're what now?" He shook his head. "I was born
and raised in this town, as was my father before me.
I'm fairly certain I'd remember you…"

She actually felt heat coming up her neck at the tone
of his voice in that last comment, though he really didn't
appear to be flirting with her in any way.

"I was born here. But I…left when I was three."

"How long ago was that?"

"Nearly thirty years."

He nodded, watching her with more than just interrogation in his gaze. "I'd have been three thirty years
ago," he told her, sounding almost as much as though
he was talking to himself.

"Which explains why you don't remember me any
more than I can remember a damned thing about this
town."

"So why are you here?"

With a long glance at him, she turned and headed
back toward her door. She needed to be inside, away
from…she didn't know what. Prying eyes.

Whatever was threatening her peace of mind.

Whatever had driven her to trespass on private property and maybe get shot at. Unless the sheriff's theory was right and the bullets had been meant for prey of the animal variety and not human. Still, she'd been trespassing without a thought to breaking the law. And could have gotten herself accidentally killed.

He followed her to the door. Inside the door. She shut it behind him. He was law enforcement. Technically, she'd broken the law. If he had questions, she'd be wise to answer them.

And...maybe he'd have some answers for her, too.

The thought took root and flourished quickly. He'd have access to records. Car accidents. Maybe going back thirty years. Maybe he'd share them with her? It would be a better start than she'd envisioned, not having a plan beyond checking the address out at the courthouse.

And hoping something triggered enough of a memory to make sense of the dreams she'd been having. There was always the same big boy crying. The one who'd been pushing her on the swing in her vision earlier. Only in her dreams, there'd been no swing. Or anything else. It had always just been him. Or the two of them. It was always about his dirty hands. He didn't like the smears of dirt. Sometimes he was trying to get it off.

Sometimes she was.

Neither of them ever succeeded. She always woke up first.

And she had absolutely no way of knowing if the dream even had anything to do with Evergreen.

"Why are you here?"

Sheriff Redmond repeated his earlier words, only this time there was no walking away from that intent gaze. Or the interest he was showing.

It was unbelievable, but she felt like she knew him.

Because they'd both been born in the same town at about the same time?

Had her parents known his father? Seemed likely.

Had she and the sheriff ever played together? Maybe in a day care? If there'd been one. And she'd attended.

"My parents were killed in a car accident when I was three," she told him. "My only known living relative was my mother's sister, who came and got me and took me to live with her in New Orleans. She was wonderful to me. I adored her…" She paused, managed not to tear up.

She hadn't known until she was in elementary school and started asking why she didn't have a father, that her Aunt Bonnie wasn't her birth mother. It was as though she'd wiped away any memory of the parents who'd given her life. Once they'd had the talk, her aunt had made her start calling her Aunt Bonnie instead of Mommy. So many times after that she'd wished she'd never asked questions.

And had felt horribly guilty for wishing that her aunt had been her real mother. That guilt was part of the reason she'd traveled to Evergreen.

"What were your parents' names? I can look them up for you."

Way beyond the scope of her plans. And the quickest way out of town—except…she needed her psyche to cooperate, too. To let her know its secrets.

"I'd like that. Their last name is Cooper. Adele and Mason Cooper. Mom's maiden name was Barker. Mine was changed when Aunt Bonnie adopted me." So there wouldn't be questions about them belonging together, her aunt had explained. "My aunt never met my father.

All she knew was that he'd grown up in foster care and there'd been no one but her with legal claim to me."

"So that's why you're here? To find out about him?"

She shrugged, not sure how much to tell him. "I'm here to find out about them," she settled with. What else could there be calling her back to a town she didn't remember? She'd been too young to have any life of her own there. "My aunt said no one knew where they'd been heading the day they died. Only that they'd left me with a sitter to go to some meeting that was supposed to last no more than two hours. They never made it back. I don't know what happened to the car. If anyone was ever charged. I'm ashamed to say I never asked some of those details. I don't know if Aunt Bonnie knew them. She, um, just died...a few weeks ago. She drowned...and..."

"I'm sorry..."

She nodded, her head tilted a little to the side. She'd been receiving condolences every day since her aunt had dived off the side of the boat, hit her head, and not come up. Love and well wishes had come from strangers and friends, in the store and out. She couldn't get distracted down that road at the moment.

"I found a key to a safe deposit box at the bank and when I went to open it, one of the things I found there was that address," she nodded toward the front pocket of his shirt where he'd stashed the piece of paper she'd given him. The original was back where she'd found it. Locked safely away. Until she knew why it had been locked away to begin with.

And then there'd been the dreams...but she was keeping those to herself.

"So...let me do some checking. I'll look up records for the address, though I can tell you that plot of land has been just as it stands now for as long as I can re-member..."

She didn't doubt him. "I was thinking maybe it was where the accident took place, though why county de-velopers would have given a separate address to a blank plot of land in the middle of an estate, I don't know..." she continued, thinking about what he'd told her.

He nodded. "I agree—the address is perplexing. I don't expect to find anything on the books, which won't help you a bit. But it makes sense, about it being the site of the accident. That road gets more than its share, being two lane, and largely out in the middle of nowhere, which prompts people to drive at high rates of speed."

Good, then. Maybe her grief really was just making mountains out of molehills and she'd only be using a day or two of her month-long lease.

"I'll stop back by with an update this afternoon," he told her, "if that's okay?"

She nodded.

He nodded.

And was gone.

Leaving her with the sense that she was actually making progress toward the next phase of her life.

Because there were going to be answers, or because the man had ignited a spark in her, letting her know that she was still alive, she couldn't say.

And she damn sure wasn't going to make another mountain out of figuring it out.

Jackson sent one of his four full-time deputies out to four wheel around the more than five hundred acres, before heading over to the courthouse himself.

As he'd expected, Jackson didn't find any tax documents at the assessor's office in the basement of the courthouse for the address Aimee Barker had given him. He didn't find any listing at all of the address in permits to build, or in deeds recorded.

But what he did find, what he noticed, because he was that kind of precisionist guy when it came to his job, was that the hard copy page he held, taken straight from the folder of planning/developer listings for that zip code, was printed on different paper than the pages directly before and after it. And while the format was exactly the same—a format that had been changed roughly five years after Aimee's parents had been killed—the line listings for the page that denoted Evergreen family property was one line shorter than the rest, leaving a noticeable, to him at least, larger space at the bottom of the page.

Feeling pretty certain that his discovery meant absolutely nothing, he made a copy of the page, as well as the ones directly preceding and following it, and headed to a different portion of the courthouse—the room holding all of the microfiche of birth and death records dating back to the time he was born. He didn't have to get access permission, or even explain himself. Being the sheriff in a small town had its advantages.

Because he'd lived in town his entire life, the only child of a tough, disciplinary sheriff, people were used to him and his penchant for crossing every t. His digging around rarely raised notice, let alone a curious eyebrow.

Looking felt different that day. He couldn't say why. Just didn't have a good feeling about what he was doing.

Maybe because he wasn't completely sure that he was doing it with good purpose. If Aimee Barker had been a man, rather than a strikingly different and noticeable woman, would he be digging around trying to find something that didn't exist just to please a summer visitor?

He wanted to think so. He called Sandra Philpot, Evergreen's one detective, and asked her to do a search of Arizona Department of Transportation records for cars titled to either Adele or Mason Cooper.

And felt a bit more justified as, sitting alone in the little room in a deserted corner of the basement, he found no death records for Aimee's parents. Frowning, he scrolled back in the film to the *B*s and checked for Adele Barker. And then checked the *A*s for Adele, the *M*s for Mason and even tried the *D*s for Dooper in case there was a typo. Two other microfiche rolls later, the years directly previous and following the year Aimee said they'd been killed, he checked all the same letters of the alphabet and still found nothing.

Not sure what to think…wondering if the intriguing woman visiting his town was more than a little confused—maybe the bullet he'd pulled out of her car had come from some other event that had scared, harmed or shaken her to the point of lying to the sheriff in a small town in the middle of miles of uninhabited desert and mountain terrain—he moved on to the locked metal container housing birth record microfiche dating back thirty-five years and working forward. Just in case of timing incongruities.

Thinking maybe he'd drive the bullet to a buddy of his at the forensics lab in Flagstaff, rather than sending it by courier, and wait for test results, just to be done with the situation.

An obviously successful, gorgeous woman showing

up in his town wasn't all that unusual during the summer months. One with a bullet in her car's frame, an address that didn't exist, and claiming parents who'd lived and died in his town, parents who also apparently didn't exist—it was all adding up to…someone who had some problems beyond his scope of diagnosing or solving.

Adjusting the backlight on the screen in front of him, he scrolled one month at a time, through alphabetical listings. Found himself.

Read his mother's name. Twenty-four years younger than Jackson's nearly fifty-year-old father, Celeste Redmond hadn't hung around long after finding out that the elder Redmond would never leave his position as sheriff of Evergreen. That he had no political ambitions or any willingness to "move up" with his career as Jackson had been told she'd put it. He couldn't speak about her from personal experience. He had none with her.

Recognizing a lot of the names of people he'd gone to school with, his mind wandering from memory to memory, thinking about the lives some of them currently lived, wondering about others, his fingers stumbled on the little roller ball that powered the ancient machine.

There she was. Born four months after him. In Flagstaff. At the same hospital. Delivered by the same doctor. Birth records naming Evergreen, both county and town, as residences.

Had Adele and Celeste known each other?

Shaking his head, he pushed that particular wondering away. Personal details had no place in the investigation. He had proof that an Aimee Cooper had been born at the time the new visitor said she'd been born. Had proof that at least a portion of her story was real.

The part she'd brought to him.

And had no explanation for any of the rest of it.

No answers to her questions.

Just a list of addresses with a possible line having been erased.

And a bullet to identify.

He had it. So, it made sense to start there.

And a trip to Flagstaff meant he wouldn't be able to stop back by Aimee Barker's rental that afternoon.

A man of his word, he pulled his phone off the case at his belt, left side, opposite the gun he always wore on the right, no matter if he was in uniform or not, and dialed the cell number she'd given when she'd first called in the shooting.

"H...hello?" The apprehension lacing the stammered greeting was unmistakable. Grabbing his keys from his pocket, Jackson nodded at Landon the security guard at the front door of the courthouse and hurried out toward his cruiser parallel parked in a reserved spot out front.

"What's wrong?" he asked, jogging down the courthouse steps.

"Nothing. There's...just...a rattlesnake outside my door. I'm sure I should have been prepared, but...wow." Her deep breath was loud and clear.

He wanted to assure her that it was probably a king snake. And nothing to be afraid of. But first things first. "Are you inside?"

"Yes. I took a nap and then was heading out to unload some things from the car, and it was right there on my stoop..." Another deep breath, as the decibel of her voice rose with panic. "It did its rattle thing at me..."

King snakes didn't rattle.

And the address she'd come looking for didn't exist.

Nor did the deaths of her parents in Evergreen.

"Stay put," he told her. "I'm just a mile away and heading in your direction."

With a call to Leon Goldberg, his second in command as deputy sheriff, he logged out for the rest of the day.

And told himself that one way or another he'd have the Aimee Barker situation resolved and off his plate before morning.

Chapter 3

Of course, the sheriff would call right when she was heavy breathing over a stupid snake. She was in the rugged Arizona mountainous desert. She knew what kind of wildlife to expect.

She just hadn't expected it to be shaking its tail at her front door.

Not quite the kind of greeting she'd envisioned when she'd woken from her nap feeling more like the capable, responsible self she knew herself to be.

In a short lime-green denim skirt, a sleeveless and flowy hip-length lacy blouse in various shades of lime green and orange, complemented by dressier orange jeweled flip-flop sandals, she'd been prepared to take control of her life. And get back to New Orleans to get on with it.

Five minutes after the phone call, her pulse had slowed

considerably, her breathing returned to normal, until she heard, through the front door, "Well, hell," followed almost immediately by, "Gerald, I'm at Blooming Bridges, cabin five. Get the snake removal gear over here. We've got a rattler on the front porch..."

Though she'd just had a lunch of the fruit and crackers she'd brought on the flight, she brewed herself a cup of chamomile tea. She'd rather be sleepy than anxiety filled. And quit pretending not to be interested minutes later as she peered out the front window and listened as the sheriff and another guy conversed as with a long pole they attempted to coax the venomous snake into a cage.

"When's the last time you saw one of these out in the open in the shade?" The bearded bear of guy she was assuming to be Gerald asked. He was in charge of the cage.

"Never." Jackson Redmond sounded tense. Not that she knew him well enough to really know how he ever sounded. Could be, irritated was his norm. He nudged at the snake, getting it closer to the open metal door.

"Can't remember the last time Burley had anything worse than ants on his property," the bear continued. "Not with the way he is about pest control and walling off the property. Can't have a little nature scaring off his lucrative city guests."

Burley... Randall Burley...the owner of Blooming Bridges...didn't seem to have a fan in Gerald the bear.

The sheriff didn't engage in Burley conversation. With a few quick moves, he had the snake in the cage. Gerald flipped the lid, took the pole in his free hand and off he went.

And a knock sounded on her front door.

When she opened the door, Jackson Redmond was

staring straight ahead, not glancing toward the window through which she'd been peeping at him.

Did he know?

Why should she care?

She cared about the frown he was wearing. "I'm heading to Flagstaff to get the bullet checked out," he said. "I'd like for you to ride along with me, if you don't mind."

There was no command in his tone. She felt completely free to decline the invitation. Didn't even think about doing so.

"Did you get to the courthouse?" she asked, as soon as she was belted into the front seat of his cruiser.

"I did." He pulled onto Main Street, and then with a quick right, headed out of town. On the same road she'd come in on. He'd take it to Interstate 40, she knew, and then it was a long hour to the town where she'd landed early that morning.

She hadn't expected to be headed back so soon. Nor had she thought to have cause to meet the sheriff and get her answers the easy way.

"And?" she asked, ready to take in whatever he had to tell her about the accident that had killed her parents. Or anything else about them that might have turned up.

Her dreams had been about the desert. And the crying big boy.

The angry voice approaching the swing that morning…making the boy cry…she'd known it like a little girl would know a voice of authority.

She wanted to know what her brain was trying to tell her. To deal with it.

It was the only way to get free from its harassment.

Jackson, as he'd told her to call him as they'd headed

to his car, was staring straight ahead. His face…flat. No indication of anything. Good. Bad. Friendly. Not.

"I found your birth certificate," he told her.

She watched him. He was giving her something in the not telling. "I didn't ask you to look up my birth certificate."

"You were born four months after I was. Same hospital," he continued. "In Flagstaff."

She hadn't known that.

About being born in Flagstaff. For all she'd known, her stop there that morning had been the first of her life. Aunt Bonnie had picked her up from social services in Phoenix after her parents' deaths.

She and Jackson had birth circumstances in common. Kind of cool. She wondered if he thought so. Didn't ask.

The muscles in his upper arm bulged at the hem of his uniform shirt. She wouldn't want to get on the guy's wrong side.

But figured being on his right one could be nice. For whoever was there.

He didn't have on a wedding ring. Didn't mean he wasn't married. Or hooked up.

Someone as hunky as him would definitely be hooked up. Especially in a town where pickings were slimmer than the big city with which she was familiar. And with his job…

Her mind wanted to meander further. She cut it off. Avoidance was not currently the key to success.

"And?" she prompted a second time. He'd hit the cruise control. She'd seen him do it, but he still continued to monitor his dash as though watching his speed.

As though she, or something about her, made him uncomfortable. A fact that kind of pleased her.

But only because he made her a bit uncomfortable, too. Turnabout was not only fair play, but it made a woman feel a bit more normal at a time when she was fighting the idea of having serious doubts about herself.

What kind of dill brain ran off to Arizona because of an onslaught of stupid dreams and a handwritten address, in handwriting she didn't recognize, in a safe deposit box?

Being shot at—for whatever reason—having a snake choose that exact morning to snooze on her rented porch—were both signs that she was on the wrong path.

What would seem coincidences to most had often played bigger roles in Aimee's life. She took the universe's signs seriously. And with a grain of salt, too. Because they could just be coincidences. In this case, most likely were.

Jackson's silence was grating on her. Dammit. It wasn't like she was out for a Sunday drive. Or on some peaceful vacation getaway in the mountains.

She stared out at the mountain peaks through which they were driving, anyway. Hoping for a semblance of peace. Of comprehension or acceptance.

"There was no record of the address you brought me ever being recorded."

Okay, so that mystery wasn't solved. Maybe it wasn't meant to be. It wasn't like she'd dreamed of a plot of land. Or any ties to an estate.

And the tree that morning…it had just sparked something because…she was there, looking, and maybe there'd been the same kind of tree in her yard…

With the same heart shape formed by the branches?

"There was also no record of a car accident involving your parents, or any fatal accidents, in city or county files during the time in question. There's no record of your parents' deaths."

What? Her neck cracked with the speed with which her gaze shot back to him.

"You're…trying to tell me my parents aren't dead?"

Was he really careening so far of course? Their deaths weren't in question. Of that she was certain.

He shook his head. "I'm telling you there's no record of their deaths here. Are you sure the accident happened in Evergreen? Did your aunt ever indicate who she dealt with to get custody of you? Or what happened to the bodies? Were they buried? And what about any insurance settlement from the accident? What about their possessions?"

Right. She knew some of those answers. "There was money—I understood it to be from the sale of their possessions, but it could have been insurance settlement, too. As I said, I have no idea if anyone was ever charged in the accident. My aunt invested the money when she got me and I used a portion of it to pay for college." She tackled the least upsetting, and most clear, first. "She dealt with child services in Phoenix. After I questioned her about my parents, and found out she was my aunt, she told me all about the day she got me. She'd seen me once before, when I was seven months old. Mom brought me to New Orleans to meet her, just a quick trip without my dad, but we only stayed one night. Anyway, she said she'd never expected to fall so much in love the day she knew I was hers…"

Her throat clogged a bit as tears pushed at the backs of her eyes. She'd let enough of them fall. It was time to move on from that place.

"From that point on we always celebrated 'gotcha'

day, as well as my birthday. And every year, she'd tell me the story of coming to Phoenix to get me and how I made her life worth living…"

"And your mom? Did your aunt ever say anything about losing her?"

"She said she lost her when she married my dad, but she never said how or why. She didn't seem to think he was a bad guy, though. She mentioned once that she'd never been in love like my mom and dad had been. Mostly, though, she talked about Mom when they were younger, and since I wanted my aunt to be my mom, I never asked questions a daughter should ask about the woman who gave birth to her." Saying the words aloud made them worse than they'd been in her head. "I sound like a selfish little creep," she said. "A woman gives birth to me, adores me, according to my aunt, and because I can't remember her, I'd rather not know about her…"

"Don't be so hard on yourself," he said. "I can't remember my mom from when I was little, either, nor do I feel any particular affinity for her."

"Your mother died, too?" Her mouth hung open. How weird was that? The man who showed up to help her was not only born the same year as her, in the same hospital, but he lost his mom, too?

"No, she split." He quashed the idea she'd been about to consider as another possible sign. "Marrying a man her deceased father's age, the sheriff to boot, had been great right up until she found out that there was no way he was going to move to Phoenix, where they'd met and courted in a very short period of time, and let her family money move him up the political ladder. I suspect she thought she loved him at the time…"

He stopped, shook his head. Because he'd never understand his mother?

Or because he'd said more than he'd meant to.

"Did you ever see her while you were growing up?"

This time when he shook his head, there was no mistaking the intent—a definitive no.

"I looked her up the year I was graduating from high school. She was married to a guy who didn't know about me. And when it became clear that him not finding out was more important than seeing me for the first time in seventeen years, I made it easy on her and blocked her number."

"Did she ever try to get in touch with you?"

He shrugged, thrummed a thumb on the steering wheel. "I'd have no way of knowing that, with the number blocked, and all."

Which had been the point, she surmised.

He could tell himself she'd tried and just hadn't been able to get through.

In case she hadn't tried.

Because, really, if she'd wanted to be in touch with him, at any point, it wasn't like he'd be hard to find. Or to contact by some other means.

She didn't mention the obvious. Something else was pushing at her.

The probable woman in his life. And the fact that she felt so…drawn to him. Like they'd been meant to meet from the days they were born.

And another similarity—his big-city mother had been so incapable of living in the remote mountain town his father wouldn't leave that she'd left her own son. And while Aimee would never walk out on any child of hers, no matter where it was, she sure could understand a woman not being able to live in Evergreen.

And one other thing...

"Why are you telling me this? You don't seem the type of guy to spill his guts. Most particularly with a stranger who comes to town with flying bullets, non-existent addresses and supposed deceased parents she can't remember, who died in a car accident that doesn't exist."

He glanced her way.

Didn't respond.

And she decided to leave him alone for the rest of the way to Flagstaff, lest she inadvertently convinced him not to help her after all.

Jackson drove because driving had always been his panacea. Yeah, he had to get to Flagstaff, but regardless of what he found out about the bullet he carried, he needed to get out ahead of whatever had come into his day. He did that by clearing his mind. Letting the facts speak for themselves.

Problem was, no facts. Or not enough of them to form any kind of conversation. In addition to his lack of findings at the courthouse, nothing had turned up on the Evergreen estate.

The rattlesnake was a problem. It rankled more than anything else that had gone on that day. More than the dual flying bullets. More even than no evidence of an accident or deaths. All of the above he could explain away between bites of a burger.

But the snake...

He'd been certain it would be a king...they were more prevalent, partially because they just were, and partially because people in Evergreen tended to want them around. They were harmless to humans and ate rattlers.

Rattlers were more active in the early morning. They'd come out to sun themselves sometimes, if the weather was cooler, which it wasn't that day. Beyond that, in his experience, they generally hid in the brush, or maybe a woodpile.

Still, a snake on a doorstep in a mountainous desert town wasn't going to make the news. It happened.

But to Aimee? Hours after she'd arrived? And been shot at?

Nothing about the situation felt right.

Including the fact that he'd shared such personal information with her. It was not like his life story was a secret. But…

What was he missing?

He debated further conversation against accepting the silence she was currently offering. He couldn't get the job done without answers.

"Do you know what happened to your parents' bodies?" She hadn't answered. He couldn't follow up on proving or disproving what had happened to them if he had no starting place.

"They were cremated." She glanced his way, and then back out the front windshield, her hands resting in her lap. Right there where her bold, bright, short skirt had ridden up a bit farther exposing more of the slim, yet nicely curved expanse of thigh, as she'd sat down. He was doing his best not to notice.

"They'd died on impact from the car crash," she elaborated. "From what my aunt said there was so much damage, an open casket funeral for my mom was out of the question. She had their ashes put together in one urn. It's in a crypt with my grandparents, and now Aunt Bonnie."

Convenient, there being no way to investigate the evidence. Or at least, with an unlikely chance that bone or teeth fragments large enough to get DNA had survived the crematory.

"Do you know who did the cremations? What mortuary she used?"

She shook her head. While he thought about the futility of trying to find thirty-year-old bank or payment records to help corroborate her story.

Still, he could check locally. And then send a query down to Phoenix. Just in case.

"And the accident? You don't know any other details at all? What caused the crash? What were they driving? How many cars were involved? Were there any other injuries?"

Again, she shook her head. "If I did I don't remember it. I honestly don't think Aunt Bonnie knew the details of the crash. She was too busy rearranging her life to become an instant single parent to a three year old, and grieving for the sister she'd just lost. My grandmother raised both of them alone after my grandfather was killed in Vietnam and she passed away the year before my mom met my dad."

"How did your parents meet?"

He needed something to go on. Anything.

"She was working as a traveling nurse, supposedly just for a year before moving back to New Orleans to settle down. She was doing stints mostly on the reservations, and lived in Evergreen. My dad was a miner. Apparently she had car trouble and he stopped to help her…"

Evergreen citizens were known to help out. Living remotely as they did, it was kind of important to know there were those you could rely upon.

"I had the impression from what you said earlier that your aunt didn't like your dad…"

"I think it's more that she didn't know him. I know she didn't like that he refused to leave Arizona which was why my mom never moved back home. According to my aunt, my mom loved Arizona, but hadn't ever intended to settle in such an out-of-way place. She was lonely for home, and for city amenities. Living in the mountains, mining…it was all so dangerous…"

It could be.

Living there could also be heaven on earth.

"Yet they died of a car accident—an occurrence much more prevalent in the big city."

He heard the hint of defensiveness in his tone. Probably because he'd just been thinking about his mother, who'd put city life over the love of her husband and child.

And, perhaps, his father had put life in Evergreen over her.

Lord knew, the old man had been a true Arizonan— fiercely independent—and he'd been adamant about having his dictates adhered to. Life with Shephard Redmond had not been easy.

Nor had it contained an ounce of nurturing that Jackson could remember.

But he'd loved and faithfully served Evergreen until his last breath.

Jackson took a deep breath. His father had believed in a more vigilante justice system…thinking he could adhere to or ignore laws as befit the situation…but he'd filled Jackson with a deep and abiding purpose—to serve and protect the people of Evergreen, Arizona. Jackson loved the town. Keeping her people safe was his legacy as well as his father's.

And he had a visitor who was rattling his door with her bad luck and unanswered questions.

Filling his day with tension, frustration, unwanted desire and a ridiculous sense that if he wasn't careful, he could lose control of everything he held dear.

He couldn't let that happen.

Chapter 4

"Why are you really here?"

It was the third time he'd asked the question and this time it clearly didn't come lightly. Suddenly feeling like a criminal, sitting in his cruiser, Aimee stared out at the seemingly unending expanse of desert landscape with gorgeous mountain peaks. They'd made it to highway 40 and would travel the mostly straight uninhabited patch all the way to Flagstaff—a city that was a quarter of the size of New Orleans.

No *call me Jackson*, or shared birth histories present at the moment.

"To find answers."

"You know there was a car accident somewhere, you now have proof you were born here, you've got your parents remains, what more do you want?"

The question was fair. More than fair.

She could see, from his point of view, how she'd disrupted his day for seemingly no good reason.

"I want to know why my aunt had that address in her safe deposit box." But that wasn't all of it. Or even a big part of it. The address had only been a stepping stone.

Something to get her there.

She was afraid if she told him the rest, he'd write her off as a woman who needed to get herself under control, and possibly suggest that she vacation elsewhere.

As badly as she wanted to go home, she didn't want to leave Evergreen.

"I need to find the parts of myself that are missing," she said aloud, not really weighing her comments as much as giving in to a need to have someone she could trust to talk to.

Maybe it was him. Maybe it wasn't.

He was the only candidate who'd shown up.

"Ever since my aunt died… I've been having these dreams…okay, nightmares. I can't seem to get a good night's rest. At first, I thought it was because of the shock and horror of losing her so unexpectedly…she drowned diving from the same boat she'd dived from a hundred times…who does that as an adult? She slipped on the step, hit her head and didn't come back up…"

"I'm so sorry…" He glanced her way several times, his gaze always quickly returning to the road. She felt… touched by compassion. And shook her head.

All of the sincere and heartfelt condolences she'd received in the past month…they were all still just sitting together on the edge of her consciousness, not really touching her.

And a simple *I'm sorry* from a complete stranger reaches inside her?

"…but the dreams…" she continued as though he hadn't interrupted "…they don't have anything to do with my aunt. They're all the same. I wake up crying… with a pain so deep sometimes I can't breathe at first…"

The words sounded even worse out loud than they did when she talked to herself. Like she needed to get over herself and move on.

Everyone had bad dreams.

You shake them off.

Except that no matter how hard she shook, they wouldn't let go.

"And these dreams…they have something to do with Evergreen?"

The man was intuitive. Or just a damned good investigator who was paying attention. She'd settle for either.

"I feel like they do. I've been trying to figure them out, racking my brain to remember anything that might be associated to them. And when I found that address in the lockbox…something clicked. Seriously… I was compelled to come here. So, maybe I'm half nuts… I don't know…"

"Tell me about the dream."

He sounded serious to her. Like he was still listening with an ear to figuring things out—not just humoring her.

"There's not much to tell. It's more like feelings. I'm not really in the dreams…or I haven't been," she amended, shuddering as she remembered that morning in the field. "There's this guy…there's this sense that he's all grown up, but he's always got dirt on him that he's trying to clean off. Sometimes I reach out a hand to help, but I can't. He rubs at himself but he can't get it off, either. I can't ever remember clothes, or surroundings…just this sense that the dirt won't leave. And always, every single time, he's crying. And that hurts so bad. When I wake up it's like I'm feeling his pain. I'm the one crying. So am I somehow the guy who seems all grown up? Yet still a kid who can't get dirt off? Have I somehow transposed myself into something else because of something I knew in my past?"

When she first fell silent, she tensed all over. Afraid she'd made a terrible mistake in saying anything at all. Afraid, period.

Feeling trapped, she focused on the dry ground whizzing past, realizing there was very little vegetation she could identify.

Which didn't help.

"Are you young in the dreams?"

She glanced his way at the question, and her gaze lingered, studying him.

Determining he might be taking her at face value, assessing her predicament as something valid, she said, "That's just it—I don't know…when I'm trying to get his dirt off I never see me. Never feel me. Just this sense that I keep trying, but can't do it. All I ever see is him…" She paused. Wanted to end there for the time being. But didn't feel right doing so.

"Until this morning," she added, knowing she had to give him everything if she wanted his help.

"You had another dream today? When you took your nap?"

She shook her head. "Before that." A long deep breath didn't release any of her tension. "And it wasn't a dream. It was more like a waking vision…" No that wasn't right. "Like a flash of memory so strong it felt real in the moment."

"You're going to tell me you had it out at the Evergreen estate, aren't you?"

She stared at him. Not sure if he was on her side or not. Not even sure what her side was. "I didn't recognize anything when I got there," she told him. "But then I saw this tree…that's why I trespassed…the tree pulled at me…and then for a second there I was a little girl, so small my fingers couldn't reach around the ropes holding up a swing. The big boy was behind me, pushing me. I couldn't see him this time, but I could hear him. And then there was this other voice. Male. Angry. Telling the boy he was going to hurt me. Crying, the boy said he would never hurt me…" She shook her head, feeling it all freshly again, as she had that morning. Shivering.

"What happened next?"

"Nothing." How could that be? If she was remembering something how could it be so clear, and then just vanish? "Except fear. Unlike anything I've consciously felt in my life. It's just like with the dreams, I'm left with a sense of fear that lingers throughout the day…"

Which was one reason she couldn't just keep living with them. She needed her joy back. At least some of it. For a few minutes now and then.

"Of course, this morning, the fear was probably motivated as much by the bullets flying by me as any memory, real or imagined." She tried to lighten her moment.

"Let's hope the bullet gives us something that can help clear that piece up at least," he said, leaving her bereft. As though he'd been humoring her after all.

"How do you see that happening?"

"Best-case scenario there will be prints on it. Someone had to load it, and even if there's no criminal activity connected to it, chances are the bullet will tell us who touched it."

"If you have prints on file."

"And if I don't, just spreading the word that I have them can trigger more information coming forth than you'd think."

He didn't expound on the statement. She let it go, wanting to hang on to the hope he'd just given her that at least she wouldn't have to be fearing for her life while she was in town. Not that she really had been.

She'd just learned not to trespass on other people's property.

And he needed to clear a sheriff's report concerning a bullet in a rental car.

"And otherwise? You think I'm nuts, don't you?"

"Actually, no, I don't." He slowed as traffic picked up. Hard to believe they were nearing Flagstaff so soon. The journey between the two towns that morning had seemed unending. "I think if I was in your position, I'd need to investigate, just as you're doing. I'm not good with unanswered questions lingering around me."

She'd never had any particular bent toward finding answers to anything. Until the dreams…

Mostly she'd gone through life taking things as they came…never really finding a deep enough sense of need to move away from what she had. The shop held her happily captive. As did her own art—floral originals made from dried blooms and twigs. And while she'd always pictured herself with a husband and kids, she'd never met anyone who awakened her enough to commit to something lasting.

"Do you have any pictures of your parents? I can show them around, see if anyone recognizes them…"

Holding up her phone, she said, "You want me to text them to the number you used to call me this afternoon?" And after he nodded, she said, "I only have one of my dad. It's all my aunt had. I have a ton of Mom, from when she was younger, but will send the one my aunt took when Mom and I came to visit. It's the most recent."

His phone binged a few seconds after she'd sent the text. He didn't look at it, but then, she couldn't blame his lack of immediacy. He was driving.

"I'll do everything I can to help you find your answers..."

She glanced at him, caught his gaze and nodded.

But wasn't sure he hadn't just been humoring her all along.

As he entered the outer edges of Flagstaff, the only town he'd ever lived in besides Evergreen—having spent four years getting his criminal justice degree there—Jackson had a lingering concern pushing at him. Boyd Evergreen. He hadn't yet called the older man to alert him to the stray bullet fired on his land that morning. He'd been avoiding bothering Boyd until he had more information to give him.

Boyd had enough on his plate at the moment.

Had had as long as Jackson had known the man.

Clearly, their summer visitor, Ms. Aimee Barker, was going to be an ongoing situation for a bit, too.

Boyd would be greatly served if Jackson could get her away from his land and onto whatever property was the potential source for her dreams and possible memories.

He didn't know that there was anything for her to find. But he sensed that there could be.

Just as he'd had enough discomfort over the double bad luck she'd had since arriving that morning—the bullets and the deadly snake on her doorstep—he hadn't wanted to leave her alone in town until he had some time to process.

And now he had to find out just how seriously she was ready to pursue her answers.

"A couple of years ago, I worked with a company that provides experts in just about every field…from forensics and finances to child development…they're nationally known…" As he talked, the idea that had just occurred to him grew in scope. "They recently provided a high profile lawyer to help with a custody case involving wealthy rescue dogs, and one of their experts worked with displaced children in the one of the hardest hit storm areas last year…"

Stopped at a light, he glanced at Aimee, wishing he knew her better. Knew if she'd be open to what he was about to suggest. Because he was pretty certain he was on the right path to help her.

"One of the partners of the firm is an expert witness psychiatrist. Her name is Dr. Kelly Chase. I've met her a time or two. I think she might be able to help you, if you'd be open to some sessions with her. And if she's available. The firm, Sierra's Web, is based in Phoenix, though the experts live all over the country…" He kept talking to prevent an immediate no from the woman who, while she appeared to be listening to him, was giving no indication as to her reaction to anything he was saying.

"The Evergreen Sheriff's Office might pay for an initial consultation, based on the fact that we have no record of your parents' deaths, but proof that you were born here, and based also on evidence of your aunt's testimony to you, and the address you found in her safe deposit box."

The light turned green. He pushed the gas slowly. They were five minutes from the lab.

"I saw Kelly do something she called a cognitive interview with a teenager who'd been targeted for trafficking but got away, and the girl was able to remember key details that ultimately brought down the ring."

Evergreen was a safe town. The mountains surrounding them weren't always so, as people—criminals preying on teenagers—could disappear in them and never be found.

"You're willing to pay to try to find out what happened?" she asked.

Jackson pulled into the lab's small parking lot. Turned off the engine, and turned toward the unusual woman in her bright, colorful clothes.

"Are you willing to do the interview?" He wanted the answer before he went any further. Before they walked into that lab.

He wanted to know they had a plan—a potential way to proceed with an investigation—before he took her back to Evergreen.

She was staring out the front windshield and he studied her for a long moment. Could hardly believe the way she'd so drastically changed the course of his day.

Didn't like not being in control…having solid leads to investigate…knowing what path to take. He was the sheriff. The one paid to determine who did what and why.

He didn't like that her facts, given to her by her aunt, didn't coincide with town records. Didn't like what he *hadn't* found at the courthouse. If her aunt had lied to her, how did he prove that?

And he most certainly didn't like the tension she created within him—professionally, and personally, too? He couldn't be sure. Couldn't figure her out.

He just knew that he didn't like the unanswered questions she'd brought to his town. Or the fact that she'd involved the Evergreen estate.

And he didn't like the way her big brown eyes became pools that seemed to want to suck him in as she turned to look at him.

"I'd like to do the interview," she told him. "I need peace."

The response relieved him, but it also sent a rock of dread to his gut. The woman was deadly serious. He had a strong sense that she was on the up-and-up. She wasn't playing some kind of game, or visiting Evergreen on a whim. Something deep was driving her.

And based on what he knew, there was very little chance that the answers she sought, if she ever found them, were going to be good.

Chapter 5

The trip to Flagstaff served one good purpose. Aimee witnessed, firsthand, the loyalty and respect Jackson Redmond earned from those who knew him. Buzz Lopez, the forensic guru who put aside what he was working on to look for DNA or any other identifiers that might possibly have survived the heat of the bullet's detonation, clearly not only respected Jackson, but was fond of him as well. He didn't owe Jackson the favor; he was just happy to help out a good friend.

Turned out they'd gone to the university together right there in Flagstaff. Had been in many of the same classes. Turned out that Jackson was godfather to Buzz's four-year-old son Julius. Also turned out that Jackson had never been married. Buzz made mention of the fact. Twice. Egging Jackson on to make him a best man and a godfather. He didn't mention any specific prospects who could help complete that journey.

The bullet didn't turn up anything. Other than it was one of the most common around, could have come from any number of make and model handguns, and with Arizona being a state that didn't require licensing to open carry a gun, tracing its shooter was going to be pretty much impossible. If Jackson happened upon a gun he thought could have been used to shoot at Aimee, he at least had bullet striations on file which could prove whether or not the bullet had come from that gun. But only if he had the weapon. There were no fingerprints or DNA.

Jackson spent a good bit of the time on the way home on the phone, hands-free with his Bluetooth earpiece, trying to get a hold of Kelly Chase, for one, but also talking to people at the station, while Aimee dealt with email on her own phone. Before she'd died, Aunt Bonnie had been in the process of acquiring pieces from a gourd artist in Arizona and the deal was threatening to go sour. Something Aimee couldn't let happen.

She was glad to have something else to focus on, though. Was glad not to have to make conversation with the powerfully compelling man expertly driving not only the car, but apparently much of the world around him. She needed to get her life in order, to give her subconscious mind safe space to emerge, not get all tangled up with someone else.

Anyone else.

To that end, she declined his invitation to grab a quick supper at the diner as they came into town, preferring, instead, to be dropped at her car still parked at the cabin so she could make a run for groceries before it got dark.

When she returned, she stopped as she first entered the cabin, certain that someone had been there in her absence. The smell…it wasn't soapy, or bad, just different from the clean mountain scent she'd inhaled when she'd first checked in. After pausing on her first instinct to pick up her phone and call Jackson, she was glad she had as she noticed the freshly laid wood in the fireplace grate. Part of the service for which she was paying.

It had been somewhat warm during the heat of the afternoon, but with the evening's chill, and her need to relax, she figured a fire sounded like a complement to the microwave pasta dinner and glass of wine she had on the agenda.

The plan worked. Right up until she fell asleep on the couch without a blanket and woke up freezing sometime after midnight. She'd actually been sleeping well, no memory of any dreams. Shivering, she sat up, was just deciding to leave the wine and plate of grape stems, all that was left of the food she'd practically inhaled, on the table until morning when she flipped on the table lamp and noticed movement by the fireplace.

No one was there. She'd have seen a person in the shadows. She stood up. Took a step. And froze. She'd seen spiders before. Not one as hairy or big as the one that was slowly moving across the floor in front of the hearth. Pulling her phone out of the side pocket of her skirt just by instinct, she stopped herself from actually calling anyone. Even the sheriff needed to sleep. And she'd been raised to do for herself. Not to think she needed to call a man to do for her.

Shaking, she stood there, keeping the creature in sight with peripheral vision, but too frozen to do anything. Even from a side view the hairy thing looked…evil.

Her best guess, it was a desert tarantula. Which meant

the venom was basically harmless to humans. But from what she'd read, the bite hurt.

She wanted to run from the room. Hide in the bath or bedroom. Slam the door shut. And if she did, she'd hover there the rest of the night, imagining the thing coming in under the door.

She wanted to call Jackson. And the force of that desire propelled her to the kitchen area of the one-room living space. Pulling a large plastic bowl from the cupboard, she marched with purpose toward the thing still moving slowly along the floor. Shuddered. Twice. Aimed. And landed the bowl on top of the creature, screaming as she did so.

Backing up, she fell against the couch, staring at the bowl. It was really light. Would the spider be able to move it? The thought had her up and moving again, back to the kitchen, where, in the bottom of the stove, she came up with a big double broiler pan—the kind Aunt Bonnie used to use to cook strawberries for jam.

The heavy pan fit perfectly over the bowl. The nocturnal visitor wasn't going anywhere before morning. She'd be better equipped to figure out what to do with it in the light of day.

In the bedroom, she couldn't stop pacing. Back and forth along the bottom of the bed. A spider in a mountain cabin wasn't reason to call the press.

But a tarantula by the wood someone had carried in only that evening? On top of a rattlesnake at her door? Was someone trying to scare her off?

Or was her angst getting the better of her? Making her paranoid?

She was out of her element. Stuck in a small town

in the mountains where wildlife had equal housing op-
portunity…

She hadn't imagined the bullet that morning. Jackson
had pried it out of her car himself.

And he and Buzz had talked about it most likely
coming from a poacher—an illegal hunter who'd not
only been on private land, but shooting toward the road.

She'd had a rough day, but it had to be because she
was in such an unfamiliar land.

Who could possibly want to harm her? No one but
the Mr. Burley who'd rented to her and Jackson Redmond even knew she was in town. Only Jackson knew
why.

It wasn't like anyone who could possibly, maybe have
known her before would recognize a thirty-two-and-
three-quarters-year-old woman from her three-year-
old self.

Her gaze landed on the round plastic laundry basket
in the corner, beneath a clothes rod with empty hangers.
Grabbing up the basket, she carried it out to the living
area, turned it upside down and dropped it on the pan.

There. She'd jailed the pan.

Feeling ridiculous, but better at the same time, she
checked her sheets thoroughly, inspected every corner
of the room and under all pieces of furniture, went in
to brush her teeth and crawled into bed.

She'd conquered one demon.

Bring on the rest.

Saturday morning came a little too early for Jackson.
The night before he'd stopped at The Monkey Bars—the
diner and pub he frequented often enough to be considered a regular—for a burger and beer and had ended

up having to arrest a guy who'd had too much to drink and was all up in another man's politics. Something to do with legalizing the use of tracer bullets for hunting which made no sense to Jackson, but then he'd never been into hunting innocent prey, either, regardless of overpopulation.

Probably because he spent so much of his life tracking down criminal lives.

Still, tracer bullets? A guy had to see his bullet heading toward the animal in his sights?

He didn't know either of the men involved in what had turned out to be one guy pulling a gun on the other. He just knew his burger had gone cold and his beer warm by the time he had the gunman locked up. Then a couple of his deputies had been called out to a domestic violence situation which they hadn't been able to de-escalate in time, and a woman he'd known most of his life was currently in the hospital.

Jackson had seen to her kids, two boys, getting them safely to an aunt's house in a nearby town while his men got the perp locked up.

Three men in custody overnight wasn't a statistic that pleased him.

But it was summer. There were six times as many visitors in town as there were residents. Just as there had been his entire life. It wasn't like he could expect it to change just because he had a cold case that was occupying a massive majority of his brain.

Brewing coffee in the kitchen of the large triangular-shaped log home he'd bought against his father's wishes—the old man had wanted him to raise a family in the house where he'd been raised—he glanced around at the thousand square feet of open living space on the ground floor, thinking about Maria's two boys, about the life they knew.

About the unused space he had. All in all, his place had four bedrooms, two on the ground floor off the main room, one which he used as an office, and then the two in the loft upstairs.

He could see himself happily growing old in the space.

Just wasn't sure he'd be as content doing it alone as his father had been. At the same time, like his dad, he was definitely married to the town of Evergreen. To her people, visiting and full-time. And couldn't see himself marrying anyone knowing he'd be asking her to play second fiddle to the town's first seat.

So…did he start looking around for a boy or two who needed a good home? Not Maria's two. They had a mother who adored them fiercely. Who'd taken a beating meant for her oldest son, and who'd sworn to Jackson that she was pressing charges this time.

But there were others…foster kids…

Something to think about.

Another day…when he didn't have a heavy list of possible sources of information to check out.

First on the list was back at the courthouse and with it being closed on Saturday, he'd have the place to himself.

On his way into town, he put in a call to Boyd Evergreen, just to let the man know there was a potential poacher about and to assure him the sheriff's office had already checked out his land, finding nothing suspicious, and would be doing extra patrols and keeping an eye on things.

Boyd thanked him, gracious as always, and let Jackson know that he'd be gone for a bit, looking into alternative possibilities for his brother's new home, and vacationing for a few days as well. He had staff at the house, but asked that Jackson contact him on his personal cell if anything else came up. He absolutely did not want anyone coming to any danger on his land. Before they rang off, Jackson asked Boyd if he'd ever heard of Adele, Mason or Aimee Cooper, and, as he'd known, the man had no idea who they were.

Feeling better about that aspect of Aimee Barker's sheriff's report, he put his mind to any and every way he could help her find the answers she needed. She was taking up far too much of his mental energy for a cold case and he needed the matter closed.

And told himself he was most intrigued, that his interest was so piqued, because cold cases in his office were rare to nonexistent.

His detective, Sandra had already told him what she'd found from the Arizona Department of Transportation website—a small pickup truck titled to Mason Cooper, with no lien, that wasn't registered after the year of his supposed death. And a car in Adele's name, with a lien, that was repossessed after her death. Still, he looked for himself. He looked not only through property records, driver's license and car registration records, but then, after making some phone calls, had access to old city services—water, sewage, trash—records. He'd already accessed criminal records, late the night before. He put Sandra on similar searches for surrounding cities, some of which were digitized so would be much quicker to find.

And he distributed copies of the photos of Aimee's parents, asking his department to ask around among people who'd been in town thirty years ago, to see if anyone knew anything about them. And by noon, after receiving a phone call from the professional organization of mortuaries in Phoenix, he headed down the street to Blooming Bridges, cabin number five, only to find Aimee Barker's car absent from the lot. He tried her door, just in case, but got no answer to his knock.

That's when he pulled out his phone and made the call he'd been avoiding since dropping off Aimee the night before. He'd hoped to keep everything less personal than calling her private line, even while recognizing that the distinction didn't bode well for him. The fact that he'd made such a distinction at all. Phone calls were a regular part of his job. Why should one more number make any difference at all?

He didn't think about wanting to call anyone else on his list all day long. He didn't lie in bed at night, as he had the night before with Aimee's number newly added to his phone's database, wondering if other people on his contact list were alright.

Or think about calling them upon waking in the morning.

Nor did his gut leap when anyone else picked up the way it had when he heard Aimee's voice. Telling himself he was just hungry, coffee for breakfast and no lunch weren't his norm, he arranged to meet Aimee back at her cabin in an hour. She was out driving, trying to see if any sight sparked a memory as the tree had the day before. And he had to grab something to eat.

A burger that wasn't cold.

Something he could eat at his desk while signing forms and checking in with his teams. All three new prisoners were awaiting arraignment—something that could happen electronically on a Saturday, but he wasn't requesting the privilege on their behalf.

And at exactly the agreed upon time, he was back at Blooming Bridges, knocking on the door of cabin five.

She was in a tie-dyed brown-and-fuchsia sundress with spaghetti straps, and black with fuchsia bling flip-flops accenting those slim, tanned feet. Reminding him of when he'd dropped into bed the night before and thought about those toes sliding up from his ankle to his calf. He'd never, not even in his pubescent youth, had a fantasy about toes.

And his uniform would be the barrier that kept him from having one now.

"You're on duty?" she asked, looking beyond his shoulder, as though seeking out his cruiser.

"I was until noon." Though his official hours only meant that he'd for sure be available, not that he wouldn't be equally available any other time, day or night, if needed. "If I'd gone home to change, I wouldn't have had time for lunch." The added explanation was unlike him. And bothered him.

He'd never felt a need to justify his actions. Not even to the old man.

Another trait he'd inherited from the former Evergreen sheriff.

"If you've got time, I'd like to run you by a couple of places." He got right to the point of his presence in her day. He could fill her in on the way.

She nodded, turned to grab her purse—a large cloth floral bag, with a wide shoulder strap he recognized from the day before—and he caught a glimpse of the room beyond her. Wasn't going to say anything.

Told himself her activities or personal habits were none of his business. As long as they were legal.

He couldn't come up with a single law having to do with pans being trapped in laundry baskets. But… "You playing some kind of game over there?" he asked, staring at the odd arrangement of household items not far from her fireplace. "Some kind of toss game?" Trying to throw a basket over a pan was a better scenario than thinking she might have used the upside down basket as some kind of step stool—with the pan beneath it so it didn't collapse?

She didn't turn to look where he'd pointed. He was pretty sure she shuddered, though she'd also been hitching her bag over her shoulder so he couldn't be certain.

"It's a problem I solved in the moment, waiting for me to come up with a more permanent solution."

Was there nothing this woman did that didn't intrigue him?

She moved toward the door, as though urging him out. He stood still, staring at the basket. "Mind telling me what the problem is?" he asked. Maybe some kind of artistic thing. Spatial. She ran an art shop. And from the look he'd taken at her website the night before— a much longer look than intended, while lying in bed unable to sleep—he'd learned that she was also an artist whose work was featured in the shop. Floral pieces. Old window frames, for instance, with dried flowers pressed between the panes of glass.

There'd been one that would…

"A spider if you must know," she said, her wild short brown hair covering more of her forehead as she frowned. "I've got it trapped and I'm growing enough of an armor around me to be able to actually get it out of here. Until then, it stays were it is."

A little spider was underneath that boiler pan and laundry basket? He grinned inside at the thought of her dealing with a lizard—something else prevalent in Arizona wildlife—and in residential yards.

"If you wait long enough, it'll die."

She nodded, moved toward the door again.

He still ignored the cue. "You want me to get it for you?"

"No." Her tone was adamant. The way she stepped back, kind of looking down told a different story. "I can do it," she said, then, still not looking over at the basket.

Which, of course, made the decision a sure thing for a guy like him. While he appreciated her attempt to make herself stronger, to face fears, and critters outside her comfort zone, this was something he could take care of without a blink.

"I figure the emotional trauma you're here to deal with will be enough of a challenge without having to face down an intruder in your space," he told her, removing the laundry basket.

"Be careful! It's huge. And hairy..."

With one booted foot on either side of the pan, ready to stomp before the thing got even an inch closer to her, he yanked the pan away. And had to stop himself from laughing out loud as he saw the bowl underneath.

"I had to make sure it couldn't get away," she said, from still over by the door. "So I could sleep."

Because she was being traumatized by nightmares that wouldn't let her go. The reminder was sobering.

"Watch your fingers," she said as he bent to the bowl. "It's big and I don't want it to bite you. I was thinking it was a tarantula, not that I've ever seen one before in my life. But I did research before I came and it looks like a picture I saw of one. It's probably some big ugly friendly thing…"

Her words stopped him just before he pulled the bowl away. He stood, looking over at her. "It's really that big?" he asked.

She nodded. "Too big for me to step on."

Finding zero humor in the situation suddenly, Jackson grabbed a magazine off the coffee table—a tourist thing filled mostly with local ads that was complimentary in most of the motels, summer homes and cabins in the area—slid it under the bowl with one quick movement and then, just as expertly, flipped the bowl over, magazine on top, trapping the spider inside.

Without a word he headed for the door, and as she stepped immediately out of the way, got the possibly poisonous, though likely not lethal, creature out of her living space.

Carrying it across the few acres of common ground in the middle of the circle of cabins, he headed toward the woods beyond. His reasons were twofold. First, he wanted Aimee to rest assured that the thing wasn't likely to find its way back inside her temporary home. And second, he needed to be able to get a good look at it.

Yes, a tarantula could have gotten inside her cabin. Could have come in with the wood. Except that there'd only been a couple of logs—and they'd both been on the fire. And the chances of finding a rattlesnake on the doorstep, and a tarantula inside the cabin within hours of each other were so slim, he wasn't buying it.

He tipped the bowl, tossed the spider onto the ground.

His heart sank as he was forced to confirmed that it was a tarantula.

Grim-faced, he headed back across the compound. Bullets. Two poisonous visitors. He didn't like it.

They could all be explained. A poacher. Snakes did appear on cement doorsteps now and then. And he'd had a tarantula come in on a stack from his woodpile once.

But all three in one day?

Had someone followed her from Louisiana? Or, knowing of her travel plans, had someone hired a local to stop her from returning to New Orleans? Maybe there was trouble there. How would he know? She'd said almost nothing about her Louisiana life. Maybe something to do with the shop her aunt had left her? Maybe someone needed Aimee gone.

Maybe his mind was out of whack for the first time in his life.

But his gut was telling him that someone was out to get her.

It was his job to find out who.

And to stop him before he did more than just scare her.

Chapter 6

Aimee was still thinking about the strong uniformed sheriff dumping her bowl of spider as she climbed into the front of his dark blue SUV in the Blooming Bridges parking lot a few minutes later. She'd been in town twenty-four hours and he'd already rescued her twice.

She couldn't remember the last time anyone had had to rescue her from anything.

It couldn't become habit.

Still, it felt good. Someone having her back.

That's why he was lingering in her mind so much more than any other man she'd ever known. Surreal circumstances.

He'd called the night before to let her know that her first appointment with the expert psychiatrist was later that afternoon, in her own cabin. Hadn't expected to hear from him again until afterward.

He'd said he wanted to run her by a couple of places. Perhaps she should have asked where and why, instead of just blindly trusting him. She would have with any other person in her life—Aunt Bonnie included.

She'd have asked out of curiosity, if nothing else.

"Where are we going?" She posed the question a little late. Pushed by her internal dialogue.

"I'd rather not tell you, if you can trust me for a bit. You've been driving all morning to see if anything sparks memories. That's all we're doing here."

"But you know something. You have someplace specific to go."

"I do." He didn't look away from the road. "But you won't know when we get there. I called Kelly a little bit ago, to ask her how best to handle this situation and she suggested just driving around. Some places we stop will have significance. Some won't. And if none of them mean anything to you, that's fine, too. We're just out for a drive."

He knew something. He'd found out something! She heard the rest. Somewhat. Eyes peeled now, she was afraid to blink, afraid to miss anything that could be the point of significance in her life. "When we're done, you're going to tell me what you found, right?"

"Of course."

"Before I meet this Dr. Chase you have so much faith in?"

She felt his glance, more than saw it. Knew the remark had been beneath her. "I'm sorry," she said. He was trying to help her.

Had absolutely no obligation to do so.

She tried to explain. "I'm just…"

"Scared." He said the word like a challenge. Daring her to contradict him?

Or to agree?

"Yeah," she said. "I'm scared. And tense, which was what I was going to say."

"You don't have to work with Kelly. She's rented a cabin on a lake just out of town, said she needed the getaway, so she'll be around if you decide to cancel, and then change your mind."

"I want to work with her."

And would he be seeing Dr. Chase, socially, while she was in town? Was that why she'd "needed" the getaway? Was Aimee an excuse for the two of them to spend more time together?

Feeling deflated, she kind of hoped that Jackson was part of Dr. Chase's reason for coming to town. Maybe then Aimee could focus fully on her purpose for being there and get the heck back out. All the wasted brain power focused on the sheriff—even lying in bed the night before wondering where he lived—would be better suited to finding out whatever it was her young, suppressed memory was trying to tell her.

Staring out the window, keeping her mind and heart open to anything that might ring any kind of bell for her, she determined that her focus had to be, not on Jackson, or his possible love interests, but on getting to know what she could about the people who'd created her. Given birth to her. And, through the many accounts her aunt had given her, her mother had adored her.

They were passing an older white home with a large front porch wrapping around it, and a detached garage with steps up the side, a landing, a door. Second-floor windows.

Longing filled her. So deep it took her breath away. She wanted that. To have a family big enough to fill that home. And overflow to the garage. A mother-in-law suite, they'd call it back home.

Her mother hadn't had a mother-in-law. Neither would any husband she might take on someday. Her mother had come to mind then. Not Aunt Bonnie.

Feeling at once guilty and somewhat…freed…she continued to watch the landscape pass by—all with no sense of recognition at all—and to think about having had a biological mother. A woman who'd been pregnant right there in that town. Who'd shopped at the grocery store—clearly not the same modern building they were passing—with Aimee in her belly. Who'd named her.

Fed her. Bathed her. Rocked her?

Gotten up in the night with her. Changed tons of dirty diapers.

Played with her? Read to her?

Loved her.

She wanted so badly to remember. To the point of tears. Her heart flooded with them, in such force she couldn't do anything but sit and endure.

As log cabins and wood-sided houses passed, the despair slowly faded, but as they pulled back into the Blooming Bridges parking lot minutes later, Aimee felt changed.

Opened and in pain in a way she'd never known.

And had no idea what to do with herself.

He'd never taken anyone on a potentially psychological journey before. Kelly had told him to remain completely silent as they drove. She hadn't wanted Aimee distracted by conversation. Rather than having her brought into the moment in his SUV, she needed to be able to look outside and go wherever her mind took her.

He was no mind guru, but he was pretty sure, judging by the expressions that had crossed her face, the paleness that had come and gone from her skin, she hadn't gone anyplace good.

He wanted, quite forcefully, to know what she'd remembered. Wanted to tell her where they'd been.

And didn't feel confident enough in his ability to have the conversation.

She didn't invite him in. At the moment, he took that as a good thing, though he didn't much like her silence.

She didn't get out of the vehicle, either.

He glanced at his watch. It would be another half hour before Kelly got there. If Aimee needed someone to sit there in silence with her until then, that was fine. He could be that guy.

"You said you'd tell me what you found out about my family?" she asked.

So much for the silence route. One he knew he could handle.

"You want to wait for Kelly before we go into that?" *Please.*

She shook her head, her hair the only lively thing about her as it bounced with the movement. "I didn't remember anything," she said.

That shocked him. "You seemed…bothered…"

Tears sprang to her eyes, surprising him, though, in retrospect he wasn't sure why they should have, considering what the two of them were doing there.

"This is going to sound irrational, but hey, what about me isn't sounding that way since I arrived in town… I feel like I just met my mother for the first time. Again. See, I told you it sounded weird. How can you meet someone for the first time, again?"

He didn't know. But… "It actually doesn't sound all that irrational. You said you basically wiped her out of your memory—that you hadn't even known your aunt wasn't your mother, at least not consciously. In reality, you did know her. For three years. Maybe now, being here, you're opening up to her existence again. Even if you don't have specific memories."

Great, now he was sounding like he knew what he was talking about. He really and truly didn't. And started to sweat, wishing the doctor would get there. Hoping she was an early arriver type of person.

"I'd like to know what you found. Please."

She had a right to know. And was under no obligation to seek professional help before or after receiving the information. If she didn't want to wait for Kelly, that was her call.

"Your father did work as a miner. In the Oracle Copper mine. He worked there from the time he was out of high school until the date you gave for his death. He owned a small truck free and clear and there's no record of it after the time of the accident. Perhaps that's what they were driving and it was totaled. Your mother had a smaller car, with a lien, and it was repossessed not long after the date you say they died."

She went white.

He stopped. Sensing the weight of emotions roiling inside her, almost as though he could feel them, too. His ability to do that was because he had compassion, empathy, one of his criminal justice professors had told him. In his job, it was good in terms of interrogation. And could be lethal if he didn't keep a handle on it.

For the first time in his career, he was struggling to keep that emotional distance.

And wasn't going any further until, or unless, Aimee demanded that he do so. A kid didn't just wipe out memories of her parents unless there was reason to do so—Kelly had told him the night before. Could just be having been taken away from her home, without her parents, had been enough to suppress those memories, considering Aimee had only been three at the time... but something had driven her to seek out answers, to travel across the country to Evergreen in an attempt to find them. Kelly was taking Aimee's journey seriously.

"Go on," she said after not enough seconds had passed.

"I found their marriage license. It's dated two years prior almost to the day you were born."

"Did it contain an address of where they were living?"

He shook his head, and said, "I found utility bills for both of your parents, separately, your mother's under her maiden name, from before they were married, and for a few years afterward."

"And then nothing? They must have had a power bill. You think they moved away from here?"

"His Oracle records still listed him as an Evergreen resident and he paid county as well as state and federal taxes, but there was no address on record for him." Which in itself had been odd. In a bothersome way. What employer, even then, didn't have an address on file for an employee? But he'd seen copies of Oracle tax records regarding his pay so he knew the man had been paid. Helped to know everyone in high places in the area.

She stared out the front windshield, though he wasn't sure she saw the cabin door in front of them.

He waited for the next question. Hoped it didn't come, but knew it would.

"That's where we drove this morning, wasn't it? By their places?"

Yep, there it was. He nodded.

"And I didn't know them."

"No real reason why you should have. They lived there before you were born."

She nodded. He wanted to ease her distress.

Was frustrated that he couldn't.

He was the fixer. The problem solver.

"Which places were they?" Her gaze turned on him, piercingly.

Something about the intensity of that look… "You have a particular reason for asking?"

"Which places were they?"

He watched her for a moment, then said, "An older motel, across from a gas station…used to be a rent-by-the-month apartment setup, that catered to miners."

"My father lived there."

"Yes."

She was frowning. "Had redwood trim along the roof?"

"The eaves are redwood, yes, but they're new. The place has been re-sided and there didn't used to be a motel sign out front, but the basic structure and parking lot frontage are the same."

She nodded. "I remember seeing it today, but, beyond that, feel zero connection to it."

"But you did feel something, somewhere, didn't you?" He'd always been a good interrogator. Good at

reading others, his old man used to say. One of the nib-
blets of praise that came so sparingly, but were always
completely sincere.

"There was this house… I'm sure they couldn't possibly have lived there…but…" She shook her head.

"You recognized it?"

"Not at all. I just felt this longing…" She shook her
head a second time, reached for the door handle.

"Which place was it?"

Hand still on the door handle, but not pulling it open,
she shook her head again. "I don't know. I'm sure I'm
just oversensitized at the moment."

"Describe it to me."

He knew every single residence in the city and surrounding area. And needed to know if something resonated so he could investigate, find out if either of her
parents had any history with the place.

"It had a place over the garage…"

"Off-white, ranch-style house, set back from the
road, an acre of grass out front, trees, stream running
behind it…" He tried to keep his tone neutral as he described it to her.

"I didn't see the stream, but yes. The garage was set
back, on the left. The driveway was gravel. Just as we
turned out of town…"

He was nodding. "The White house. We drove by it
specifically." He'd been watching, but hadn't noticed
any reaction from her at the time. "Your mother rented
that garage apartment. She didn't move out until almost
a year after you were born."

"I lived there with them?"

Mouth left hanging open, she stared. Then, as he
nodded, she closed her mouth.

Said nothing. Her eyes teared up.
Her hands were trembling.
And, thank God, Kelly pulled up beside them.

Chapter 7

Dr. Chase looked younger than Aimee had expected. With loosely curled blond hair that graced her shoulders down to midback, and kind blue eyes, the woman seemed like a bizarre cross between angel and rescue worker as she stood outside the passenger door of Jackson's SUV, waiting to greet her.

"How'd it go?" the woman asked before introductions had even been made, glancing first at Aimee, and then across the hood to Jackson, where her gaze lingered.

"That's for you to determine."

It was obvious, by the quick, abbreviated exchange of words between the two professionals that they'd spoken that morning as Jackson had indicated.

Anything else between them, she couldn't determine. And couldn't think about at the moment. She felt like she was coming out of her skin. Losing her grasp on reality.

And at the same time the drive to let go of her grasp wouldn't stop, as though she had to hurry up and get wherever she was headed.

No matter what.

She didn't like no-matter-whats. Period. Her life was built around plans and sticking to them. The success of the shop, of her career, of her aunt's ability to become a fabulous overnight single parent, all stemmed from making plans to handle a situation as soon as it presented itself. And, while being flexible to their change, sticking to those plans.

Inside the cabin, she glanced at the laundry basket and pan still in the middle of her floor, the bowl on the little table just inside the door. Picking them up, a bit embarrassed for the psychiatrist to see them there, she then quickly deposited the two smaller items in the basket and slid it just inside the bedroom door, while Jackson asked Dr. Chase if she'd settled into her cabin okay.

She couldn't tell if he had any plans to join her there. But then, neither of them would let on to something like that with her.

And it wasn't like it was going to hurt her case if they did. Jackson had done Aimee a huge solid, getting an expert to town overnight, just to help her find answers. Any private relationship he had with the woman wouldn't conflict with that.

She still didn't like the idea. For no good reason.

But for a not good one.

She felt drawn to the sheriff and didn't want to share him during her time in town. She didn't want to sleep with him, either, though, so it wasn't fair or even kind to want to deprive him of companionship with the beautiful psychiatrist.

And…she was stalling her own thoughts, distracting them, and she knew it.

An activity that absolutely did conflict with her reason for being there.

Feeling awkward as she joined them, she asked if they'd like some tea or bottled water. Both declined. Did she show them to the living room? Was Jackson going to leave?

The home was hers. The party was about her. But she wasn't the one throwing it.

The psychiatrist formally introduced herself, telling Aimee to call her Kelly.

"I'd like to stay, on an official capacity, just for this first conversation, since I'm the one hiring Sierra's Web services," Jackson started in, still standing by the door.

Kelly, in dressy-looking black shorts and a white button-down short-sleeved blouse, stood just off his right and nodded. "I told him that I'd only agree to his presence if you were okay with it," she said to Aimee.

Aimee nodded. Relieved.

Why she'd want him there, she couldn't explain, other than that, in Evergreen, she felt best with him around.

They all three sat then, her picking the only armchair in the room, first, and the two of them settling on opposite ends of the matching big dark brown leather couch where she'd fallen asleep the night before.

A table made out of knotted pine logs sat in front of them.

"Sheriff Redmond filled me in on what's transpired since you arrived in town yesterday morning," Kelly, who just seemed to establish by her presence that she was the hostess of their little shindig, started. "Is there anything you want to add, before we talk about what part I might play in helping you find your answers?"

Did she talk about the near-psychotic-feeling space-outs she'd had since arriving in town, at this point? The swing incident and the longing she'd felt that morning? Or did she wait for a private session?

She'd never seen any kind of mental health professional.

She looked at Jackson, who, while he couldn't have any idea what she was thinking, nodded.

"Jackson told you about the memory I had yesterday morning out in that field?"

Kelly nodded.

"So…this morning…we were driving by this house… I know now it was where I lived with my parents right after I was born, but I didn't know that then. And I didn't recognize it at all…" She needed to get that right out there. She didn't want them thinking her episodes were any more than they were. Didn't want to waste everyone's time.

She really just wanted to know where her parents died, why there was no record of the car accident, and go home.

Or, that was what her brain wanted, at any rate.

Two sets of professional eyes were trained on her. "Seriously," she blurted, letting out a breath and following it with her brightest, friendliest smile. The one she used for customers at the shop who clearly weren't interested in buying anything, but kept reaching out to touch and handle one-of-a-kind, breakable pieces, in spite of the signs instructing them not to do so. "I'm happy to speak with you, Kelly. I'd love any help you think you can give me, but I don't want you here under false pretenses, like there's something serious going on, some mystery to solve. And…" She glanced at Jackson, "I told you I'd pay Sierra's Web's bill. This isn't anything the city of Evergreen needs to take on…"

The whole thing…it was getting out of control…

"We've got the disappearance of two people who we can trace back to living in this town until your aunt took custody of you," Jackson said. "I've heard back from the morgues and mortuaries and no one has record of your parents' bodies. Your aunt was told by social services, I'm assuming, that there was a car accident, and yet there's no record of one…but we've got record of both of your parents owning vehicles that were registered in Evergreen. The tags were last renewed just months before the accident was said to have happened…"

"Sheriff Redmond has asked me to see what I can help you remember, in the hopes that it could help him solve a missing persons case," Kelly said.

The words struck her heart like a painful bolt of lightning. "My parents aren't missing," she said. "They're dead. Their ashes are in a vault in New Orleans…"

"Until there's some record of them, some proof that those ashes really do belong to Adele and Mason Cooper, we…"

"It's them," Aimee said, feeling a little dizzy with the rate that things were spiraling. "We had DNA tests run a few years ago…there were fragments in the ashes, tooth or bone, and…we spent the money to have the testing done. I'd been talking about not knowing my father's ancestry and…my aunt had it run as a gift to me. You know, from one of those new DNA ancestry places."

"Then I need to know how they died without there being a record of it," Jackson said. He looked straight at her, then at Kelly. "I need to know that whatever happened…truly was an accident."

"You have reason to believe it might not have been?" Aimee got the words out through a dry throat.

"I have reason to question when records can't be found."

Okay. That made sense. She sat back. Took a deep breath. Was surprised at how emotional and overreactive she was getting.

"Right," Kelly said. "So for now, I'm working for the Evergreen Sheriff's Office. Do you still want to meet with me?" Her glance was kind, nurturing and completely straightforward, too.

"Yes." The response was unequivocal and just flew out.

"If, as things progress, the sheriff department has all it needs, but you want to continue our sessions, we can talk about a different payment arrangement."

Her nod came easier, with less tension from the cords in her neck. "Thank you," she said. Glad to be dealing with forthright business. She was good at it.

"You were talking about a house you drove by this morning…"

She hesitated another second and then gave in. If her reply sounded woo-woo and out there, and as though it bore no validity, better that they all found out sooner rather than later. "I had no idea I had any connection to the place," she started slowly, her gaze glued on the doctor now. "And didn't feel any sense of having ever seen it before…but as I looked at the place, this lovely big elegant home with a mother-in-law suite over the garage… I felt such an incredible longing to someday own a place like that. And… I identified with my mother all of a sudden, was overcome with sadness that she wasn't there, that I didn't know her...which sounds perfectly natural, considering I was orphaned so young, except that it's the first time I've ever been aware of feeling that way. To the point that, when I realized what was going on, I felt guilty, like I was betraying my aunt..." She sounded like a bad soap opera character. Creating drama where there needn't be any.

Should she lie down on that couch? Close her eyes and give her mind up to being scientifically studied?

Or maybe just suck it all up, head back to New Orleans and quit laying her guts out in the open in front of strangers...taking up time better used for real criminal and psychiatric work.

Jackson's glance at Kelly blew out any other thoughts from her brain, as she watched the silent exchange between the two. Personal, professional, she didn't know, but she was done being their guinea pig. She was going to...

"Do you mind answering a personal question?" Kelly asked. "It's something I'd generally ask in a confidential session with just myself and the client present, so we can wait if you'd rather..."

She shook her head. Another session seemed highly unlikely at that point. Might as well give them whatever they wanted, if it could help Jackson get on with real sheriffing work.

And justify the expense of Kelly's presence in Evergreen.

"I'd like to know about your personal relationships."

"What about them?"

"You were close to your aunt...obviously...since you

felt guilty experiencing feelings of longing for your mother."

"I didn't know until I was in fourth grade that my aunt wasn't my mother." She heard the defensiveness in her tone, wondered at it, but couldn't take it back. "So, yes, we were close."

"Would you say soul deep close?"

"Yes." Absolutely. Soul deep close.

"And who else are you close to?"

She shook her head. "I mean… I have so many friends…people my aunt and I know together, share holidays with, artists we work with, a gang from college, another one from high school…"

"And you're soul deep close with all of them?"

"No. Of course not." And soul deep, what was that? Certainly not a psychological term.

"So let's talk about those friends. The ones you're deeply heart connected to…"

Not one name sprang to mind. Because there were so many of them. Her life was full. Lovely. Or had been until Aunt Bonnie's accident.

"I'm the type of person who has a ton of friends, who's open to so many people," she said. "Not the type who only has a few close friends that she tells everything to."

"What about a romantic relationship?"

She shrugged. Uncomfortably aware of Jackson Redmond sitting there, watching her, listening. She tried to ignore his presence as she said, "Nothing serious." She shook her head. "Not because I'm opposed to it or anything," she quickly asserted. "I've always thought I'd get married, have a family. I'd definitely like that. I just haven't met the right guy. And I know it wouldn't be healthy to settle…"

She'd been busy with the business. And her art.

"I date regularly," she added, not wanting her current problems to seem more than they were. "I'm open to more…it just hasn't happened yet."

Yeah, she'd pretty much said that already. Fell silent.

She'd lobbed the conversation back to Kelly, and was leaving it there.

After an intolerably long and uncomfortable few seconds, Aimee was ready to pack her bag, turn in her rental car and jump on the first plane that would take her someplace else.

"Here's what I think." Kelly's voice was like a rock against glass. It shattered whatever peace had been left in the room, filled her with fear and garnered Aimee's full attention.

"I think what could be happening here is that you witnessed something when you were three, that you are starting to slowly remember what it was, for any number of reasons, but most likely associated with your aunt's sudden and tragic death, and that whatever it is has to do with your parents in some way. I think this could, in part, be why you've failed to form deep connections with anyone else in your life, other than the aunt who saved you at the time."

Okay, that was just a bit over-the-top. There was nothing wrong with her relationships…

"You think, somewhere inside, she knows what happened to her parents?" Jackson's voice brought her gaze back to him. She let it stay there. Giving her something upon which to steady herself.

"It's possible. It could also be something as simple as

being present during an argument between the two of them the day that they were killed in the car accident. A three-year-old mind would see the argument as the hugest, most horrible thing she'd ever experienced, and then them not returning could have solidified that that argument was the end of life as she'd known it. Ordinarily, a three year old isn't going to remember an argument, but one with a major life change attached could hang around in her psyche."

It could be that simple? An argument. And her ability to have healthy relationships was just fine.

Then why in the hell didn't she just remember the damn thing? *Come on, younger kid me, cough it up.*

"It could also be something horribly tragic. Until your mind shows you, we can only guess…"

"You think there's valid reason for you to be here?" Aimee asked the question, afraid of the answer, either way.

"I do."

Then she had to follow this through. "So when do we start?"

"We can start now if you'd like. The first thing I'd like to do is a cognitive interview about yesterday's memory…"

She was nodding, sitting forward before the woman even finished the sentence. Anything. Whatever it took.

Jackson stood. "I'll be heading out…"

"No!" Aimee had no conscious thought of deciding to stop him. The outburst was purely reactionary. So unlike her. And yet, not to be denied. "I'd like you to stay. In case…you've been here your whole life. And we were three together. Maybe you'll relate to something…"

The justification was clearly bogus.

He glanced at Kelly. Who shrugged. "That choice is between the two of you," she said to Aimee, and then included Jackson with a quick glance.

Aimee looked up at him. "You can go if you'd like." She had no business keeping him.

"No." He sat back down. "As long as I'm not in the way, I'd like to be here."

Her old self would have smiled. Thanked him. Offered him another shot at tea or water. Her current self just sat there, glad that he was sitting there, too.

Chapter 8

He should have felt awkward, out of place, sitting in that small cabin, witnessing an intimately personal moment for a woman he'd just met. Or, at the very least, had the wherewithal to shield himself in professional immunity.

He didn't even realize his lapse until his heart leaped in his chest and he got a visual of himself sitting forward, completely engaged, and more emotionally tuned in than he could ever remember being.

"That voice...the angry one...do you recognize it?" Kelly's question came gently, but with soft authority, as she sat perpendicular from Aimee, who sat head back, eyes closed.

"Yes."

"Can you see who it is?"

"No... I can see the branches and leaves. They start in a vee at the trunk and go up and form a heart shape right above me. Hearts like on the bottom and ear of my teddy bear. The white one, with the red hearts…" Aimee's response took on an almost childlike quality, but in the voice he recognized. He didn't want to move, felt as though even a breath inhaled or released too strongly could interrupt what was happening before they found out what they needed to know.

"Where is that teddy bear?"

"In the house. In my big girl bed. He stays there and plays and waits for me to go to sleep with him."

Aimee opened her eyes. "What was that?" She looked only at Kelly.

"It's okay," the psychiatrist said, as though calming a child. "Close your eyes and tell me about the voice."

A second or two passed, and then Aimee's lips moved, but emitted no sound. They moved again, and, "It's getting louder."

"Because it's getting closer?"

"Yes."

"And you recognize it."

"Yes."

"Who is it?"

"It's Daddy." The response was so matter-of-fact—stating something in a way that expressed surprise that there'd been any doubt—that Jackson was taken aback.

Had she known all along?

Even as he had the thought, Aimee's lids popped open again, her gaze wide, her brow lined with pain. "It was my father!" She looked at Kelly. "My father was coming toward us. He was making the man cry."

"The man?"

She shook her head. "The boy, man, it's never really clear. It's like a really big boy. I don't see him, other than the dirt on his hands, or his clothes. There's never a face…"

"Are you afraid of him?"

"No." Closing her eyes again, Aimee shook her head, her mouth pinched, her hands clasped with one thumb rubbing up and down the other, over and over again.

"But you're afraid of your father?"

Another shake. "I was then, but… I think that's what scared me."

Kelly was so focused, as though she was only aware of Aimee in the room, as though she was watching the past unfold right along with her. "I don't understand. You were scared because he scared you?"

"Yeah," Aimee said. "I think he didn't usually talk like that. It's like he was a stranger right then, but I knew him."

"And you're sure that whoever was pushing you, perhaps so high your father was reacting with an alarm you weren't used to, was crying behind you?"

"The voice made him cry." Aimee didn't even hesitate. "Or the words. He said he'd never hurt me."

"Do you recognize that voice?"

Aimee's head shook slowly. She opened her eyes. "Maybe I do. From my nightmares. It's always the same one."

"A boy's voice?"

"I think so. I can't ever tell."

"Is it deep like a man's voice?"

Amy shook her head again. "I'm not sure…"

Kelly's tone compassionate, she asked, "You ready to take a break?"

Aimee nodded. "I remembered my father." The tone was a cross between awe and despair. She seemed so lost. A grown woman and a three year old all rolled into one moment.

He wanted to hold her hand, to tell her that she was safe.

And he didn't know that she was.

To the contrary, his gut was telling him that she hadn't been—which could mean that she wouldn't be when she had the answers she was seeking. The father's fear…the boy man…her parents seeming disappearance, her memory block, the way things had been going wrong for her since she came to town, none of it boded well. He had a bad feeling. A driving force within him to investigate her parents' deaths until he was satisfied that justice had been done. No matter how they'd died. No matter the cost. And suspected that, whether it had anything to do with his investigation or not, whatever her memory was hiding from her could cause more pain than the knowing would be worth to her.

Kelly suggested that Aimee take some time off after their Saturday noon session. She'd recommended something that would help her relax, that felt good to her, warning that if she tried too hard, if she pushed things, she could end up burying deeper whatever memories appeared to be trying to surface.

And so, leaving the sheriff and the psychiatrist talking in the parking lot of Blooming Bridges, she got in her car and drove downtown. The main strip was a lovely mile-long piece of eye candy to her—eateries and, more importantly, artist shops. She'd read about them before coming to town, and visited websites, and was eager to drop in. To, perhaps, find wares for her own shop and unexpectedly successful online business.

She spent hours walking the strip, disappointed at the touristy feel of a few of the shops, the cheap trinket gifts for sale, but was delighted with the majority of them, the unique, handmade wares, including some paintings and jewelry by two different Native American artists previously unknown to her. She talked to store owners, handed out business cards, received some as well and got artist contact information. For the first time since she'd packed her bags at home she felt in control. Confident. Happy.

As far as anyone knew she was Aimee Barker from New Orleans, not Aimee Cooper who'd been born in Evergreen, and the relief of just being herself was palpable.

One of the shop owners she'd met, a woman named Cynthia, suggested that she try a chimichanga for dinner, from a family-owned, trendy little pub on a corner in the middle of town. She treated herself to a margarita as well, almost able to convince herself that she'd made a huge big deal out of something that was going to turn out to be the dramatic recollection of a three year old, and that, in another day or so, with Kelly's help, she'd be heading home with a psyche in sync with itself.

The whole cognitive interview thing…she'd heard about them, of course, from television…but doing one in real life…it had been intense…but pretty cool, too.

She'd remembered her father's voice. Which meant that there had to be other memories of her parents inside her, too, right? She was kind of excited to find them.

To get to know the people who'd given her life out of their love for each other.

The rest…the crying boy…the dirt she couldn't help him wash off…

That part still made her uneasy. But only because she didn't have the explanation for it, yet. Once she knew what her childish self was trying to tell her, she'd be able to reframe things from an adult perspective and put it all to rest.

And Jackson Redmond?

Her instant negative reaction to him leaving her interview? Her inexplicable desire to have him stay?

He'd saved her from the tarantula. And the rattlesnake before that. She'd been off her mark. Afraid. Feeling insecure and needy.

And had left him alone with the beautiful psychiatrist on a blissful, warm, breezy Saturday afternoon, so any wayward chance there might have been for him and Aimee to have a moment had been nipped in the bud.

Satiated from a wonderful meal, relaxed and ready to tackle life again in the morning, she headed up the mountain half a mile and around the corner to the Blooming Bridges, and noticed the work truck outside her cabin before she'd even pulled in. A big white truck with A & E Plumbing emblazoned on the side. A couple of men, Mr. Burley being the only one she recognized, stood outside on the sidewalk leading up to her door, which currently hung open.

She hadn't called for a plumber.

Or had any need of one.

After pulling into the closest guest spot, she was out of her car and heading toward the door of her cabin in seconds. "What's going on?" she asked her landlord as he approached.

"Problem with the sprinkler system," the older man said, his craggy, weatherworn face seeming almost complacent. Like the problem had happened before?

"You must have left a spark in the fireplace which smoked up the place while you were gone. Set off the system and it didn't shut off."

Which meant, what?

"The place is soaked. It's going to need to dry out and then we'll see the extent of the damage," he continued. "Mattress, furniture, all saturated. I have no idea what damage there will be to the floor." He shook his head, his mouth tipping in not quite a frown, as he stared at the door. "I'm sorry to say, but there's no way you're going to be able live in it. Or anywhere else in Evergreen. As I told you when you first sent in a request, you were lucky I had a cancellation. Places around here…we book up months, even a year, ahead of time for the summer season. I just called around, hoping someone else had had a cancellation, but we're all booked up. Might need to head back to Flagstaff even to find a place for the night…"

She was barely comprehending. Stared at the bit of soaked floor she could see. "My stuff…"

"Mostly ruined, I'm afraid. Anything that was out. I saw some clothes in the closet, but the door was opened and they're soaked. Whatever was in drawers was probably okay, but the leather bag doesn't look like it fared well."

A college graduation gift from Aunt Bonnie. Eight years old and still rolling along just fine…until then.

"I need to go in and get it all." If he thought he was there to stop her, he was wrong. She had her phone and credit cards in the bag she carried with her, but she wanted her things. Clothes could launder, toothpaste containers were likely waterproof…her makeup was in a zipped pouch inside the medicine cabinet…

In bits and spurts, thoughts of her belongings came to her until they propelled her up the walk and through the front door.

Everything was indeed saturated. An inch of water stood on the floor, though she heard a vacuum going in the bedroom area—a wet vac, she assumed.

A spark she'd left? As in, he was trying to blame the mess on her?

The Blooming Bridges website said that staff cleaned the fireplace and set the evening's fire every night.

The spark could have smoked before the late afternoon cleaning, except that she'd carefully put out that fire.

Her cute little cabin...

With the tarantula and the snake...

Without looking any farther around, she went straight for her suitcase, found it virtually ruined, grabbed the grocery bags she'd stacked in a kitchen drawer and started throwing her stuff in. What clothes wouldn't fit she shoved inside the sweatshirt she'd brought, using the arms to tie the bottom off well enough to get it out to her car.

Her laptop was fine—she'd shut it in the nightstand drawer—but the case was not. Her makeup was fine. The blow-dryer wasn't.

With each piece she owned, she mentally catalogued, packed—wet with wet, dry with dry, ruined or not—and moved on to the next.

Where was she going to go? The sun was setting. It would be dark soon.

The drive to Flagstaff...forty-five minutes of it would be across desolate desert land that would be pitch-black.

It wasn't like there'd be streetlights. Or homes in the distance. Nor were there exits with gas stations. Or anything else emulating human civilization.

Longing for home, for city life, feeling trapped and claustrophobic, she told herself she'd be fine. That it was for the best, really, as she should never have come in the first place. Talking with shop owners that afternoon, being back in her art world…she'd come back to herself. Seen who she was. She'd been good.

And good was enough.

Taking one last look around, her glance fell to the chair she'd been sitting on early that afternoon with Kelly talking softly to the memories deep inside her.

She remembered her father's voice.

And if she went home…the dreams would start again.

After what she'd learned and seen in Evergreen, they'd probably be worse. If she wanted peace, and to move on with her life—could Kelly's inference that she didn't have close relationships because of something she'd buried deep in her psyche be right?—she had to see this through. Had to help her little self find her way out.

Maybe Jackson would know of someone who'd let her stay for the night. And she'd figure out the rest in the morning. Make the hour and a half commute back and forth from Flagstaff each day if she had to. Making sure she did all driving during daylight.

Filled with anticipation at the thought of calling him, she hesitated to pull out her phone. All she'd been since the moment they met was one disaster after another.

Seriously…what were the odds of a spark smoking

from an extinguished fire to the extent that…just hours after a tarantula…and before that a rattlesnake and bullets…

Someone didn't want her there.

She'd stayed upbeat, in a positive frame of mind, as long as she could. Being soaked was the last straw.

Upon picking up her phone, she dialed the sheriff on his personal cell, as he'd instructed her to do if she needed to reach him before morning.

Squelched at the thought of interrupting private time between him and the psychiatrist. But didn't hang up.

He'd said to call if she needed him.

She needed him.

And didn't know who else to call.

Chapter 9

Jackson was sitting out back with a beer, waiting for his owl family to appear for their nearly nightly sojourn together when his phone rang.

He grabbed it quickly, not wanting the jarring sound to interrupt Hoot's journey to him, and was pleasantly surprised to hear Aimee Barker's voice. He'd changed from his uniform into jeans and a black T-shirt and was ready for some downtime.

By the time she'd finished apologizing for bothering him, he was feeling like a creep because the sound of her voice had turned him on.

Most particularly when the tone of her voice reminded him why he'd given her his number. Not for pleasure—whether he'd wanted to do that or not—but out of professionalism.

She was calling the sheriff who just happened to be

sitting at home in jeans drinking a beer. She wasn't calling the man himself.

"I'm on my way," he said as soon as he heard that
there'd been further trouble at the cabin. Already up
and inside, he was putting on his gun, and heading toward the door.

"Wait."

He didn't.

"I'm not there," she told him. And then he waited.

"I got my stuff out. I just…don't have anywhere to
go. I'm parked outside the pub where I had dinner. I can
drive to Flagstaff, but it makes me nervous to do that
in the dark and I was hoping you'd know someone who
could put me up for the night. As a favor, you know.
I'd gladly pay…"

He could come up with half a dozen places without
trying.

The women's jail, for one. There were currently no
inmates.

And she'd be safe.

He wasn't putting Aimee Barker behind bars. No
matter how much the idea of her being locked in safe
seemed like a good one at the moment.

"You can stay here." As soon as the words were out,
he jumped on board with them. "I've got an entire upstairs…well, it's got angled ceilings so the rooms are
kind of unique and you have to watch your head…but
there are two bedrooms and a bathroom up there that I
don't use. You're welcome to the entire floor."

"I can't put you…"

"…at least for tonight," he interrupted her. "Something is going on here. No one has so many seemingly

natural disasters or mistakes befall them in a single twenty-four hour period…"

"I could be a klutz for all you know."

"This isn't you doing things, well, other than the trespassing incident. Overall, these are things happening to you, and frankly, I'd feel better knowing you were under protection. At least until we have time to figure out what's going on."

"Okay, then thank you."

Her quick compliance kind of surprised him. Until she said, "I know I had that fire out, Jackson. I poured water on it. Like you, I've kind of come to the conclusion that someone doesn't want me here, which makes absolutely no sense at all."

Her words did nothing to calm the unease rising inside him. "Stay put," he told her, not liking that idea, but not wanting her driving on dark mountain roads alone, either. "I'm coming in to get you and you can follow me home."

Home. His home. Not hers.

And he better damn well keep that designation firmly locked in his mind every second that she spent in his personal space.

Whether it be at his house, or anywhere else.

"Who knows you're here in Evergreen?" Jackson, looking so good in those jeans and black T-shirt, like a regular, hunky man, rather than the youngest sheriff she'd ever heard of, sat hunched forward on the edge of his couch. Aimee was sitting in the armchair across from it—both pieces of furniture in a light brown leather covered with small darker brown decorative inscriptions—trying to wrap her mind around what was happening. To help him figure out what was going on.

"No one but you and Kelly know I have a past here," she told him. He'd shown her his place, including the washer and dryer in a little room in the back where she could do her laundry, given her time to get settled upstairs and then asked her to meet him in the living room to discuss her situation. It had all been very businesslike. With a bit of small-town welcome, and her awe at his unique and very lovely home, thrown in the mix. "And no one but Mr. Burley knew I was coming to town before I got here," she added, thinking of the shots that had been fired the previous morning. Surely those couldn't have been directed at her.

Had that only been a day and a half ago? It seemed like weeks.

"What about in New Orleans? Surely someone there knows where you were headed for vacation. Maybe someone who has a beef with you got a hold of the information and is after you here where, feasibly, they wouldn't be a suspect."

Made sense. Except that, "I can't think of anyone who'd want to hurt me, but that aside, I purposely didn't tell anyone where I was going. Just that I needed some time away to myself. With my aunt's sudden death... everyone was understanding, sympathetic, telling me to take what time I needed."

Everyone being the shop's employees. And her next-door neighbor who was also her closest friend and was watering her plants while she was gone.

She frowned. "And it's weird stuff. Was the snake supposed to bite me? You don't die from rattlesnake bites, from what I read. At least not often, and not if you get medical attention right away. Same with tarantulas—they can't open their mouths wide enough to bite deep enough to get enough venom in you…" She broke off when she saw his brows raise. Then said, "I did a lot of reading about the area before I left home, kind of hoping it would trigger memories without me having to make the trip out.

"And the sprinklers," she continued. "It makes no sense…except to force me out of town, maybe." And then it hit her. Wide-eyed she stared at him. "Unless Mr. Burley knew my folks. Knew my aunt's name. Recognized my name when I contacted him for a cabin reservation…"

Her voice grew in momentum until she saw him shake his head. And she realized…if he'd recognized her name, and wanted her gone, he'd simply have told her he didn't have accommodations for her.

"He's only been in town about a decade," Jackson said. "I was already on the force when he and his wife moved here."

"He has a wife?" She'd been under the impression Burley lived alone, ran the place by himself, with hired help for cleaning.

"She died a few years back. This was their retirement dream, coming to a place like Evergreen and opening Blooming Bridges. She's the one who named the place."

She was trying to draw from his calm. Wasn't completely succeeding.

"If someone is sabotaging you, and I'm at the point of going with that theory, then it could be anyone who's ever had access to that cabin. The door opens with a regular key that hangs on a board behind Burley's desk. Someone could have had a copy made. For that matter it could be someone who stayed there and for some reason doesn't want you, or maybe even someone else there."

"I got the place because there was a cancellation…" Could it be that simple? The weight on her chest physically lightened. "Maybe these are just outlandish pranks meant for someone else." All but the gunshots. Those had been alarmingly real. But probably not meant for her. Not if they were the work of a poacher.

"I'll check with Burley in the morning to see who was supposed to have been renting the place. And look into whoever had it before you…" Jackson sat back as he spoke, seeming to relax a bit more, too.

They'd dealt with the cabin for the moment. Seemed likely she wasn't in danger as they'd initially been thinking that evening. And they still had her past looming in front of them. "I'm meeting with Kelly again in the morning. We were going to do it at the cabin so I'll need to call her…" Hopefully the psychiatrist would be willing to do the session at her own rental. And, if Jackson had had dinner with her, she'd been imagining, then he probably already knew about the appointment.

"I'll be at the station for a bit. She's welcome to come here."

Meaning he didn't want to observe, as he had that afternoon? In a way, she was relieved. More comfortable with the process, and with Kelly, and yet, tense in a whole new, very private way. What would come up out of her?

And did she want the sheriff knowing about it the second she did? Before she had a chance to process. Or determine what part of her inner workings she wanted exposed.

"I called the current owners of the white house," he

told her, bringing her attention immediately back to current conversation. "Used to be owned by Evelyn and Barney White, but they died about twenty years ago and the place went into probate court and was eventually purchased by William Granger, who sold it to the current owners, Penny and Stan Palmer, five years ago. They had no idea a young couple with a child had ever rented the place above the garage."

She nodded. Had figured the original owners were long gone. Still…another connection severed.

"I also looked at census and school records this afternoon, searching for boys ten to eighteen who lived in the area when we were three. The most logical theory as to why you remember this other voice as a confusion between man and boy is because he was a boy going through puberty. His voice was changing. It's only a guess, but we have to start somewhere. I have my detective, Sandra Philpot, cross-checking the list I came up with against any of the places we know your father was associated with, anything to do with the mine, or the addresses where we know for certain he resided. Obviously, based on this guy's appearance in your nightmares, and in yesterday morning's memory flash, his role in your life held some significance for you."

"A babysitter, maybe?" she asked, coming at the dream from his angle for a moment. Looking through his perspective. Completely outside anything within her.

His gaze sharpened. "You think he was your babysitter?"

Did she? She wanted to. She liked the idea. It made sense. And she was there for the truth. "I have no idea." There was nothing more attached to him. Just dirt they couldn't get off and his tears. What if she was imagining the whole thing?

Wasting everyone's time...

Except, the memory of her father that afternoon... that had been bone-deep real. She'd bet her life on that one.

And...where was the record of a car accident that killed them? Or of any death they'd suffered? Except the nearly three-decade-old ashes she knew were theirs?

Where had they lived from the time she was one until she was three? And why wasn't there any record of it?

"I'm not imagining this," she finally said softly. "Something's off about those last couple of years I lived here."

"Enough so that I'm not going to stop looking until we find answers. We've had no hits on your parents' photos, so far."

Emotion welled up within her and she couldn't speak. Just looked over at him, thankful that he was there. Feeling safer than she'd felt in a long time.

Which made no sense to her. She didn't go around living in fear. Hadn't been aware of being afraid of much as she went about her days, until the dreams had started. They'd left a sense of lingering fear, but nothing attached to her real life. She didn't suffer from anxiety or panic attacks. So why, suddenly was she noticing a resurgence of a sense of safety she hadn't known she'd been without?

"I need your help, Aimee. It's possible you've got the key to all of this locked up inside you and until we know one way or the other... I'd like you to hang around. Close, not in a hotel in Flagstaff. Kelly advised that the more you immerse yourself with the area, the better chance we might have to help resurrect your memory..."

"Like with the white house with the garage apartment." She understood his request. And figured she probably needed the answers much worse than he did.

"Exactly. And the flash that the branches of a tree brought to you. Even if it's not the same tree...there are so many similar ones the area...anything that triggers something can potentially break the case open for us."

Nodding, she hoped he was right...wished there was some way to communicate her desire to remember to whatever part of her was holding her hostage to the blankness in her mind where her parents were concerned.

But she'd remembered her father! Only briefly. A voice. But he was there.

"All that said," Jackson continued, sitting forward again, elbows on his knees, "I'd like you to stay here. Because we have so little understanding of what's going on, because of the 'pranks' that could be more than that, the bullet in your car... I'd feel better if you were here, rather than staying with someone I'd asked to give you a room. The upstairs can be yours for the duration. I won't step a foot on even the first stair..."

She wanted to stay. Badly enough that she probably shouldn't. But what he'd said about asking someone else...he'd been spot-on. At the moment she didn't want anyone else involved, not in her life, her past, and certainly not in anything that might come in the next day or two. Prank or not, meant for her or not, negative things had been happening to her since she'd hit the outskirts of town, and she sure didn't want to involve anyone else in that karma.

"Thank you," she told him, standing up so she wouldn't let herself stay there and sit with him as long as he was willing to have her in the living room with him. Sleep seemed an impossibly far way off at the moment. After all that had happened. And everything on her mind. Spiders and snakes included.

"You want to talk to an owl?" Jackson stood, too, facing her.

She stared, feeling his heat, his closeness, wanting to be closer still, to kiss those lips that had just moved, to lose herself in good feeling and nothing else, and not at all sure she'd heard him right. "I'm sorry, what?" Praying he didn't know what she'd been thinking.

"Hoot. He and his family live in the woods and come to visit most nights in the summer months. We sit out back. The fam hangs out, moving from branch to branch. I drink a beer. It's all pretty laid-back. It's where I was when you called." With a nod of his head, he motioned to the sliding glass door that he'd said led out back. "You want to join me for a few?"

Yep. She just did. Without analyzing, thinking, trying to figure out rights, wrongs or anything at all. Except, "How do you talk to an owl? And can I have a beer, too?"

Didn't matter what answers she got, whether she could join in the conversation or had nothing to drink, she was heading outside with him.

What in the hell was he doing? Aimee wasn't his houseguest. Wasn't his anything. She was in his home for professional reasons and he needed to get a grip.

Not let the moon and stars and cool evening air lull

him into feeling like she was a date. The best one he'd ever had.

He'd never so much as told anyone about Hoot and his family. Let alone invited anyone to share the sacred communication he shared with the other owners of his land.

On his phone screen he touched the Go button in his birdcall app, playing the owl call sound again, and watched Aimee's face as she peered up into the moonlit portion of a branch where Mrs. Hoot was currently perched. The mama owl didn't answer, but Hoot did, giving out a loud call as he swept in to land not far from his mate.

"That is the absolute coolest," Aimee said softly, an almost serene grin on her face, her eyes wide as she continued to watch the birds.

If he'd been alone, he'd have asked Hoot where the kids were, but he wasn't ready to expose himself quite that much.

Instead, he played sporadic owl calls. Answering Aimee's questions. Content to sip beer in the cool air, watching Hoot and the Mrs.

"How long have they been coming here?" Her attention was still all on the tree off to the left of her. Jackson was on her right. All was good.

"Three years that I know of. There are a couple of little ones, but they probably won't be allowed to show themselves with you here."

"They know I'm here?"

He shrugged. "To my way of thinking they do. It took weeks of trying before Hoot would even show himself to me. I'd hear his call, but he kept himself hidden. Then Mrs. Hoot came. Then the babies. It's like he has to check out the situation before he'll join the party. And then more so for his family."

At that she turned her head, looked over at him, her face in shadows, but his was currently lit by the moon shining in his eyes. "You spent weeks earning the trust of a bird."

It was what you did when you'd dedicated your life to others. You made family out of what you went home to. But... "I wouldn't put it that way. I could hear him and just wanted to see him. I was out here to relax and have a beer." He never should have brought her out.

There was a reason he kept his private life...private. He didn't like being put under a microscope, having to explain his actions in his own home. Lord knew he'd had to do enough of that growing up.

And to get her attention off him, he segued into a trail guide's quality dissertation about the wildlife in and around Evergreen. The mountain lions who could occasionally be seen coming in to find water when it was blistering hot out, or there'd been a drought. The bears who wandered in for reasons known only to them. Antelope, deer, jackrabbits, coyotes and quail families...he knew it all.

"You really love it here, don't you?" The question was filled with something akin to envy, or so he thought.

"This place is as important to me as breathing," he told her honestly one of the things he knew for certain about himself. One trait he'd inherited from his father. "The months I was away at college each year... I'd get sluggish...and then drive the hour and a half home for the weekend and be energized again..."

Something else he'd never told anyone. Not even the old man who'd have understood.

Aimee was definitely bringing out the *different* in him. While pointing out to him just who he was and wasn't. The whole situation with her seemed bent on making him take a look at himself.

Because they were practically born together? Because they'd been alike in the beginning and their lives had traveled such drastically different courses just to have them cross again in such an absurd way?

Because he'd been present when she'd been completely, honestly, painfully open—giving him a glimpse of the three year old she'd been? Showing Hoot to her didn't rate anywhere near that level of vulnerability.

"Tell me about your father. You said he was old enough to be your mother's father, which would make him more like a grandfather to you. I'm imagining the two of you were best buds while you were growing up, the way you know so much about this town, about the wildlife, and the way you've followed in his footsteps."

He'd told her his father had been sheriff before him. And, yeah, that bit about him being older than his mother. The rest…

Taking a sip of his beer, he thought about himself researching every inch of her parents' lives, looking at pay stubs proving that her father had barely made enough to survive let alone support a family…

She was only in town for a few days. And if him giving her a bit of his past helped her through whatever was immediately ahead, it was a small price to pay.

"Living with my father was like being at a strict boys' school with no summer vacation and you as the only student and the headmaster your only family." He said it like it was, a matter of fact. Took another long sip of beer. Thought about having a rare second. And thought about growing up with no memory of a parent at all.

"He provided well," he continued. "He wasn't abusive," he added, thinking back to some of the stereotypical boarding school horror stories from movies. "There just wasn't a lot of room for error."

"I'm guessing you didn't make many."

He'd had his share. Some of them on purpose, just to show the old man who he was.

And when punishment had been meted out, he'd done the penance without argument, to show him who he wasn't, too. He was not a guy who thought it was okay to break the law. Or who thought he deserved to get away with wrongdoing. He was a guy who had to think for himself and if the rules seemed unfair he had to test the boundaries. And then be accountable to what he'd done.

"You knew he loved you," the soft voice came from beside him, and he considered the point she'd raised.

"I knew he cared for me," he said. "I trusted that he'd always be there, that I could always go to him." But love?

He wasn't even sure what that was. Not really. He saw it in the movies—the compulsion to be with someone above all others, a drawing to one another. He'd just never felt it.

He hadn't cried when the old man died. Hadn't shed a tear since he was a kid and his dog got hit by a car and his father told him to go bring wood up from the pile down by the tree line to the shed outside the back door for winter fires. Because death was just another part of life and the living kept going. He hadn't known until later that Shephard Redmond had buried the dog up by the road. Probably would never have known if a neighbor hadn't seen him doing it and told Jackson about it.

Whether or not the old man had realized he'd sobbed the entire time he'd carried the wood was something Jackson would never know.

"My father would have died for me," he added, thinking back to a time he'd nearly fallen over a cliff up on the mountain when there'd been a landslide and Shephard had dived to save him, thrown him back to safety, and had gone over the cliff himself. He'd managed to grab a root, to hang on, until he was rescued and had shrugged the whole thing off, but that had been Shephard Redmond. Nothing moved him to the point of overt emotion.

Jackson kept wondering when he'd get that tough. The old man would certainly not have been caught dead talking to an owl, much less let anyone know about it. Old Shep was probably turning over in his grave right about then.

"He'd have died for anyone in this town," he added then, not even sure she was still listening. Other than to take a sip or two of her beer, she hadn't moved, that he'd noticed. He hadn't looked over in a while. Almost hoped she'd gone off in her own thoughts.

Maybe remembering something else about her time in Evergreen with her parents?

The idea was to enmesh her in Evergreen life. To help her feel what living in Evergreen was like. He could continue to ramble…to build a framework for her to jump into.

He could tell her how his father's justice was more vigilante than his own. That he and his old man had clashed there near the end, because Shephard, who'd been semiretired by then, had wanted Jackson not to arrest a man who'd gone on a drunken binge, destroying property, after his wife had died. No one wanted to press charges. Everyone understood the man's pain. And Jackson knew the only way for everyone to live in society together, to see true justice done, was to make the law equal for all. And to do the man any good, he had to hold him accountable. He'd arrested him. And then talked to the judge on his behalf.

There'd been no jail time. Just a mandate to stay sober.

And damage to pay for, over time, as he could.

The alternative could have been giving him a ride and risking him sinking into a habit of drunkenness from which he might never have escaped.

He could have told Aimee all about it—and so much more—but, instead, he pushed the owl call button and let Hoot do the rest of the night's talking for him.

Chapter 10

Aimee awoke to the smell of bacon, and glanced at the clock. After nine? Seriously? She glanced toward the window, having left the blinds open the night before because, up on the second floor outside town, no one but Hoot and other birdlife could look in on her.

The sun was well up from the horizon. It was really nine o'clock? Feeling like a sloth, she flew out of bed and into the shower next-door to her room. Her appointment with Kelly was at ten.

How could she have slept so late? She never made it past seven. Or sunrise. Whichever came first depending on time of year. It wasn't like she'd been up late the night before. A few minutes after Jackson had grown strangely quiet, she'd figured she'd outstayed her welcome in his private time and excused herself to bed.

Those moments she'd spent with him, though…they'd

stayed with her through the night. Waking and not. She'd lain awake for more than an hour, listening for him to come inside. Imagining him down there on his deck, getting sustenance from his owls.

He was an enigma. A heart wrangler. And, in a secret world, a huge turn-on.

Strong and intelligent, with a whole town relying on him for their safety, the man was also sensitive enough, patient enough, to develop a companionship with an owl family. He knew what he wanted, and yet, he'd seemed almost lonely as he'd sat out there, talking about a father who'd been there for him, yet he'd fallen short of mentioning any love between them.

Her heart had opened to him, and hurt for him, this birth mate of hers whose life was so vastly different from anything she'd grown up knowing.

And the rest…as she'd fallen asleep…dwelling in that place where you were aware of your surroundings, but were floating mentally, too…she'd fallen into a dreamy glaze of want. Imagining her fingers on his chest, the hair, the muscles, and soft skin, too. The trail of black hair that would line down from his belly button, and the hardness it led to. Those lips doing far more than talking…

In the shower, it all came back to her with a heat that had her sweating beneath the spray until she had to adjust it to a more cooling temperature. The thought occupying her mind as she'd drifted off seemed to have stayed with her on and off throughout the night. Vague memories of hands on her body filtered through, but when she tried to grasp them, slid away.

Still, they were so different from the nightmares that

had been plaguing her sleep for so long, she was glad for their existence.

You couldn't blame a woman for helping herself through a hard time with a little fantasy on the side. And when the main character in your private little tableau was an all-Western mountain man secret softie, gun-toting hunk like Jackson...

Maybe you took a little longer than normal to wake up and face the life waiting for you.

Wearing a spaghetti-strap, tie-dyed calf-length cotton dress, brown with slashes of burgundy, purple, greens, blues and yellow, with burgundy-studded flip-flops, she descended the stairs, knowing that she couldn't have picked a safer man to crush on. Jackson was so professional, so assured and so bent on serving his town and solving her case that there was no way he'd be open to a sensual liaison with his summer visitor.

Besides, for all she knew he could have something going with Dr. Chase. Or someone in town. Just because he lived alone didn't mean he didn't have a full-time, monogamous companion.

He was standing at the counter, in uniform, his back to her, as she came quietly down the winding wooden staircase, but he turned.

"I was just getting ready to call your cell phone," he said, his eyes seeming to light on her, but then he turned and started in, all business, as he grabbed an oven mitt and pulled a plate out of the oven with a burrito on it. "I have no idea what you like to eat, but I figured if you're hungry, this will do." He slid the plate on a cloth placemat at the table. There was a matching set of four mats, one at each chair, that were printed with what looked like maps of Evergreen.

She was hungry. And sat down, eager to fill her mouth so she didn't have to hold conversation just yet. Not until she had herself more firmly rooted in reality.

"I stopped by Blooming Bridges," he continued, barely giving her another glance. "Burley turned over information on both the previous occupant of your cabin and the one who cancelled, and I've got an officer following up on both of them."

"Thank you." He was thorough. Conscientious. And clearly dead serious about helping her. Like him, she needed to keep her mind only on her business in town. No matter how difficult it might be to dwell only in that place.

The burrito smelled heavenly and she turned her attention to it.

"Oh my God, this is delicious," she blurted after barely swallowing the first bite. "What's in here?" Eggs and sausage, she could identify, some cheese and onions; but...

Other than those few things, his refrigerator had been pretty much devoid of anything but condiments and beer and milk when she'd loaded it with her stuff from the cabin.

"My father's recipe," he told her. "I fry up potatoes for the bottom layer and also add a bit of sour cream to the eggs. The salsa I get from a shop in town—it's all homemade there."

All said, as though she was a customer in his diner, while he brewed one cup of coffee, set it in front of her and put another cup, empty, in the dishwasher.

She wasn't a coffee drinker. But she was focused on his butt in those pants... "You don't have to cook for me," she told him when she started fantasizing again.

"I was actually planning to get something in town before I headed to Kelly's." She'd texted Kelly Chase the night before and they'd agreed to meet at Kelly's cabin which was on the other side of Evergreen.

"Kelly's coming here for your session," he told her, folding up a kitchen hand towel and hanging it over the oven door handle. "I'd have arranged it through you, but with the trouble you've been having sleeping, I didn't want to bother you…"

She didn't care where she and the psychiatrist met.

"I ran into a guy this morning, Wayne Burns. He was a friend of my father's. He actually called out to me when I was heading into the station. He owns a shop across the street, Bear Claws—sells trinkets, Arizona souvenirs, that kind of thing, and his wife's homemade bear claws…"

"Right at the beginning of the main section of shops," she said, remembering the place. Though she hadn't known about the pastries.

"He told me about you *nosing* around town, as he called it. He's under the assumption that you're checking out the area for a potential shop ownership, and is worried that you're going to come in with your nationwide artist pool and that local artists—as well as current shop owners—will suffer. He says the pie's already sliced too thin for our current economy."

Wow. She'd had no idea…and had thought they were all having so much fun the day before, visiting artist to artist. "The people I met, they all seemed so friendly…"

"They are! Including Wayne. But until I can ask around, and see if this is just one older gentleman feeling threatened and talking to me about it because he's known me since before I could walk, or if there's some

threatening sentiment going, I'd like you to stay put. I'll
have my answers by the time you're done with Kelly."

She should be losing her appetite, but had to swallow another pleasurable bite before she could say, "You
think he, or some of the other owners, is behind the
snake and spider and sprinkler mishaps at my cabin?
Burley knew who I was. He checks credentials before
he rents his places. Maybe he said something to someone…"

Made her kind of sad, after her enjoyable afternoon
downtown and with all of the business cards she'd collected, but what a relief it would be to know that her
mishaps had nothing to do with her parents or the past.

"That's what I intended to find out," he said. "Right
after I got back here and made sure there was something for you to eat since I to ask you not to go anywhere just yet…"

The man truly was thoughtful.

And the way he was making her feel could be allowed only in her fantasies. Those weirdly soft emotions absolutely could not become a part of real life.

No one in town was out to stop Aimee Barker from
setting up shop in Evergreen. To the contrary, several of
the shop owners were excited about the potential part-
nership with their artists, their unique, one-of-a-kind
pieces, and her hugely successful online store. None
of them had known she was in town until she'd shown
up in their shops the previous afternoon. So the snake
and the spider most definitely couldn't have come from
any of them. None of them recognized the people in the
photos he showed them of her parents.

The response he got to his inquiries not only had him

concerned all over again regarding the mysterious bad luck she'd been having, but had him back at the station, looking up Seeds for the Soul, the online version of the shop she owned in New Orleans. Having heard, also, that she was a quite talented and well-known artist herself, specializing in pieces made from flowers pressed in glass. He spent more time looking around than he had to spare, finding several pieces that he'd like to have for his home.

He'd known the basics from her website, just hadn't clicked on the store link. And he'd had no idea how well known, and well respected she was. He'd known she was unique. That she ran a shop that apparently supported her, at least one employee, and until recently, her aunt. He'd had no idea the kind of clout she carried in her world.

Or of the kind of money she must make.

More in line with his mother's family, than any life he'd ever lived.

Absolutely none of which had to do with her case. A mystery he had to solve before someone did more than just scare or inconvenience her.

A mystery he had to solve as soon as possible so she could get back to the world in which she lived, before he started falling into his father's shoes, falling for the wrong woman and wondering if someone who didn't belong there would hang around a little longer. For the summer, maybe.

He spent the rest of the morning visiting people he'd known all his life, trying to find anyone who remembered a young miner, his nurse wife and their baby girl who'd once lived in the White house. Asking about tree swings they might remember. Or a young teenaged boy who'd done any babysitting. No one he spoke to seemed to remember the couple—which wasn't all that surprising. Neither Adele or Mason was from Evergreen, and the townspeople were used to having people around they didn't know. People who came and went. It was all part of living in a city whose population exploded several times its size for part of every year. Add to that all of the wealthier young families from Phoenix who owned property in Evergreen and came up for weekends during the winter as well...

Neither Mason nor Adele had worked in town, so they wouldn't have become known that way. And as young as Aimee had been, she wouldn't have attended school yet. They didn't have parents or family in town. Unfortunately, they'd been able to just pop right out and no one seemed to have noticed.

That kind of bothered him, too. There had to be someone still in town who'd met them. He had a call in to the ob-gyn who'd delivered both him and Aimee, but the man, who now lived in Scottsdale, Arizona on a golf course, was on a cruise with his wife. His practice had long since closed. As had a lot of the small practices in town after the medical conglomerate had come up north from Phoenix and built a hospital and medical complex for three of the small neighboring towns to share—Evergreen being one of them.

He was just checking in with his people on the school records and Burley rental information, was receiving headshakes from his deputies, when his cell phone rang. Pulling his phone out, he glanced at the screen. Kelly Chase.

"I think we're on the brink of something here. Can

you get away?" the psychiatrist asked, her tone soft and yet managing to convey an immense amount of urgency.

"On my way," he said, already grabbing his keys and heading out the door. He'd intended to stay on the call while he drove, to be filled in on what was going on, but as soon as the woman had confirmed that she was still at his place, she'd hung up.

Leaving him to wonder whether or not the emergency was more violence or otherwise. She'd have said if she needed an ambulance—hell, she would have dialed 911 first if that was the case—or if there was immediate physical danger. Didn't mean there hadn't been some.

The emergency number would have dispatched whatever patrol car was closest. Kelly wanted him specifically.

Adrenaline was pumping through his veins as he pulled into his land, and had his foot on the ground before he'd even had his SUV fully stopped and off. Everything looked fine from the outside. Kelly's small rental car parked in the circular gravel drive. All windows intact everywhere he could see. Pushing in through the front door, his gaze went immediately to Kelly, who stood at his entrance, her finger to her lips, as she nodded toward the table and a completely different-looking Aimee than he'd left hours before. Her hair was damp around the edges, as though she'd been exercising. Her face was flushed. And the look in her eyes, as she glanced over at him, seemed…vacant.

And he understood what Kelly had meant by being on the brink.

"You ready to go back?" Kelly asked her, her tone professional. Respectful.

Aimee's immediate nod belied the completely lost look about her.

"You're sure? We can be done if you want to be."

She didn't speak, but the shake of her head was solid. Firm.

Pulling over another chair from the table, Kelly sat right next to Aimee, leaving him to stand there, wondering what on earth he was supposed to do.

Obviously, Aimee had remembered something. Or had been about to. And either she or Kelly had wanted him there.

Which was all that mattered. Thinking of the day before, when Aimee had specifically asked him to stay for the session, he pulled out the chair on the opposite side of the table from Kelly, the one closest to Aimee, and sat.

He was there as a cop. Wanted to be all cop.

Wasn't sure that was the case. A cop wouldn't likely have had to fight himself not to grab the subject's hand.

"Okay, close your eyes and let's go back to the house you saw yesterday. Just that house, again. Let go of the rest and just let yourself feel what you felt, driving by yesterday…"

"I'm…happy." Aimee's tone was soft, as though she was reciting. Like it had been the day before, and yet different, too. More aware. Less fearful. And reticent, too. She didn't fear the process, but seemed to not be as sure she wanted to go where it might take her.

A sign that she'd remembered something significant?

"No…no…" Aimee shook her head, her brow furrowed above closed eyes. "I'm…longing… I want it so badly…"

"What do you want?"

"To hear my mother's voice again."

She'd heard her mother's voice?

Jackson's brow rose as he glanced at Kelly, who met his gaze and nodded.

The doctor was scientist all the way. Though there were many around town who'd be willing to do psychic readings and bring people back from the dead, Kelly wasn't one of them. With her call to Jackson, she obviously believed that Aimee was remembering something.

"So listen. Tell me what you hear."

"Laughing. It's soft. And…it makes me giggle more until I can't stop because I don't want her to stop."

"What are you doing?"

She shook her head. "No, she's doing it, and I'm laughing."

"What is she doing?"

"She has bubbles on her hands…she's blowing them and they go up in the air. I'm trying to catch them."

"Are you outside?"

Still frowning, Aimee shook her head again. "No, I don't know. I can't see her, really, I just…know she's blowing the bubbles. I'm watching the bubbles, not her."

"Can you see the sky?"

Aimee shook her head.

"Just relax. Do you feel air on your skin?"

Another shake of the head, as Aimee shrugged.

"Relax, Aimee. You're okay. Don't worry about what you don't know. Just try to be in that moment. Is it bright? Do you see any colors?"

"No. No, I'm sorry, I…" The words seemed to be filled with tears, as though Aimee was on the brink of crying. It took every ounce of self-control Jackson had to just sit there.

"Don't be sorry. It's okay. Your memory isn't going to let you go any further with that today. You're afraid of what's coming aren't you?"

Aimee's head movement, a nod, was barely perceptible that time.

"You said you were ready to go back."

"I am." The beautiful artist sounded certain.

"Then go."

"The laughter. It's the same, but I'm someplace different. And there aren't any bubbles."

"Are you laughing?"

"I don't know. I don't think so. I can't see her. I don't know where I am. It's like I'm in a cloud or something. I can't see anything. I just…"

"Just what? This is where you stopped last time. If you need to stop again that's fine."

Aimee's hair bounced about her head with the force of her headshake. Her hands on the table clenched into fists. He could see the veins in her neck and shoulders, left bare by the spaghetti-strap dress and unlike that morning, this time there was absolutely no thought to her beauty, or what the sight of her did to him. This time, all he could see were the lines of tension in the cords of her neck, the way her veins were more prominent. And still she sat there, eyes closed.

"Can you tell me what's next?" He hadn't intended to speak. The words just came. As though she'd pulled them from him. Which made about as much sense as the rest of what had happened since she'd rolled into town.

"There's nothing," she said. And then stiffening, slammed both of her hands against her ears, shaking her head vigorously, back and forth over and over.

Tears pushed through her closed lids, and Kelly asked, "What do you hear, Aimee?"

"Screaming. Mama's screaming and…" She shuddered. Dropped her hands. And opened her eyes, wiping them as though just becoming aware of the tears she was shedding. "I'm sorry." Abruptly pushing away from the table, she went to the sink, washed her hands. Splashed her face. Wiped both with a paper towel. And stood there, her back to them.

"I remember my mother screaming." Her voice was low, almost as though she was talking to herself. "I don't know where, or why. I don't know where I am. I don't know anything about any of it, but I am one-hundred-percent certain that that scream was real. And that it was hers." Her shoulders hunched and he could tell the tears were still coming.

Jackson started to stand, to go to her. He couldn't just let her stand there, taking it all alone. Kelly reached out a raised hand, shaking her head.

And he clenched the edges of his chair with both fists as he did her bidding. He'd hired her. It was his job to make certain she could do hers. Not to impede her.

All three of them in the room were there only for one reason.

To find the truth.

He just hadn't figured what that truth might cost.

What it was going to demand of Aimee.

Or of himself.

He should be chafing for more information, intent on getting it in spite of the cost. Pushing to have her continue. Clearly something awful had happened at some point in Aimee's young life. Whether or not it had to do with her parents' deaths he couldn't say, but his instincts were leaning more and more strongly in that direction. And in the direction of Evergreen. His town.

The town he'd die for.

So why was he suddenly wanting to stop the memory process, take her in his arms and gently kiss her tears away?

Chapter 11

Aimee needed a break. To get away. Not far. Not for long. She was on the brink of something huge and she owed it to herself, to little Aimee and to her parents, to stand up to whatever it was. But she had to take some deep breaths. To be among flowers and find the spirit that lived so strongly within her.

Jackson didn't want her out of his home, or out of protective custody. Not without explanation for the natural threats that seemed to be following her.

Gunshots aside. Nothing natural about that one. And no guarantee that the bullet in her car had come from a hunter's rifle. But if someone had wanted her dead, he'd had plenty of chance to get the job done. Which was what she'd said to Jackson when he tried to insist that she not go anywhere alone. Adding that he now knew the shop owners in town weren't out to get her, either.

She'd insisted she was just going for a drive and had

walked out of his lovely log home, leaving him and the doctor alone to discuss the irrational person she'd turned into.

Her assessment, not one they'd indicated, in any way, that they shared.

She wasn't making this up. She knew that. And knew they knew it, too. Her brain had been storing some pretty potent information for three decades and was apparently now willing to share the goods. If she was willing to do the work. So Dr. Kelly Chase had explained to her this morning.

Why now? Her own question to Kelly replayed in her mind as she took a winding road out to a nursery she'd found online. And the psychiatrist's answer, *There's no way to know for sure, but my best guess is that your aunt's death was the catalyst. Because of the stress, the shock of it, you being all alone, but also perhaps because as long as she was alive, your surrogate mother, you felt guilty about needing your biological one. Or maybe having your aunt alive just made it easier to hide from whatever you're suppressing regarding your birth mother.*

Her birth mother. The words hadn't felt right. Something deep within her had revolted against them. Birth mother implied she'd been given up. That her mother had had her and let her go.

That's when she'd had the memory flash of laughter. Her mother's laughter.

Driving on the expanse of two-lane road winding through northern desert terrain, and small stretches where the road butted straight drop-offs, too, she smiled, remembering that laughter. The bubbles. Kelly had helped her find the bubbles. She'd tried for more, too, and that's where the frustrating part came in. She'd been feeling so good, floating in happiness, and slam. She'd heard that scream and hit a hard, black wall.

Seeing a sign for the nursery on the left telling her the business was three miles ahead, she slowed some. Feeling better even before blooms were in sight. She had two good things out of the morning. The sound of her mother's laughter. And the bubble memory. She could readily access both of them. Anytime she wanted. Apparently once she let the memories come alive, they couldn't go back into hiding.

Kelly had explained it all in much more scientific terms, but the gist of it was…good or bad…what she brought up was going to be with her to stay.

She had to be ready.

Flowers would help. They'd take her brain to a creative place where beauty appeared, where she could express feelings with color and shape, capture and frame them, and in so doing, bring peace to her life.

And… Jackson Redmond was helping, too. Over and beyond his duty. Some knowingly, like letting her stay in the luxurious upstairs area he'd turned over to her. And some completely without his awareness—the fun fantasies she was building about him to distract her when panic got too close.

Thinking about that butt in jeans…she smiled, rounded what had to be one of the last corners, saw a long stretch of straight road with only one vehicle, a dot in the distance, in the opposite lane. Probably going to turn in to the nursery as well, her brain formulated, as she continued, taking in the beauty of such starkly natural surroundings. GPS told her she had about a mile to go. Being out, with no homes, no stores, no evidence of human occupation to mar the earth, other than the road on which she drove, she had an idea of why Jackson was so dependent on Evergreen for his sustenance. Growing up with the power of nature, the peace of it, being aware enough to hear and respond to the hoot of an owl…

The vehicle must not have turned in to the nursery. She still had half a mile to go and it was close enough that she could make out that it was a blue pickup interrupting her sojourn with the sun's glare bouncing off its bumper in blinding spikes. Adjusting her sunglasses, she turned her gaze as much to the right as she could and still see the road in front of her, but the piercing silver was still there, more there, right in front of her there. The truck was in her lane! Coming right at her!

Slamming on her brakes, swerving to the right, only then seeing too late that she'd reached a spot in the road that led to one of the mountain's infamous drop-offs. She swerved again, back to the left, facing the oncoming vehicle, but not fully head-on. They were going to crash. Heart pumping, she prayed she didn't go over the edge, saw the road turn away from the drop-off just ahead, pumped the gas and then swerved, bouncing off the road, running over cacti, brakes fully engaged, before coming to an abrupt halt against rock mountain wall.

Sitting there with the airbag in her face, Aimee fought back panic. She hadn't hit her head. She could breathe. And ached around the midsection. No stabbing pain. Stinging in her left collarbone area, like open skin, where the seat belt dug into her shoulder bone. Reaching up her fingers came away dry. No blood.

And she was all alone.

The truck hadn't hit her. Hadn't even stopped.

Shaking, afraid to move and to stay there, a sitting duck with a bashed and smoking front end, she pulled out her phone. And called Jackson. He'd know who to send, who could get to her the quickest.

He'd tell her what to do in the meantime.

And she was going to follow every edict. His and Kelly's. This thing…she was in over her head. Someone in Evergreen was out to get her.

And she had a feeling whoever it was had been out to get her parents, too. The thought wasn't grounded in fact. Or science. It might be completely irrational.

But she believed it.

As much as she believed that Jackson Redmond would do everything he could to help her find out the truth.

They could scare her silly. They could even hurt her. But as long as she was alive, she was going to find her missing pieces. Her parents deserved to have their fates known. And to be known to her.

She wasn't leaving town without finding the past her mind had buried. Jackson got the message loud and clear. No amount of him promising to stay on her case until he got answers convinced her differently. Being in Evergreen had awaked memory flashes and Aimee Barker wasn't going to take a chance on slowing the process.

She'd also used his own words against him. Just the day before he'd asked her to stay, believing that accessing her buried memories could be the key to solving the mystery of her parents' deaths. At the time he hadn't thought it could also be at the risk of having to bury her.

Getting that call from her…hearing the shaky frightened voice telling him she needed his help…he'd been reliving those horrid seconds over and over in the hours since. He hadn't been first on the scene. He hadn't been closest. But he'd been there within fifteen minutes, half the time it should have taken him.

He had his own people working on the description of the truck she'd given. Searching department of motor vehicle records for blue pickup trucks and tracking them down. Unfortunately, Aimee had no idea who'd been driving or if the truck had any passengers, due to the blinding bumper glare, so unless someone with a registered blue truck didn't have an alibi, or admitted to being on Harper Road that morning, they didn't have much chance of making an arrest. Still, Sandra was gathering what security camera footage there was from the area. Maybe something would pop there. He'd also put a call out to the tribal police chief, and officers were searching for the truck on reservation land as well.

With his adrenaline still ratcheting up, he'd convinced Amy to ride in the ambulance to the nearest hospital, half an hour from Evergreen, and then to let him take her back to his place, where she promised to stay, while he went to head up the investigation into her near death. While it was unfortunate that the rental car was no longer drivable, he saw the circumstance as a blessing in disguise in that she had no way to take off on him again.

He couldn't keep her hostage. And wouldn't even want to try. If she wanted to go, he'd see her safely out of town and be done with her—though he wasn't going to rest well until he found out what had happened in Evergreen thirty years before. Under his own father's watch.

But while she was in his county, her safety was his responsibility.

As was finding out what in the hell was going on in his town. Things were always more chaotic in the summer with the town's population exploding like it did, but he'd never before had any trouble keeping the peace.

Or keeping their visitors safe.

And now he had a cold case on his hands. Every theory he had about Aimee's parents, every avenue he explored, all came to dead ends. There'd been no record of a car accident in town, no record of the deaths of Adele and Mason Cooper anyplace in the state, no address for them for the last two years that Mason had worked at the mine. Sandra had found no evidence of Mason or Adele Cooper residing in any town close enough for a work commute to Oracle. She'd found no connections between any of the names of the men who'd been full-time resident teenagers in Evergreen thirty years before with the mine or Mason or Adele, and not one of them to whom they'd spoken remembered the Coopers or even just Aimee. Members of the Evergreen Sheriff's Office had called as far as Upstate New York during the tracking-down process. Neither Burley's former tenant, nor the one who'd canceled raised any suspicion, and Jackson had spoken with both of them himself, that morning after the session with Kelly had ended.

While Aimee had been out driving her way to near death.

He shuddered again, as he waved off Leon in his driveway, letting the deputy sheriff know that he was good to go as Jackson pulled his own car into the circular drive. All hands were on board now, protecting Aimee, trying to solve the current malfeasances. What might have started as pranks had risen to the level of attempted murder half a mile from the nursery. No one but Leon knew of Aimee's ties to the past, though his detective, Sandra Philpot, had probably figured that his request for teenaged boys in the area thirty years ago might have something to do with the summer visitor staying at the sheriff's house. He didn't usually involve himself in the hands-on investigative work.

And he'd just done the checking on Burley himself. Running a full background search. Which was why he'd had Leon at his place, making sure no one got to Aimee who was supposed to be inside resting.

She was in the house, but whether or not she'd rested he couldn't even wager a guess.

Nor did he have anything on Burley, except the knowledge that the man was as clean as Jackson had always thought him to be. Other than a simple assault charge that had been the result of a run-in with a bookie before he'd ever moved to Evergreen—and for which he'd never been convicted—there'd been nothing to find. Not even a traffic ticket. A bit of gambling in a man's youth would hardly raise eyebrows in Evergreen. And there'd been no evidence of a continuance of the habit since the Burleys had settled in northern Arizona. To the contrary, Burley wouldn't even let the bus that took visitors to the closest casino stop at Blooming Bridges. Leon was going to follow up the Burley background check with some real-time inquiries, just to be sure. With three of the five incidents involving Aimee happening at Blooming Bridges, they had to be thorough.

Still, there he was, the great sheriff, with a thirty-year-old cold case which was probably tied to a current attempted murder and he had nothing.

Except Kelly Chase—thank God for Sierra's Web and the work he'd done with the firm in the past, or he'd never have thought to call in an expert psychiatrist. His father would have laughed him out of the house if he'd suggested such a thing when the old man had been alive.

Almost as though thoughts of the woman brought her to him, Kelly's small rental pulled into the drive before Jackson was even out of his car. Except that he'd been expecting her momentarily. The three of them—him, Aimee and Kelly—were going on a field trip. Kelly's suggestion.

He'd thought of showing Aimee junior high and high school yearbooks from thirty years ago, to see if she recognized any of the young men, but Kelly had advised that, in her opinion, it would be better if Aimee could bring up images on her own. If her mind could release them to her, they had a better chance of finding out a whole lot more than a mere recognition might give them.

So, his suggestion had become plan B.

First, they were going to try a series of things to stimulate the feelings that seemed to be bringing back flashes of memory. Starting with the old White house. Aimee had felt a longing as they'd driven past the place. Nothing as concrete as a memory, but Kelly seemed to believe that Aimee's feelings were the best portal into her memory bank. The current owners, Penny and Stan Palmer, had agreed to give them access to the garage apartment, but had warned that it had basically been little more than a storage barn since they'd taken ownership.

Jackson was going on the outing for Aimee's protection more than anything else. She'd said that other than a bruise or two, she felt fine, was moving fine, but he wasn't taking any more chances with her safety.

And reminded himself of that fact as the three of them climbed out of his SUV in front of the White garage, Kelly having ridden shotgun after Aimee went straight to the back passenger door from the house. She'd changed from the tie-dyed dress to a short-sleeved cotton one that fell to just above her knees. It was tie-dyed, too, blue and white, and he wondered if she dyed her own clothes. And what her closet full of them looked like.

Then quickly reminded himself that he did not and would not ever have access to the woman's bedroom. She was a victim. He was a cop. Period.

Watching their surroundings, Jackson fell immediately behind Kelly and Aimee as they slowly approached the staircase leading up to the garage apartment. The grass had been freshly mowed—maybe even after his phone call to the Palmers that morning.

"I'm going to hold your hand," Kelly was saying softly, "and I want you to close your eyes as you walk up the stairs. Concentrate on the smells, on the sounds of feet hitting the stairs, maybe the touch of the rail against your skin…"

Aimee nodded, but didn't speak. She hadn't when she'd come outside to meet them, either. He'd intended to go in for her, to ask how she was doing, but she'd come out while he was greeting Kelly and gotten into the backseat of his vehicle. Kelly had been the one to call Jackson and tell him the field trip plan. He didn't know if the psychiatrist had seen Aimee since the near-fatal crash or if they'd only spoken by phone, but he watched as the two of them took the first step, with Kelly slightly in front going up to the second step to make room for Aimee on the first.

He was right behind them, close enough to feel Aimee's body heat, ready to catch her if, in her blindness, she stumbled.

Close enough that he was shielding her from any attempt on her life, though he didn't think anyone from Evergreen would be bold enough to try something with him standing right there.

And with the security cameras the Palmers had installed keeping them in plain view.

But there were about thirty-thousand people staying in the area who he didn't know...

"I do it."

He heard Aimee's voice. Didn't recognize the tone. Froze, looking to Kelly.

The psychiatrist had one foot perched on the step above her and one on the step that Aimee occupied. She was looking at Aimee, but her expression gave him nothing. Frustrated that he couldn't see his summer visitor's face, he waited.

"What did that mean?" Kelly asked. Not in her cognitive interview voice, but, rather, as though she and Aimee were just conversing, leading him to conclude that Aimee must have opened her eyes.

"The steps," Aimee said slowly, sounding confused. Or...stunned. "I wanted to walk up the steps by myself."

"Here? You were only one when you left here." Clearly Kelly wasn't putting a lot of weight in the current memory flash.

"No," Aimee shook her head, still standing on the

step, holding Kelly's hand. "Not here. I don't know where. But the grass…it smelled just like this grass does. And there were steps. Up to a house, I think. I just had a flash. A deck maybe. There weren't very many of them. The steps. My mom was holding my hand and I wanted her to let go. To let me walk up the steps by myself…" Her tone grew in confidence, the more she spoke.

"What did they look like? Were they cement?"

"No, wood. Like these only wider and there were rails on both sides instead of just one."

"What color wood?"

"White."

"And what about your mother? What was she wearing?"

Aimee shook her head. "I don't remember. Just a sense that she was holding my hand."

"What did her hand feel like? Was it soft? Or more rough, like a working man's?"

"No, her fingers were soft. I liked to rub my thumb against her thumbnail when she held my hand. It was short, but smooth. It was my mother. I don't know how I know that, but I have no doubt about it."

Again, Jackson only had Kelly's expression to go by, but the doctor seemed pleased.

"You want to close your eyes, keep going?" Kelly asked then, and when Aimee nodded, they continued on up to the door leading into the apartment. Jackson had the key and leaned around Aimee to let her in, his arm brushing hers as he did so. He felt the warmth of her skin, wanted to linger, glanced at her to see if she'd noticed, but she'd already stepped away, inside, and he felt like a clod out there, thinking that a simple touch could possibly matter to her in the midst of such a traumatic time in her life.

They spent several minutes in the apartment. Walked down and back up the stairs. And in the car, Kelly had Amy close her eyes again and try to go back, to get more of the brief moment she'd remembered, but to no avail.

Still…he had something. A good possibility that after moving from the garage apartment, the Coopers had lived in a house with stairs up to the deck. Just a few stairs. Front steps. Made out of white wood. Could be hundreds of places that would have matched that description thirty years ago. No guarantee those steps had even been in Evergreen. But it was a start.

More than he'd had.

And something he and Aimee could talk more about as they shared Sunday dinner at his kitchen table. He invited Kelly to join them. It was the right thing to do.

She declined, saying she had a friend from Phoenix driving up to spend some time at the cabin with her.

He shouldn't have been so pleased about that.

But he was.

Chapter 12

She'd remembered her father's voice. Her mother's laugh. And the touch of her mother's hand! Such an incredible gift. Who'd ever have thought such a small thing could feel so incredibly life changing. Giving her life, her entire existence, added depth. It was like she'd been black and white and suddenly her picture contained a little color. And with each addition, Aimee became more driven to find the treasure trove she'd become certain was locked inside her. To feel her true colors, to wear them naked, not just in the clothes she put on her body.

Thoughts of naked bodies were definitely prevalent in her psyche since coming to Evergreen. And the types of naked thoughts she'd been having didn't go hand in hand with parental thoughts. At all.

So like her to challenge herself on opposite ends of

the spectrum at the same time. She'd been doing it with her artistic expressions all of her life—deeply emotional and bright and flowery at the same time. With her fight for independence, getting a place of her own, at the same time that she'd officially gone into business with her aunt...

Add in a little possibility of death threat and she was really tipping the barrel.

But still standing. In Jackson Redmond's great room— a huge two-story space, directly inside the front door that contained both living room on one end and kitchen on the other. With the whole evening stretching out before them. She couldn't leave. He wasn't going to leave.

And as off-kilter as she was, she wanted nothing more than to walk into his arms and ask for a hug. A long one. A really, really long one. That might entail offspring hugs, in various positions...

"I'm calling The Monkey Bar for take-out dinner," he said, pulling out one of about twenty drawers in the huge kitchen with a double-sized counter island in the middle of it. "Here's a menu—just tell me what you want..." He handed her a well-used, straight from the pub, based on its leather jacket, listing of Monkey Bar offerings. Including an impressive array of salads she'd like to try.

But... "You don't have to pay for dinner." And, with his fingers having just brushed against hers, she was suddenly in desperate need of something to do. "I brought all that food over from the cabin. We can make something here."

We. Him and her. In the kitchen together. She should have thought things through a bit better...

"You must have noticed my refrigerator when you

made your deposits," he said, with a bit of a shrug. "You had the sum total of my culinary skills this morning."

An incredibly delicious breakfast burrito. And yes, she'd noticed the bareness of his refrigerator shelves, but she'd glimpsed a freezer in the garage when he'd given her the tour of the place, and there were all those cupboards...

He was grimacing at his lack of cooking skill. She smiled at him...

"So, I'll make dinner," she said, looking away abruptly, as she forced her brain to a mental tally of the meals she'd planned to fix for herself—New Orleans' specialties that she didn't actually consume all that often at home, but had wanted to have to remind her of home. "You want a po' boy sandwich or red beans and rice with sausage?"

She couldn't just sit with him and wait for a delivery. And was fairly certain she couldn't trust herself to remain upstairs in her room. Not without driving herself silly.

"Kelly said I should relax as much as possible, and I find cooking relaxing." Truth.

"Then go for it. I'll have whatever you prefer." He grabbed a beer from the refrigerator. Held one up to her, and, when she nodded, opened it for her.

One beer. She could have one. Any more than that could push her struggling inhibitions beyond their limit. He asked if he could help. She needed him out of the immediate space. No more smelling his outdoorsy scent or feeling his hotness. She was overheated enough as it was.

He pulled out a stool on the opposite side of the island, facing the kitchen, apparently intending to watch her work. Aimee's lower belly gave another flood of sexy wanting.

"Can you go back to the white wooden steps leading up to the deck?" His question, a definite splash of cold water in the face, zipped her right back where he wanted her. Where she most needed to be. In the memory. Funny how she didn't lose them once they'd presented themselves to her. She could remember exactly what she'd seen and how she'd felt in the snippet she'd relayed to Kelly outside the White house.

And was trying so hard to do as the psychiatrist had said and not get discouraged over the complete and utter failure of the rest of the outing. Lest she block her progress with negativity. She had to trust her mind. Give it safe space in which to reveal itself. And the patience her toddler self apparently needed.

"I already described everything I've got to Kelly," she said, flooding with disappointment in spite of the admonition, the reminder, she'd just given herself.

"You described steps up to a deck. In trying to narrow down what kind of place we're looking for, as property records from thirty years ago haven't been digitized, I'd like to know more about the deck. Doesn't have to seem significant to you. Anything you can give me might ring a bell here."

She went over the memory again in her mind. Looking around the action in the forefront as Kelly had encouraged her to do with her questions. Didn't notice anything different from what she'd already given them.

"So, for instance, we basically have three kinds of decks here that would have steps leading up to them— the kind that come with manufactured homes, which aren't ground set, but rather sit up on jacks that are actually set underground on the foundation. Second, the kind that are added to mobile homes, trailer homes, that kind of thing. And third, the kind that are added to the fronts of homes that are built into the terrain, like mine."

His house was set into the mountain terrain. There were three steps leading up to the deck, and yet the house itself was built on solid ground, not up off the ground.

Up off the ground…

She'd been cutting shrimp, getting it ready to dip in the premixed seasoning she'd bought and then into a cornmeal mixture she had yet to make. She'd make the remoulade sauce while the shrimp was frying…

Up off the ground…

"What?" Jackson was looking at her. His question brought her an awareness of the fact that she'd just been standing there, knife in hand, over an overlarge piece of shrimp.

"The house. I think the whole thing was up off the ground," she said, talking fast lest the words steal the memory away. "I remember something being underneath the floor once. There was scratching…" Closing her eyes, she tried to see more. To know more. And saw nothing but the darkness behind her lids.

"A raccoon could have burrowed a hole in the dirt…"

She shook her head. That wasn't right. Because… "Someone went under there…a person…"

"To get the animal that was scratching…"

Nothing. She got nothing.

"Who went under there?"

More nothing.

"Was it someone you knew? Your father, maybe?"

"No." She had no proof of that. No way of knowing. And yet, "It wasn't my dad."

"Did they get the animal out?"

"I'm not even sure it was an animal."

"Did the scratching stop?"

Shrugging, she stared at him, feeling inadequate. And hating it. "No clue."

He must think her unstable. Definitely not a woman he'd find in any way attractive.

It shouldn't matter.

It did anyway.

Mostly what she hated was that regardless of what he thought about her, she felt like a head case.

Kelly had said to expect snippets to return over the next hours and days. The doctor had assured Aimee that what was happening to her, while understandably disturbing, was also completely natural. The mind had a way of protecting itself—and releasing information when the protection was no longer needed—or somehow ripped out of place. Kelly had also warned that everything could return all at once if a dam burst inside Aimee. She'd warned Aimee to be prepared. As though the sudden burst would be devastating.

Standing there preparing dinner for the sheriff, a man she found utterly beguiling, one who'd been born in the same town, the same year, and delivered by the same doctor as her, Aimee prayed for the dam.

She wanted to be as whole as he was.

She wanted her life back.

Leon called just as Jackson was heading out to the front deck to call his second in command. He didn't want to taint Aimee's memories with his suppositions, but at that point, with so little to go on, he had to follow up on every single one of them.

"I got something, Jack," Leon said, his tone as unflappable as always, and yet with an uplifted sound Jackson had come to covet, just the same.

"Give it to me."

"Burley…he didn't just used to gamble. He ran a card game over in Halston…one that was fairly popular." Halston, another one of the many small northern towns that dotted the top half of the state. And it sat apart—a good hour's drive from the closest town to it. "From the way I hear it, that old aggravated assault charge wasn't him being beat up by a bookie, but him maybe being one, going after someone who owed him. Either way, charges were dropped, and there's no record of who he hit…"

Instinct perking up, Jackson let his thoughts go wherever they wanted to take him. Trusting they'd get him where he needed to be. At the moment, he wasn't getting that upbeat note in Leon's tone. How did a regular card game from a decade, or even two, ago, or a past arrest of a local business owner, have anything to do with anything they currently cared about?

"Some of the guys from the mines used to play," Leon continued, laying it all out clearly, in his time. As was his way.

"And someone knew Mason Cooper." They were going to find the guy in a roundabout way? Through someone they knew who knew someone who knew him.

"I'm not sure. The guy I talked to had never heard of him. But he'd only joined the game later. Wasn't exactly sure when it started. But I was figuring this was enough to go at Burley again. I'll head over now, with your go-ahead."

"Go. But…hold on just a second. See if you can find record of a fatal wreck near Halston thirty-years ago. And also, have Sandra or someone run a report on mobile and manufactured homes titled in the area thirty years ago. Give me a three-year span, both sides. And, obviously, it can wait until morning." Mobile homes were as common as stick-built-from-the-ground-up ones in Evergreen and other towns like her, with so many people being summer residents, but owning homes elsewhere. And the way Aimee had described the deck she'd been walking up to with her mother, not like the stairs leading to a deck at the White place…added to the fact that the Coopers hadn't been well-off, wouldn't have likely been able to afford more expensive real estate…

"And when you get a chance, will you do a search of old case records…flagging anything that has anything to do with a perp hiding out, or dead body being found, underneath a manufactured or mobile home?"

"She remember something else?" Leon asked.

He'd had to let Leon in on what was going on when he'd asked the man to guard Aimee that afternoon.

"Yeah, but just enough to further convince me she's got more in there. And that we need to know what it is."

"We'll get to the bottom of it," Leon said, probably unaware of just how much that *we* meant to Jackson. Leon was a great cop. Had been a great partner when they'd both just been deputies for the Evergreen Sheriff's Office.

Jackson's second in command, who'd been in Evergreen a couple of decades and was ten years older than Jackson, had been hired by Redmond Senior, but had sided more often than not with Jackson when father and son were at odds. He'd also been the only one who'd ever seen how autocratic Jackson's father had been with him. How impossibly high the standards had been set.

Standards which had made him into a good, decent, hardworking man, he reminded himself as he headed back inside to the mouthwatering smell of cooking shrimp.

And reminded himself that the woman cooking in his kitchen was not there for personal reasons. He couldn't stem the flow of disappointment that followed the thought. He'd had women in his home before. Had never had any sense of even an inkling of wanting one to cook in his kitchen.

Or a single thought of how sexy it might be to have any woman cooking in his kitchen.

With a firm command to keep his libido in check, he still couldn't stop the thrill of anticipation that charged through him as he glanced over to the kitchen, to see her and…

The woman wasn't cooking in his kitchen. A thread of condensation came up off the pan on the stove. A glass bowl that had been a gift and had only ever held popcorn was sitting on the counter with some orangish-looking batter or sauce, with some condiment bottles sitting out with their lids still on them.

His gaze took it all in…even as his focus was on the woman sitting on a pulled-out chair at the kitchen table, slightly hunched, her blue-and-white tie-dyed dress filled with big spots of blood.

He got to her in seconds. Knelt down, bending his head farther and at an angle so he could get a look at her face. The eyes turned toward him, but didn't give him anything. They were shell-shocked.

"What happened? Where are you hurt?" The way the blood dotted her dress, he couldn't be sure. There weren't any holes, any stab or bullet rips. How bad was it? How had someone gotten to her when he'd been right there?

Why in the hell had he stepped outside? Was the threat still on the premises? Thoughts flew without allowing answers. He pulled out his phone—911 was his first priority.

"I'm so sorry. It got on the floor before I realized. I tried to stop it..."

Aimee was speaking. The voice didn't sound like hers. He didn't like the way she was shaking. Put his hand to her cheek. Her forehead.

She was clammy.

"What's your emergency?" The voice played into the room. He'd put the phone on Speaker and dropped it to the table to grab his gun, ready for whoever might attempt to reenter the room.

"No." Aimee blinked. Met his gaze head-on. Shook her head. "There's no emergency. I cut my finger."

"Sheriff?" He recognized Corrine's voice, the dispatcher who'd been hired straight out of Evergreen high school.

"We're good," he told her, ringing off, sure he was going to be embarrassed in a moment or two at his supreme overreaction. But still assessing Aimee. Something was off about her.

And all that blood all over her dress...

"I'm sorry," she said again, sounding more like herself than when she'd said those same words moments before. "Your beautiful wood floor…" She nodded toward the spot in front of the cupboard directly below where the bowl sat. "I was trying to mince garlic with the chopping knife you had and I sliced my finger…"

He noticed as she said the words that she wasn't just clenching her dress. She had the material wrapped around the index finger of her left hand.

"As soon as I saw a drop hit the floor, I used my dress to catch the rest of it, but…"

"I don't give a damn about the floor." He couldn't hold back the emotion coursing through him, no matter what position he held. He'd thought she'd been stabbed. A shot he'd have heard unless there'd been a silencer and…

He'd been truly scared.

Fear hadn't been a part of his life since long before his father died. Fear weakened a man.

"You look like you've seen a ghost," he told her. Was she one of those who lost her stomach at the sight of blood? He wanted to get a look at her finger, but didn't want to make things worse.

"I remembered something…" The tone was still her, with a note of vulnerability creeping in. And with that tone, understanding dawned on him. The fear he'd read in her, the shock…wasn't immediate.

"Tell me about it," he said softly, still down on his haunches in front of her. While he spoke he gently took hold of her left hand, then removed the dress from around her finger to get a look at the wound. It was clean. And just deep enough to bleed like a son of a gun.

Antiseptic and a Band-Aid would take care of it.

Aimee hadn't responded to his statement. "Did

someone get cut?" he asked, following the procedure he'd witnessed from Kelly Chase.

"No." The word was a little thick, as though her throat was dry. She licked her lips. Took a deep breath that ended on a shudder. "The cut didn't trigger the memory," she added then, sounding more like herself. "I cut myself when I got the flash of memory. I wasn't paying enough attention to what I was doing…"

Did he press her to tell him? He had to know. Where was Kelly when he needed her?

At her rented cabin on the lake enjoying a Sunday evening with a friend, he hoped. He could call her.

And would if he had to.

"The smell of the shrimp… I've smelled it my whole life… I don't know why it would get to me…but it wafted over and… I had this flash… I tried to stay with it as long as I could. I can still feel it. I just can't…"

She leaned over, her arms resting on her knees, dropping her head.

Jackson stood. Turned off the heat under the well overfried shrimp. Didn't look like those puppies would be sitting on any bread anyone would be eating that night. Collecting a first aid kit from the end cupboard above the long counter by the sink, he quickly tended to Aimee's wound.

The way she let him take her hand, tend to it, without saying a word, touched a chord deeply within him. He had no idea why. He just felt kind of choked up for a second. And quickly recovered. Then taking her elbow, led her over to the couch.

He'd wait as long as it took, all night if that was what she needed. He wasn't going to push, but he wasn't leaving her to sit in her darkness alone, either.

Didn't matter if it was the best way to the answers he sought. Didn't matter if it was professional. All that mattered was sitting with her.

So she didn't have to face demons alone.

Chapter 13

Aimee needed more. So much more. And couldn't seem to help herself. What kind of life hack made it so that you had all of the answers you needed, but wouldn't give them up to yourself?

It was like a horror movie. Only worse, because it was real.

She stayed in the space between past and present—feeling the past while not fully reentering the present—as long as she could. Afraid that if she didn't hang on to the feelings she'd been experiencing over by the counter, she'd lose something she might never regain.

If she hadn't cut her finger, she'd have had more. She was sure of it. For a second, it had been like she'd been transported back in time. The memories had been so strong it was as if she'd actually been there.

Which she had been, of course. So long ago.

If she'd just had another second to look around…but she sliced herself with a knife.

Because she wasn't ready to know what had been waiting for her to see?

The idea had occurred to her almost immediately, which was part of the reason she'd tried so hard not to let go.

The couch sank beside her as Jackson sat down— not too close, but not a full seat away, either. She shuddered. A residual from the way the voices in that other kitchen had made her feel. It was almost as though, with Jackson close by, she could more easily let go of the hold her mind was keeping on her past.

But was her heart, already aching from the loss of Aunt Bonnie, ready for onslaught? It wasn't all going to be laughter and bubbles. She'd known that from the beginning. Her father's voice had been angry—unusual for her to hear, she now knew, but still angry.

And the nightmares…they'd always been awful.

But she wasn't going to stop reaching. She had to know…

Maybe whatever she was hiding hadn't been all that terrible. She'd been three. Minutia could seem catastrophic to a toddler. She'd already figured that one out on her own before Kelly had mentioned it to her.

"My mom was making fried shrimp. It feels like she was making po' boys, but I'm definitely not saying she was. Makes sense, though, since she was from New Orleans. And maybe wanted to bring a piece of home into our home." It was what Aimee had done. Buy New Orleans fare to prepare in Evergreen. When she didn't even do it at home.

Because her mother had done it there?

counter behind
_ed some pickle juice for the remoulade
I'm not all that fond of pickles."

Good Lord. She was cutting off her nose to spite her face. Shooting herself in the foot. And kicking that hand that fed her all in one. What in the hell was the matter with her brain? She wanted it to spill so why did she keep prevaricating?

"I'm actually not all that fond of them, either," Jackson said. "Though I like dressing with pickle relish in it."

"Or pickle juice," she concurred. "I put it in the mayonnaise dressing I make for coleslaw."

"I've never made coleslaw in my life. I like it, though. On barbecue pork sandwiches. The Monkey Bar makes a killer pulled pork sandwich."

Were they seriously going to sit there and talk about food? She glanced over at him, sitting there so proper in his uniform, the gun he'd pulled over at the table back in his holster.

She huddle
very much."

"What do you hear?"

"My mother. *Those dirty hands.* She just keeps say
ing that. Or I just keep hearing her over and over having said them once." She couldn't be sure. Were they
reverberating in her little-girl brain? Had they really
been said over and over?

"Who was she talking to?"

"My dad." Oh. Her dad. She hadn't known that.
Hadn't asked. Her mother's tears had been so…dev-
astating.

"I don't think I'd ever heard her cry before."

Which made sense. And could that be all it was? That
her little-girl self had been knocked so far off-kilter because she'd heard her mother cry? She looked over at
Jackson. His vivid green eyes vibrant as they focused
on her, that thick short reddish hair of his giving him a
safe aura even while his gaze touched her too intimately
for a sheriff and a victim.

Could her little-girl brain have known such a thing? That the food was from her mother's hometown?

She just didn't know.

"I'm sure it was fried shrimp," she reiterated, as much to herself as anything. "The scent is very specific, and the spices in the po' boy fried shrimp—the combination of cayenne pepper, black pepper and garlic... puts off a strong odor...and it's just something I know."

Enough with the shrimp already. He didn't need to know about the shrimp.

"I like shrimp," she said. "It's the only kind of po' boy I ever order." Uh huh. "Not that I order them all that often. They have pickles on them." The jar she'd purchased was sitting out on Jackson's counter behind her. She'd needed some pickle juice for the remoulade sauce. "I'm not all that fond of pickles."

Good Lord. She was cutting off her nose to spite her face. Shooting herself in the foot. And kicking that hand that fed her all in one. What in the hell was the matter with her brain? She wanted it to spill so why did she keep prevaricating?

"I'm actually not all that fond of them, either," Jackson said. "Though I like dressing with pickle relish in it."

"Or pickle juice," she concurred. "I put it in the mayonnaise dressing I make for coleslaw."

"I've never made coleslaw in my life. I like it, though. On barbecue pork sandwiches. The Monkey Bar makes a killer pulled pork sandwich."

Were they seriously going to sit there and talk about food? She glanced over at him, sitting there so proper in his uniform, the gun he'd pulled over at the table back in his holster.

"My mom was cry-ing." Her throat caught as she said the words aloud. And emotion slammed through her with a force that took her air. Just as it had over at the counter. She tried to stay with it. To let it take her. The wave knocked her so hard she couldn't move. Couldn't think. Fear. Hurt. She was crying, too.

And then… "I ran," she said, her eyes closed as she relived another small tidbit of her life. "I hid. Under something. In something. I didn't open a door or anything. I just ran. I hid. It was dark."

"Was it cold?"

"No. I don't think so."

"Can you still smell the shrimp?"

She huddled there in the darkness. "Yes. But not very much."

"What do you hear?"

"My mother. *Those dirty hands.* She just keeps saying that. Or I just keep hearing her over and over having said them once." She couldn't be sure. Were they reverberating in her little-girl brain? Had they really been said over and over?

"Who was she talking to?"

"My dad." Oh. Her dad. She hadn't known that. Hadn't asked. Her mother's tears had been so…devastating.

"I don't think I'd ever heard her cry before."

Which made sense. And could that be all it was? That her little-girl self had been knocked so far off-kilter because she'd heard her mother cry? She looked over at Jackson. His vivid green eyes vibrant as they focused on her, that thick short reddish hair of his giving him a safe aura even while his gaze touched her too intimately for a sheriff and a victim.

"Was your father's voice loud?"

With her eyes closed again, she remembered being huddled in the dark. Was sitting on something hard.

"No. His voice was soft." She could remember that particular tone. It resonated and she knew it. Soft. Gentle. It was how he'd always spoken to her. And to her mother. "Normal."

"Normal?"

"It was normal. Like how he always talked to us. I feel like he's kind. And… I'm sitting on something hard."

"What's your father saying?"

She tried to listen. To remember. "I don't know."

"Because you can't hear it? Or can't remember?"

Her shrug, the shake of her head, was the only answer she had.

"Was your mom angry with him?"

"She was upset. It doesn't feel like mad. It feels like…it made me cry."

"Upset with him?"

"Maybe. It kind of seems that way, but not completely. She was mad at those dirty hands."

And there she was, right back where she'd started. The nightmares. Faceless, nameless dirty hands that could never get clean.

"Whose dirty hands?"

"I don't know." She could feel the despair and frustration roiling up out of her and opened her eyes, staring at her hands. Why wouldn't she let herself have the information she so desperately needed? She could be holding information inside that was putting her life in danger. She wasn't ready to believe that. It was all so bizarre. And someone who wanted her dead wouldn't have bothered with a snake and a spider. Would they?

"Is anyone else there?" Jackson's tone calmed her. She closed her eyes. Tried again. Could quickly access what had already been given to her. Made herself feel the full force of emotions, hearing her mother cry, but, as Kelly had taught her, trying to focus on other little things in the picture her mind was presenting to her. The color of the floor. She didn't know. Was anyone else there?

"I don't think so," she said aloud, inanely. "It seems like we're at home. And it's just us. It's that feeling, you know, when you're where you live and it's just who you live with."

"So do the dirty hands belong to your father?"

"Maybe. I don't know."

"Are they yours?"

"No." She opened her eyes with the emphatic response. Stared at Jackson. "They're not girl hands," she said. "I can't tell you how I know that, but I'm certain of that. They're male hands."

"Adult male?"

Frowning, she wanted so badly to give him the clue he needed to figure it all out. "I wish I knew. In my dreams, they're not little kid hands, but they aren't, say, as big as yours."

How the comment could have any sexual charge attached to it, she didn't know, but suddenly, sitting there with him, so exposed, and trusting, having just come through such an incredibly intimate experience, just the two of them…she looked at his hands and felt a flood of desire down below.

Segueing to the safe fantasy she was allowing herself

to get through what was turning out to be the toughest time in her life. She understood the reaction almost immediately.

And would have excused herself to the kitchen to make some kind of dinner out of the mess she'd left there, if Jackson hadn't chosen that exact second to take her hand in his.

The sight of Aimee's smaller, smoother, softer hand in his muddied Jackson's emotions. He'd reached for it with good reason. And for that first second, lost view of what that was. He wasn't just a cop experiencing normal cop emotions. He was a man who was drawn to a woman in a way he never had been before. Not even close.

He was a man with a job to do—a job that had to take priority. He had a life to protect.

"Feel my hand," he told her, out on a limb, but following a hunch. "Close your eyes and feel my hand like you did Kelly's this afternoon. Put yourself back in that memory. Or the nightmare."

He wasn't a psychiatrist and while he'd sat in on a seminar teaching law enforcement about cognitive interviews, he hadn't done enough of them to be anywhere near adept at it.

She closed her eyes. Left her hand hanging loosely in his against the seat of the couch between them. Sat quietly. He could feel a slight tremor in her fingers, but the rest of his assessment came up blank. Was she ready? Had she accessed the memories?

How much time did he give her?

How long could he hold her hand without clasping

his fingers more firmly around hers, linking them together as nature was prompting him to do?

She'd remembered her mother holding her hand while taking her mind back to the past. "The dirty hands. Did you ever hold them?"

No answer.

"Is there any sense that they're as big as mine?"

Again, nothing.

Glancing from their clasped hands back up to Aimee's face, he started as his gaze locked with hers. Eyes wide open, she was looking at him.

Aimee pulled her hand away and said, "This is going to be completely inappropriate, but the feeling I get when you hold my hand precludes any chance of slipping back to the past. I'm sorry. I know you're trying. I know you need me to get on with it and figure this out, especially now that there's an actual incident with me being run off the road, but... I'm sorry."

She was sorry?

And...the question battling for release, "This feeling you get when you hold my hand, can you describe it to me" couldn't happen.

"Aimee, first and foremost, don't be sorry." Holding her gaze, he gave her an intent look as he added, "For anything." Most particularly for not getting a feeling when she held his hand.

It could mean that she was feeling the same intense connection to him that he'd been feeling for her. Analytically, it could mean that. Made sense, considering that whatever was happening to him where she was concerned was so extreme and quick and completely new to him that she'd be feeling something, too.

But for the moment, he had to stay on track, no matter how hard his lower body tried to sabotage him. Her life could very well depend on him. Based on the memory she'd just shared with him, they could be on the verge of something and he needed information. Some real-time information.

For once, he was thankful for the supreme sense of self-control his father had instilled in him as he continued. "I'm asking about the hands for specific reason." He had to swallow. Look away. Those big brown eyes of hers were swallowing him in. He needed to take her in his arms, to hold her while she received information.

And that wasn't his role.

Just as taking her into his bedroom, shutting out the world and spending the rest of his life in his bed with her sounded fabulous.

But wasn't realistic.

Though if they went in and never came out, it could keep her alive. If neither of them pursued their current course where her life and past were concerned, it might all just go away…

The thought was there, and as he dismissed it, he was reminded of who he was. A man who put the law, his city and the safety of the people in his care first.

It had never been harder to do.

"The dirty hands seem to be a key to whatever you've locked away," he told her. "Them coming up again tonight…for you…it's probably just more of the same… but to me…"

He looked her in the eye again. She held his gaze, her expression filled with interest—and trust. He valued that trust even more than Leon's.

Did it come with the hope that he'd find her truth?

Or that he wouldn't let her get hurt?

Because he didn't think it was going to be possible to do both.

Either way he looked at things, he was setting himself up to lose. But only hesitated a second before saying, "I need to know the exact details regarding your reservation at the Blooming Bridges." From scratch. Her version without any preconceived notions. If what he was thinking was true, not only was Burley's life being ruined, by Burley himself, admittedly, but the town was going to feel painful reverberations for a while to come. Randall Burley was a member of their year-round family. So many people knew him, trusted him. Had grieved right alongside him when his wife had passed away.

Dirty hands. Not dirt from the earth, as Aimee had assumed from her dreams, but from gambling? Had Randall Burley known her father? Was that their connection between then and now? Had Aimee's father had a gambling problem?

Something like that, those dirty hands—his hands for holding the cards, the hands of cards themselves— would easily make a wife cry. And could require a man to speak softly, reassuringly, if he was trying to save his marriage...

Looking a little confused now, Aimee said, "I filled out a form on the visit Evergreen website," she told him. "It's for lodging in the area..."

"I'm familiar with it," he said, his heart sinking. "Many of the locally owned places formed a consortium and arranged with the city council to have the form added to city's official site."

And every consortium member received copies of all forms as they came in. Conceivably, all visitors filling out the form would receive lodging offers from every member who had something to offer that fit their particular specifications. It made things somewhat competitive among members in town, but it also seemed to have improved everyone's business overall as it made the process of coming to Evergreen much easier from a visitor's perspective. It was first come, first served. Whoever grabbed the reservation first was the only one who saw it. Unless the deal didn't go through, then it went back up on the portal.

"In the summertime, you're lucky if you get any offers at all," he said aloud, already seeing how things could have played out.

The couple who'd cancelled, allowing Burley to have the cabin to rent, had told him personally that they'd changed their mind because the cost was more than they'd counted on. Which hadn't raised an iota of suspicion at the time. Evergreen summer rates were steep. They had to be to support the business owners during the off season. It wasn't uncommon for someone to book a room far in advance and when it came down to figuring total cost of the trip, determine that they couldn't afford as much as they'd thought they could in terms of boarding.

But what if Burley had contacted them with a higher price than originally agreed upon? It could have been as simple as them booking over the phone and him informing them later that his prices had raised. If they hadn't already paid for the room, or put money down on it...

And Jackson could be so desperate to find something that he was grabbing at straws.

He had to grab at something.

And keep his hands off from Aimee, too.

"Mr. Burley was the only one who responded with an offer. He said he'd had a cancellation, and that it was the only cabin available in the area. I was really surprised at the price he offered. It was so reasonable..."

Again, nothing at all wrong sounding about that on the surface...and Jackson's radar was squelching off the charts. Burley would have seen her name come through on the request. Aimee spelled with two e's instead of y was memorable. If Burley had ever had reason to know the spelling. Or if Burley had known Adele's maiden name, or had kept track to know that Aimee's aunt had changed Aimee's name...if he'd had reason to keep track...like maybe he knew a three-year-old child had witnessed something horrific?

But why would Burley want her to come back if he had something to hide?

To know what she had to hide? Or if she knew anything?

"Why are you asking me this?" Aimee's frown was growing.

She was there to find the truth. How did he tell her that he thought her father had had a potentially serious gambling problem? And that he suspected, and as yet had not one iota of proof, that it had somehow gotten him into trouble that may or may not have resulted in her parents being killed.

Maybe run off the road, just as she'd almost been?

"We found out some pieces of information during our various investigations today that, when all put together, seem to be making a cohesive picture. And while I have no intention of keeping you in the dark on any of this, I'd rather speak with Kelly Chase before I reveal my theories to you, in the advent that I would lead you to discern something that might or might not be real."

"It's best that the memories return to me on their own," she agreed with a nod. But her brows were still creased. "Did you find out something about my parents? Is it bad?"

"I did not," he could truthfully assure her. "We just found some connections with other people and the mine that might come into play." Again, truthful. Without giving her more than he should.

"Randall Burley. He's a part of this, isn't he? But then, why rent me a cabin if he didn't want me around?"

"That's something we'd need to find out."

"It makes no sense, renting the place to me and then trying to drive me off as soon as I get here. But if he wanted me out of town, that would explain all the bad things happening at the cabin." He watched the expressions crossing her face, question, answer, confusing, making sense. "But then, why try to run me off the road?" she continued. "If he wanted me dead, why not just stage some accident at the cabin that would kill me?"

"One theory would be that he figured he could handle whatever he had to handle by getting you to leave. If you stayed somewhere else, he'd have no control. Getting you to his place…he knew he could run you off. But maybe first, find out why you were there at all. Find out what you know. Then, today, I question Randall Burley, and suddenly your life is in real danger. My instincts tell me that we're onto something. But again, there's no proof of anything. And Burley has an alibi for the time of your crash."

"You think Burley knew my dad?" Her eyes, wide,

her tone so hopeful, he really, really wanted to stop. "And for some reason, wanted me at his place, rather than staying somewhere else in town, so he could get me out of town?"

"I think your father and Burley might have had connections in common."

The way she was studying him…intently, seriously… if he didn't know better he'd think she was reading his mind.

"Bad connections."

He shrugged. She nodded. Stood. Said she was going to get changed out of her blood-spotted dress and get some kind of dinner on the table for him. No histrionics. No drama. Just trust and acceptance. He'd seen tears in her eyes, though.

A couple of seconds later, Jackson stood, too. Followed her to the kitchen. Got them both fresh beers.

And figured, if it was possible, he might just have fallen into a serious, monogamous kind of like.

Chapter 14

She was the one who asked if they could go out and sit with Hoot after dinner. The darkness would hide much of what was going on inside her. It had been a long hard day. While she wasn't all that sore from the accident, she was feeling more and more stiff and knew that it would probably be worse in the morning.

Stiffness, a sore finger and shoulder, she could handle. Easily. Knowing she wasn't safe hanging out in town, or being on her own, was definitely working a number on her already stretched emotional resources.

Yet, she felt safe with Jackson. A feeling that wasn't totally logical. Yeah, he was sheriff, but he wasn't Superman.

Still, if she could just be with him. Soak up a bit of good feeling before going upstairs, maybe she'd actually be able to sleep. It had sure worked the night before.

Had it been only that morning that she'd slept so late? And enjoyed the delicious burrito he'd made for her? Hard to believe that someone who could prepare such a great breakfast couldn't cook anything else.

"I'm guessing you don't want to cook," she said, sipping from her second beer, as they waited for Hoot to show up. Easy, innocuous conversation. Nothing about death—hers or her parents'. No past, no future. No squirrelly landlord, or miners or unanswered questions.

"Why do you say that?"

"You fry potatoes to perfection. Scramble eggs. Chop onions. Get just the right amount of everything else… which tells me you *can* cook. You just don't want to."

"My father made me stick at it, every morning, for an entire school year," he said after a longish moment. "Whatever I managed to do with it, we both ate. We had cold potatoes. Soggy potatoes. Burnt potatoes. Mushy eggs. Rubbery eggs. Probably blood in the onions, a time or two as well. It wasn't cooking. It was a different kind of lesson that just happened to take place in the kitchen. You stuck at something until you got it right. Don't accept mediocre out of yourself. And if, after you master it, you don't want to do it anymore, or don't like it, *then* you walk away."

"Don't quit." She'd learned some version of the same lesson somewhere along the way, too. Assuredly from Aunt Bonnie, though she had no specific recollection of having it brought home to her.

"*Don't quit* on steroids," he said with a humorless sounding chuckle.

"How old were you that year?" Fifteen? Sixteen? Rebellious teen, for sure.

"Nine."

She looked over at him, could only distinguish a partial face due to the moonshine and shadows. "Did you say nine?"

"Yeah. Nine."

"And you haven't cooked since?"

He continued to study the landscape above them, as he had the night before. "Not unless I have to."

She thought about that for a few seconds. And then, still frowning, "But you didn't know I'd be staying over until yesterday, and those things were in the refrigerator when I moved my stuff in…"

"I like the burritos."

He didn't cook anything else. But he still made the breakfast his father had forced him to perfect. Something about that touched her heart. Softly. Deeply.

Each new thing she learned about the man…there were so many parts of him—a puzzle with a million pieces—and each one, as it presented itself to her, seemed like a gift.

She itched for flowers. For her work board. Needed to express the feelings he raised in her in the only way she knew. To make a floral portrait of him. Something that would be a forever reminder of how she felt when she was with him.

Which brought up another point she'd been mentally avoiding, telling herself it didn't pertain to her because her feelings for him were only fantasy. Except that they weren't.

And, back there, inside, the hand thing, she'd told him her feelings for him existed.

She was pretty sure he'd told her not to be sorry about that.

"You have a girlfriend tucked away somewhere,

Sheriff?" Her use of the title established firm boundaries, she hoped. Was pretty sure, as she heard the lilt in her voice as she'd said the word, that it had done exactly the opposite.

Obviously, since Kelly had invited a friend up from Phoenix to hang out with her, she wasn't looking for alone time with Jackson, but that didn't mean there wasn't someone who was. Someone who was alone that evening because Jackson had to protect Aimee...

"No."

"It's fine if you do, of course. It's just, I should have asked last night, before I agreed to stay, only to insist that it's okay with her that I'm here." Shut up. Shut up. Shut up. "Not that there's any reason it shouldn't be okay with her, if there was a her, just..."

His hand covering hers on the deck chair silenced her. She didn't dare look at him. Didn't dare move forward. Didn't know how to go back.

And then his free hand lifted. He was pointing to a tree directly above them.

Barely eight feet above their heads, Hoot sat perched, his bright eyes and hooked nose pointed straight in their direction.

Giving his blessing?

Or warning Jackson to get rid of her?

Jackson used Hoot shamelessly, figuring the owl would be glad to help his friend out of a tight spot. As an immediate subject change, it worked. Beyond that, not so much. Sitting there in the dark with Aimee, in the private space and with the raptor friend he'd never shared with anyone before her, he was hard as a rock and fighting himself from taking her hand again, and leading her straight into his bedroom.

In the tie-dyed spaghetti-strap dress again, her shoulders gleamed nearly naked underneath the moon's glow.

If he was getting her signals right, and he was pretty certain he was, she'd lead the way if she knew where he stood on the matter. Completely erect.

She had the hots for him. Because he was her protector and one of the two professionals helping her through a very vulnerable emotional situation. Psychiatrists were more likely to deal with transference issues, but he'd seen it happen more than once with cops, too.

Even if it was more than that, even if she was experiencing some of the same bizarre pull toward him that he was getting from her, and he acknowledged it could be, chances were it wasn't going to end well. A little girl didn't normally mentally bury happy memories that came back to attack her in nightmare form.

And gambling…followed by death…didn't bode well, either. Any way he looked at things, he was going to be the bearer of bad news. If they were extremely lucky, he'd find details of a car accident, but he was having a hard time believing that was the case. And not just because he couldn't find any record of it.

Why would a thirty-year-old car crash be a threat to anyone? Unless it hadn't been an accident? He hadn't heard back from Leon on the Halston accident reports, but if the town wasn't any better digitized than Evergreen was, it could be later on Monday before he knew anything there.

And how could a car crash explain Aimee's nightmares of a boy/man? Or any of the memories that had been surfacing? Why wasn't there any evidence of where her parents had lived from a year after her birth until their deaths?

How was she going to feel about him if he had to tell her that her father had worked for a gambler or gotten into trouble gambling and either or both had resulted in him and his wife being killed?

And why did his body so badly need to be moving inside her? He'd always had a healthy libido, but had never had trouble keeping his desires under control. Mentally or physically. He'd learned self-control before he'd learned to walk.

Okay, probably not literally, but it sure as hell felt that way.

He played some owl calls. Talked softly to Aimee about antics he'd witnessed between the family over the past couple of years, answering her questions about the nine-to-ten-year wild owl life expectancy, about the insects and mammals upon which they typically fed and about them generally staying within the same territory year-round. Grateful for the distraction, he tried to focus on answers he knew by rote, instead of the sexy sound of her voice on the dark night air.

And then Mrs. Hoot showed up, and all he could think about was mating again.

"The great horned owls, which is what they are, mate for life," he blurted, still as part of his lesson. And not. He had mating on the brain.

Jackson held off on sipping any more from the bottle of beer he'd carried out with him. Told himself to get his ass inside. And locked in his office. Focus on the case.

And no way he was leaving her outside alone. Or forcing her to stay locked upstairs in her room. She'd asked to come out. He understood so well needing fresh air to breathe, needing nature, to help sustain calm during times of stress. He couldn't deny her that.

And couldn't turn his head in her direction when he felt her looking at him. Had his voice just sounded as strained as it had felt?

"I think I'll turn in," she said, which did suck his gaze right to her. The moonlight on the bottle of beer she held showed it half-full still.

He stood with her, only half facing her, and that same moon glow was like a spotlight on the crotch of his work pants—a thinner cotton than the jeans that would have contained him more firmly. She wasn't even pretending not to notice. Just stared straight at the evidence.

"You want some help with that discomfort, Sheriff?" She was grinning, but didn't sound like she was teasing. More like she was as emotionally charged as he felt.

"In another place and time, you bet," he told her. No point in denying what was standing right up there between them.

She didn't turn toward the door. Or even take a step away. He felt like, if he did, he'd show her how weak he really was on the matter. How little it could take to get him to change his mind. How hard he was struggling to maintain the professionalism that was mandated between them.

"I...um... I'm not a woman who takes sex lightly." Her words were near whisper. "I've actually only ever slept with a couple of men. I just...you seem to... I don't really even know you, and yet I feel..."

"Transference." The word was mostly strangled as he finally got it out. She'd only ever had two other lovers? He'd be only the third?

"No." Her frown even turned him on. She was look-

ing up at him completely without guile and yet that short
dark sassy hair gave him wild thoughts. "I felt it the first
time we met. Before you knew anything about me or
my parents. Not that that means anything, or is meant
to sway you. I just…being with you feels good. In what
seems like a purely physical, healthy way. If there even
is really such a thing. Purely physical, and healthy."

He'd had some one-night stands that offered pleasure
to both parties and left both fine to walk away without
looking back. This wasn't that.

"I know it's inappropriate for you, in your position
with the sheriff's department, to come on to me, but
what are the rules if I ask for some moments of distraction from you as long as you're mutually engaged
in the effort?"

He choked. Gulped beer. By the time he'd recovered,
she'd stepped back a pace or two. But was still there.

Jackson reached a shaking hand out to her face, ca-
ressing her jawline with his palm, igniting fires inside
him with the feel of her softer skin against his. "How
about if we table this for a day or two," he said, his internal battle probably obvious in the less than steady
tone of his voice. He'd meant to tell her no. And maybe
to add that he wished things were different.

She studied him in the semishadows, then slowly
nodded. She didn't look away. Didn't act as though she'd
been rejected. It was like she could read him. Like she
truly understood.

And he had no idea what to do with that. He'd grown
up in a universe where everyone had known him since
before he was old enough to remember them. His place
in the world, who he was, his role in life was taken for

granted. Everything was at face value. No one needed to look deeper.

He'd never been aware of wanting them to.

He wasn't turning down her offer. He was putting it on hold. That knowledge lingered, seemingly clear to both of them. Accepted by both of them.

Jackson wasn't ready to say good-night. To watch her walk away. He needed some kind of seal on the mostly silent deal they'd just made.

Not to have sex. But to revisit the idea of doing so.

Something magnanimous had just happened.

An understanding that there was mutual heat between them, that might be more, and a choice to not rush into cheapening it. An agreement to be there, in that place of mutual attraction, together.

Or some such.

He couldn't stand there and rub her face forever. Even if she'd let him. He had to drop his hand. To end that moment of their spell.

And he leaned forward, closer and closer, until his mouth was touching hers. Softly. Gently. And then... what was meant to say "Hold on" changed.

His lips opened.

Hers did, too.

He tasted her and lost thought. Let his tongue do to her mouth what his body couldn't do lower down. He took her tongue eagerly, too, when she plunged it into his mouth. Accepting the passion her lips spread to him. Answering it.

But when his hands reached for her waist, he used the grip to steady himself. To hold them apart, not pull them closer together as he lifted his mouth from hers.

"Until we revisit," he said, somewhat shakily, but firmly enough, too.

"Thank you." Her gaze was wide open. He had no idea what she was thanking him for. Kissing her? Stopping? Being willing to revisit?

"I'm going to do a perimeter check and then I'll be in. If you need anything during the night, or hear anything, make a noise, or push that speed dial I set on your phone and I'll be right there."

Her smile was tender. And still so sexy. "I know. And I will. Good night, Jackson."

His entire body felt slammed the way his name rolled off her lips. Hit by a sense of nurturing he'd never known. He was pretty sure he said good-night.

And positive that he wasn't going inside until he'd given her time to get her butt upstairs.

He wasn't going to make a mistake in what could turn out to be a turning event in his life. Meeting Aimee Barker was certainly proving to be the most unusual thing that had ever happened to him.

That didn't make it right. Or the best. His old man had once described his mother as having such a head-turning effect on him. So much so that he'd not only ignored their financial and age differences, he'd missed the part where she couldn't exist in a small town.

Aimee was also a big-city girl. And Jackson was Evergreen through and through. Everything else aside, he couldn't ignore simple facts.

He was his father's son in many ways, but he was not going to repeat the old man's mistakes.

Chapter 15

Maybe she'd made a mistake, being honest with him about her attraction to him. Aimee tried to convince herself she was just overwrought and not thinking clearly—allowing as how being nearly murdered that morning could do that to a body—but in some ways, she felt as though she'd never had as much clarity as she'd had since the crash. Seeing death right in front of you…some things gained importance, others that seemed big didn't matter at all.

Honesty mattered. Truth mattered.

Jackson needed her to be open and truthful with him. For her, that came with an all-or-nothing caveat attached, apparently. Because of having to open up so completely in the cognitive interviews.

Telling him how she felt…it felt right.

And boy had it brought with it some unexpected consequences.

He felt the same way about her?

Stunning.

To say the least.

A turn-on, for sure, but to what end? She'd allowed herself to go with the attraction because it was only fantasy, thinking there'd be no way it would ever be anything but fantasy.

So now what did she do?

Except get more and more turned on while she was staying in his home, waiting to revisit the idea of them sleeping together? Like she wouldn't spend every minute wondering if they would. And what it would be like?

Every minute that she wasn't engaged in real life, that was. Which could turn out to be far too much time since she wasn't free to roam about, to try to follow her senses and see if they took her anywhere familiar. To drive aimlessly and see if she recognized anything. Other than her interviews, and trying to relax, she wasn't sure how she was supposed to fill the next day or two.

Before the revisiting.

Jackson and his team would continue to investigate any angle he could find. Any clue she might happen to inadvertently hand to him. And go about the rest of their Evergreen sheriff business as well. With someone assigned to watching over her.

Not at all as she'd envisioned her time in Arizona.

She didn't sleep nearly as well the second night in Jackson's home, too aware of him downstairs wanting her. In the morning she gave him plenty of time to have a detail officer stationed outside the house and leave for work before exiting her room. Showered, and in a peasant-style lace-trimmed black-and-white tank that flowed to her hips with a stretchy black skirt that ended just above her knees, and black flip-flops studded with faux diamonds, she allowed that thinking of Jackson in bed had only partially kept her awake long into the night. That had been the good stuff she'd focused on every time the day's events replayed themselves, the memories replayed themselves and panic ensued. Over and over. Panic, Jackson. Panic, Jackson.

Maybe he was right and there was some transference going on. He sure seemed to be the panacea to a fear that could easily eat her alive…

Turning on the winding staircase, she was one step away from being able to see over to the floor below when she heard the doorbell ring and stopped. As far as she knew, once the officer was stationed outside, she'd be in the house alone. That was how it had been explained to her, and how it had played out, the day before.

She wasn't to answer the door, of course.

But no one was supposed to get as far as the door, either. The officer outside was supposed to make certain that didn't happen.

Hiding behind the wall, heart pounding, she pulled at the phone stuck in the waistband of her skirt, having to yank twice as the phone stuck to the sweat starting to bead on her stomach. Before she could even get the phone unlocked the door opened.

Oh, God. Was she seriously going to die?

"Sheriff? I'm sorry to bother you—I didn't know it was yer' day off…" The voice was male. Elderly sounding.

But… What?

Breath came in staggers. Jackson was still home?

She sank down fully, her butt hitting the step.

"I'm not off, just working from home this morning." That voice. Relief flooded through her. Jackson *was* home.

Weakness in every fiber of her being caused tears to form. Or the lack of strength to hold them at bay failed to prevent them.

Thank You, God.

Mother Fate.

Angels.

And anyone else who could possibly be looking over her...

Not wanting to interrupt his business, she sat there, assessing her chances of crawling back up the stairs to her room undetected. He was working.

He might not want people knowing that he had a woman staying at his place.

Evergreen sheriff business, this citizen's business with the sheriff, was out of her jurisdiction. She shouldn't hear...

Was considering staying quietly where she was, plugging her ears, when the older man spoke again.

"Your detective, the one come asking about mobile homes, she didn't seem to know much about the place she was asking about, not the owner, not nothing. She just had a copy of a permit I got to move it once. I answered her questions right, but I might know something about something she didn't ask me about. About another time I moved it. I'm sure she's right good at her job, but I don't know her, and can't say as that I really know you, either, but I knew your dad. He done me good and I'd do anything for him, same as I would you, being his son...which is why I called and insisted on speaking only to you."

Mobile home. Detective asking an old man—who might have been around thirty years ago—about a mobile home. It had to be her case…

"Mr. Landing, come in." Jackson's voice was toned down. Because he thought she was asleep upstairs? Or because he didn't want her to hear what the man had to say?

He was letting the man in the house. Aimee took that to mean that Jackson wasn't trying to hide anything from her.

The old man hadn't wanted to speak to a detective he didn't know, and would likely feel even less comfortable speaking in front of someone who wasn't even a cop. She didn't want to spook him into clamming up. And remained quietly where she was.

Did she know the man? Had he known her at three? Would she recognize him? She didn't risk exposure, and losing whatever he had to say, by trying to get a peek at him.

"My detective was looking through all of the ADOT files pertaining to mobile homes during a certain time frame. You said on the phone that you might know something more about one of them…" Jackson's voice sounded calm. Reassuring. But still commanding respect. The man reeked confidence.

And based on Evergreen's crime record, which she'd also looked up before leaving New Orleans, he ran a safe town.

"I live over in Tello," the old man said after a slight pause. She couldn't tell if they'd moved farther into the home. Their voices seemed a little more clear, a little louder. "Back thirty years ago, I ran a rig that was licensed and outfitted to move mobile homes. Some what they call manufactured homes these days, but I didn't do none that was permanently affixed.

"Sheriff Redmond, the other one, your dad, calls me one day back 'bout the time your detective was asking about. There was a single wide off the side of the road. Some bonehead tried to move it without enough axels under it and didn't tighten 'em right. Thing came right off one of 'em and there it sat, blocking the road. Nearly caused a pileup. Guy didn't have a permit. Took off. Sheriff needed me to get it out of there."

Everything felt shaky inside her. Nervous energy pulsing at mock speed.

It could be nothing to do with her, she reminded herself, hands clasped together between her knees. A mobile home mishap.

Or the accident that had killed her parents? The old man didn't know that Jackson's detective had been specifically seeking information about the possibility of a particular couple owning or renting a mobile home. Without record of paying electric, water or phone...

"Did the sheriff say where the home had come from? Who'd been hauling it?"

"Nope. I got the sense he didn't know, neither. Time I moved it before...was a old couple. In Halston. No idea what this one was about. Guy probably took off before anyone knew he'd been there. Unhooked the truck and hightailed it. Me, I think maybe it was a long haul, folks not from around here buying it." The man's voice lowered then, and Aimee had to listen hard to hear what he said next. "If I had to guess... I'd say they was from Phoenix. Maybe used it up here for summers."

"Why do you say that?"

"'Cause something happened inside it. I was told not

to go in. But there weren't nothing about any bad stuff in the news up here." Aimee could make out the words more easily again, but didn't relax even a little bit. What happened in it? Her mind screamed the question.

And she wanted to hightail it upstairs, too. She was done with eavesdropping. Wanted to stick to the business she was there to conduct. Getting her memories back.

Easing her psyche so she could get on with life.

Finding her parents? Getting to know them, again, through memories from the first three years of her life?

Yeah. She wanted that. And took a breath or two.

Her parents deserved to have their daughter know them.

The old man had been talking about the big city. Kinds of things you heard about happening there that didn't much happen "up here." "Hell, you get a fight at The Monkey Bar here and it's on our news in Tello."

Not making a sound, Aimee continued to listen.

"So's I told the sheriff, I'd get the thing off the road, and he tells me to take it to that 'ol gravel pit five miles up Easter Road. You know the one…was still part of Oracle back then…"

Part of the mine. She sat straight up, still hidden by the wall, but completely present now. Tense. Focused.

"Why would you take a mobile home to an old gravel pit?"

"That's what I asked. He just asked could I do it. I says yes, but respecting him and all like I did, I still wasn't doing it until I knows what's up. That's when he tells me they're going to burn it."

Burn it? A broken-down mobile home?

"Says that's what he was told to do when he called

the owner about the wreck. Owner didn't know nothing about it being moved—guess it was a rental—but said with the way the sheriff described the thing, he didn't want it. Sheriff knew someone at Oracle and made a deal, paid 'em some, to use that old pit for the burn. I wasn't privy to all the legal stuff. Just know what the sheriff said. And that 'cause it was an emergency, I didn't need a permit to get it off the road."

"So you moved the mobile home, we assume it was burned and that's it," Jackson summed up. She couldn't tell if the slight impatience was due to the old-timer's drawn-out way of telling the story, or by the lack of any information that could give them any proof of anything, instead of just add supposition to theory.

Like, was it just coincidence that a mobile home was set on fire on the property of the company for which her father had worked?

But with Sheriff Redmond involved, there wouldn't have been foul play. The man was iconic if you did any Evergreen research. He'd even died a hero—had earned a commendation from the governor of Arizona, or so she'd read.

"Basically, that's it," the older man said. "But with your detective asking, I figure you might be wanting to know about what happened inside the house which was why it was being burned."

"You know?" Jackson's tone changed completely. Was staccato and intense.

"Yep. Wasn't moving it otherwise. I gotta' know what I'm getting into. Couldn't have some guy up from Phoenix after me." The man's voice lowered again, and Aimee leaned forward. "Was really sad, that one was," he said. "They was burning it because of all the blood inside it.

A couple. Murder-suicide. Saddest part was, they had a little 'un. A girl. Just three years old…"

Nooooooooooo!

Throwing her hands over her ears, Aimee pressed tight, arms moving back and forth as she shook her head. *Noooooo!* It wasn't right.

It wasn't right.

Rigid inside, frozen and shaking, she closed her eyes and saw nothing but darkness.

Noooooooo! She rocked forward and back.

It wasn't them.

It wasn't them!

He wasn't right.

Every nerve in Jackson's body went on alert when he heard the sound on the stairs. A slight brushing against the wall. A small creak of wood.

Aimee must have heard. He had to get to her.

"Your dad, the sheriff, he was really concerned about that little girl. You could tell it was bothering him bad, the way he was so intent on getting the place off his road and down to the pit. Burned it that same night. I know 'cuz I was bugged, too, after talking with your dad, couldn't quit thinking about it and drove by the next day, to see the place, but there was nothing but ashes…"

Aimee.

Needed as much information as he could get for her.

And, he was first and foremost the sheriff of Evergreen County, with jurisdiction over the town of Evergreen. He had to do his job. Aimee was right there. Safe.

"Anyways…" The stooped old man in his gray beard and mostly bald head, raised his watery blue eyes to meet Jackson's gaze. "I wanted to let you know there'd

be an official report on it ifn' you want to look it up,"
he said. "I asked the sheriff for a copy so's in case anything ever came up about me moving the place without a permit I'd have my evidence why. Don't have my
copy no more, not since I sold the rig. But as I'm remembering, it was all there, 'cept the stuff about the
blood inside, where I took it or about burning it. Just
said abandoned, totaled and junked. Far as I know, the
driver hauling it was never caught."

Murder-suicide. Three-year-old girl. An untrace-
able home that would have been set up off the ground.
Any porch would have been disposed of before moving, but...

"Did you see the steps? Were they still attached?"

"Nope. There'd been a deck... I know cause I tried to
get a peek in the front door, and 'bout stabbed my hand
clear through leaning on the board left from attaching
the thing to the house, nail sticking straight out of it.
They was lining the whole front of the place."

"What color were they?"

"White. That one, with a red splotch from my hand.
Kept reminding me that house was a bloodbath." The
man shuddered. "I moved a lot of them things. I don't
remember 'em all. But I'll never forget that one."

He listened for sound behind him. Willed Aimee to
be strong. Or be upstairs in her room, unaware.

He knew better than that, though. He'd heard her.
She was there.

And should not be alone. His arms ached to hold her.
To let her know...

What? What could he let her know?

His job was to find the truth. His best gift to her

would be that. So she could get back to her life and heal. Or mourn.

"I've got one more question for you," he said, still facing Wally Landing. "Do you remember anything about how the house might have been hooked up? Any evidence of electrical wires, maybe?"

The man's gaze focused even more; he stood up straighter, like he felt more important. "I know for sure they'd been running it on propane," he said. "I could smell it coming from the hose when I was boltin' up the axels. I told the sheriff about it, said he was going to need to blow that out with an air hose before he lit fire to the thing or he'd have him some fireworks way bigger than Fourth of July."

Propane—no electric bill. And a tank that could be filled any number of places, paid for in cash. And if it had been on a well…no need for city services. No records. No bills for him to find.

Even if his theory was correct, he was still missing something. Some reason someone might not want Aimee poking around.

"That report, anything about the couple who'd been killed? Did the sheriff ever mention any names?"

"Nope. Heard him talking to one of his officers, though. Said something about John and Jane Doe who died in the house."

John and Jane Doe?

Not Adele and Mason Cooper?

Thanking the man, he asked him to call his private cell if he remembered anything else and showed him out. His mind reeling.

John and Jane Doe.

Someone had to have known who they were—if indeed the couple who'd met their tragic deaths in that home had been Aimee's parents. Someone had known who Aimee was. Had contacted her aunt. Someone had cremated the ashes—gotten them to Bonnie Barker when she came to pick up her niece.

He glanced toward the stairs. Giving Aimee a second to come down. Hoping she came down to him.

Maybe her parents hadn't actually been in a car accident. Maybe their *home* had been in an accident—axels had come off, stranding it.

Was it possible the couple had still been in the home when it had been burned? Had someone collected some of their ashes for their daughter?

And his father, being the commander who always thought he knew what was best and had the power to change his portion of the world as needed, had simply made all the evidence go away so the little girl could think her parents died in a car accident?

Was he losing his mind, reaching for something so far-fetched?

No sound from the staircase. He moved slowly toward it.

Aimee remembered her mother crying. Her father there, trying to placate. She'd run to hide. What if Adele had found out about Mason's gambling? What if the man, in debt to the point of having a bookie after him, had panicked? Killed his wife, and then himself?

And, what if, to spare the child, Jackson's father had told her only living relative that the couple had died in the accident, not before? It was just the kind of thing he'd have done.

The kind of thing Jackson would never do. The kind of thing they fought about the day his dad had been killed. Shephard's vigilante justice was for the best reasons, but societal laws existed for good reason. Following them was the only way for diverse peoples to live peacefully together.

One man didn't get to choose to play the game his way...

Rounding the corner of the staircase wall, dreading the sight he expected to see...a devastated Aimee unable to stand...he stopped short. The stairs were empty.

And her door, at the top of them, was tightly shut.

Chapter 16

"Look, my job is to help you retrieve memories that are starting to surface—that's it. Sheriff Redmond's job, his responsibility to Evergreen, is different. He has to investigate suspicious activity, to follow up with any pieces of evidence that turn up and to make his own assumptions that have nothing to do with me. And yes, he's hired me to help with a particular piece of evidence—your mind—but that's my only role. To help you remember. I have no part in, or effect on, any of the rest of his investigations. Okay?"

Sitting on the solid, shiny hardwood floor in the corner of her room at Jackson's, holding her phone to her ear, Aimee's eyes filled with tears. "Okay." She was shaking from the inside out.

"You want to tell me what's going on?" Kelly Chase's patient, reassuring voice came over the line and another wave of sweat popped on Aimee's skin. "You don't just call and ask me whether I'll be unbiased in my assessment of you, or be swayed by Jackson, without reason."

"I need to know what you honestly think about my situation. Am I kidding myself here, trusting that the images and impressions I'm getting are real?" Heat continued to suffuse her body. "Do you believe it's really possible for me to remember something that far back? Assuming it's there to remember?"

"My professional assessment is that the memory flashes you're having are real. You knew there was significance at the White house before Jackson told you there was. That's why I wanted him to take you by places of significance before you knew what they were. If you hadn't remembered anything, didn't mean you couldn't or wouldn't, but because you did, it convinces me that your mind is telling you something…"

The hot flash passed, and Aimee shivered. Her equilibrium hanging entirely on the psychiatrist's voice.

"My opinion is that you've suppressed something traumatic," Kelly continued. "And that it's coming to the surface. Traumatic events can do that."

Aimee had always been such a calm, take-it-on-the-chin type person. Where all these deep emotions were coming from…where they'd been all her life…

Even her intense attraction to Jackson that went so much deeper than body parts.

She was finding it hard to feel like herself.

"So, you don't think I'm losing my mind?" She had to be absolutely sure. Because she was trusting herself even while she was hiding things from herself.

"Of course not."

Aimee sat with a pause on the line after that. Trying

to keep at bay the panic emanating from the part of her mind that was hiding from her, while she processed what she had at hand. She wanted the memories to come. Was prepared to handle them, no matter what they brought. But she wasn't going to lose herself in the process.

"You ready to tell me what this about?" Kelly's question came at seemingly the exact right moment. "If you've remembered something…"

"No." She hugged her knees up to her chest with her free hand, trying to stem the nervous energy running through her. "And that's part of the problem. I just overheard a conversation, an elderly man speaking with Jackson. He'd come to the house." She told Kelly, in as few words as possible, about the mobile home, the bodies that had been found inside, the little girl. "Jackson's dad was there, handled the whole thing. He told the rig owner that the couple had died as the result of a murder-suicide…" She gulped as tears threatened again. Swallowed. All she could get out was little more than a whisper, "I know it's not true."

She didn't have any memory to substantiate knowing. "I have no proof. Nothing I can give him. But I'm as certain that one of my parents did not kill the other as I am that I'm sitting here talking to you. It screams from inside me that it's not true."

And she did sound a bit hard to believe. Even to herself. How could she possibly hope that a man like Jackson, one who seemed to make all of his decisions based on the information at hand, who was seeking proof to call truth, could believe her?

"Have you talked to Jackson?"

"No. He doesn't know I overheard…"

"I'd expect him to investigate what he was told, and if it's not your parents, he'll find that out."

Right. "And what if there's nothing but more dead end?" She had to get busy. No more holding the hand of her three-year-old self. "I need you to push me," she said. "What can I do to make this happen faster?"

"There's no guarantee you're ever going to remember what happened in full, Aimee. We talked about that in the beginning. You may never get more than these snippets."

She wasn't willing to accept that. "I have to know."

"And I think that need is what will get your mind to open up to you. But it's not something you can force."

Okay. She took a deep breath. Kelly's words rang true. Made total sense.

"Is there something we can do to coax the memories out safely?"

"If we knew any place you'd been, any place that could be familiar to you, it could help," Kelly said. "Like the White house. But truthfully, your mind is going to give it up when it's ready. My suggestion would be to try another cognitive interview this afternoon. Let yourself settle from this morning. Otherwise we're probably just going to frustrate you. I know it's an impossible ask, but at least try not to force things…"

"When I came here my idea was to be out and about, seeing the area, smelling the air, hoping for triggers…"

"Where do you most want to go?"

"Outside. I want to walk."

"Maybe we do a cognitive outside after lunch…"

"That sounds good."

"I'll talk to Jackson…"

He was going to tell Kelly that he suspected her parents had been victims of a murder-suicide. She didn't like the idea of them talking behind her back. Which was ludicrous since, technically, Kelly was working for him and she'd agreed to the plan.

Still…

"Can I talk to him first?"

"Of course. I'll be here and ready whenever either of you need me…"

Aimee wasn't feeling any happier when she disconnected the call. But she was calmer. And that counted for a whole lot.

With one last deep, strengthening breath, she stood up, pulled the skirt back down to her knees, straightened the hem of her blouse at her hips and opened her bedroom door, her heart catching immediately and then speeding up to double tempo.

Jackson stood, halfway up the stairs, leaning against the wall, scrolling through his phone. He turned her way as soon as the door creaked open, and the sheriff she'd expected to see there, who had his theory that he was going to prove, didn't seem present at all. Instead she met the warm, green-eyed gaze of a man who cared.

And she cared, too.

Even though she knew they were on different sides.

"You heard."

She nodded. Started slowly down the stairs. "You did, too—my conversation with Kelly?"

He shook his head. "As soon as I heard your voice, I hung out down here." He didn't know what to say to her. How to help. And had so much to do. First and foremost, get to the station and look up the report of that mobile home accident, and the emergency move permit. He could ask Sandra to do it. Or any of the other people who worked for him.

This one he wanted to do on his own.

But there he stood. Didn't go up. Or down, either.

"You knew I was there?" She nodded to just below where he stood.

"The middle of the sixth stair creaks. And you brushed against the wall." He glanced at her, and away. Feeling like he let her down, when he knew that he'd done the right thing. His job. He'd had a feeling it was going to come to him bringing bad news into her world. "You wanted the truth."

"I still want it." As she came slowly down the stairs toward him, his chest got tighter and tighter, until he finally had to head down, too. Ahead of her. She was getting too close.

Maybe he was, too.

In the living room, he turned, knowing he had to get moving. But needing to do something for her…to help her…not as a cop, but as a friend.

"We knew it probably wasn't going to be good," he started, struggling not to take her in his arms in an attempt to wrap her in comfort. He couldn't even imagine the pain she must be feeling. The shock. And more…

How did you ever come to grip with knowing that one of your parents killed the other?

If, indeed, that was how it all played out. The certainty seemed inevitable to him, but… "I need to follow up on the information Landing gave me," he said. "To verify what's true. Starting with getting a copy of that accident report…"

"My parents didn't die in a murder-suicide." Her

solid tone brought his gaze straight to her. She didn't blink.

"You remembered something?" That possibility hadn't even occurred to him. And it should have.

She shook her head. "I just know, dead certain, that that wasn't them."

His heart split at the obstinate set of her shoulders, her adamant expression. Split and bled a little. Making him damned uncomfortable.

He wasn't a bleeder. Ever.

"Let me follow the facts, Aimee."

"I'm not stopping you. In fact, I want you to, but I'm telling you that it wasn't them."

His gut told him she was wrong. He couldn't pretend otherwise. "You need to be prepared…"

Her nod cut him off midsentence. "I am prepared. And I'm not saying their deaths weren't horrible or tragic. I'm just letting you know what I know. The second I heard those words, even before I'd fully grasped them, I knew they weren't true. I was in a tailspin. I couldn't breathe. And I knew they weren't true."

His nod was out of respect.

"Kelly wants to do another cognitive, after lunch. Outside, maybe a park. Just something that gets me outside in the Evergreen air."

He needed air.

"Just because we seem to have gotten closer to solving the mystery surrounding your parents' deaths, we still don't know who's after you now," he told her. "I can't hold you hostage, but I'm going to strongly request that you allow me to continue to offer sheriff's protection until we have all the answers we need."

Like confirmation that Mason Cooper had fallen

prey to a gambling habit that had put him and his family at risk, made him desperate enough to end his life. And take his wife with him.

Had the man purposely taken his daughter to a sitter that day, knowing that when he hugged her goodbye it would be the last time he saw her?

Even with no kids, and no family prospects on the horizon, Jackson could hardly fathom that one.

Maybe Mason hadn't known. Maybe it had been a crime of passion. And maybe the dead couple in the motor home with the three-year-old girl weren't Adele and Mason Cooper.

He just didn't yet have a clue what a gambling habit from thirty years ago could have to do with Mason's daughter in town now.

There was still a critical piece missing.

One Aimee most likely held locked inside. "It seems obvious to me that whether you know something or not, someone thinks you do. Or that you could. And whatever that something is, is worth killing you over." He didn't want to scare her, but he needed her to understand the seriousness of her situation.

If for no other reason than so she'd help him keep her safe.

She nodded. And then said, "You need me to remember, Jackson. Kelly and I both think that I need to be where I feel like I need to go, to expose myself to different parts of the area, in the hopes that, like the White house, something will trigger."

She had him there. "Unfortunately all of my available personnel are busy, either helping follow up on leads from all of this, or working other things."

"I'll be careful."

She wasn't getting it. And he didn't have time to argue. "Come to the station with me now, hang out for a bit while I do what I have to do there and then I'll take you and Kelly anywhere you want to go."

It wasn't ideal. He needed to be questioning people. If Landing was out there, there were likely more just like him. People with information they had no idea was key—and dangerous. And he needed to follow up on Burley himself. Leon had already reported in that morning, letting him know that he'd gotten absolutely nothing more out of Randall Burley. The man was sticking to his story.

And didn't seem the least bit nervous or worried.

According to Leon, Burley seemed to be telling the truth.

Jackson trusted his second in command completely. Knew that Leon could read a subject as well or better than Jackson could.

Had never, ever questioned his judgment on a case before.

And still, he wanted a go at Burley himself.

Because he was making this case personal?

He couldn't dismiss the possibility.

Nor could he walk away from Aimee or finding the answers to all of the questions surrounding her.

"Fine." She'd been standing there silent for several seconds. It took him another one or two to realize she'd just capitulated. Agreeing to remain in protective custody.

"You mind if we get breakfast sent over when we get there?" he asked, eager to get her safely into the station so he could get to work.

When she shook her head, he could have pulled her into his arms and kissed her again.

Except that she'd run upstairs to get her purse.

First time a small leather shoulder bag had ever saved his life.

Chapter 17

Aimee thought it would be awkward, walking into the sheriff's office, the temporary ward of the sheriff, with so many of the people there working on a part of her life she didn't even remember. People she'd never even met, no less.

But the way everyone smiled at her as she was introduced to them individually—Deputy Sheriff Leon Goldberg, and Detective Sandra Philpot—and yet treated her with respectful distance, she felt more relaxed within a few minutes. Jackson showed her to a large conference-type room that also seemed to serve as a mini cafeteria, based on the refrigerator and vending machines at one end, and next to the sink, a counter with a coffeepot, a towel with dried mugs turned upside down on it and a sectioned-off metal tray holding various condiments, plastic tableware and napkins.

She couldn't help being a bit distracted as she caught a glimpse of his office, watched the way his staff treated him and took in the atmosphere, furnishings, rooms with which he was surrounded every day. From what he'd told her, she figured he'd pretty much grown up within the station's walls and she liked seeing all the different sides of him. Imagining him there as a child. Drawing on the chalkboard at the end of the conference room opposite the kitchen area.

Thinking about a young Jackson, taking in the daily life of the grown man, distracted her from the things that were all seemingly out of her control for the moment. Allowed her to think about something other than her parents, to feel something besides worry for them.

And for herself, too.

Why would someone want her dead? What hornets' nest from the past had she inadvertently opened up by coming to Evergreen?

And how would it all end?

She knew it made more sense for her to get the next flight out of Flagstaff and head back to New Orleans. And she knew there wasn't a chance in hell she was going to do so.

Who knew whatever beast she'd awakened wouldn't follow her to the ends of the earth to shut her up. Whoever was after her apparently hadn't been worried about a grown-up three-year-old girl. But now that she'd come to town, that grown-up girl, she'd made him afraid that she knew too much. The only way she got on with her life was to help Jackson find the truth. Past and present. Because it was pretty clear that somehow the past led to the present.

And likely that whatever her brain was trying to

show her was something someone in town didn't want her to remember.

The thought should probably have scared her. It didn't. Well, of course it did, but not enough to change her mind about finding out her buried secrets. To the contrary, it made her more determined to find them. The whole thing was making her feel more connected to her parents. She could no more walk away from that than she could go back to being who she'd been before Aunt Bonnie died.

With her earbuds in, she listened to her favorite soft pop station, going through work email on her phone, for the first half hour or so. Kelly had told her that the best way to help herself remember was to relax, to let her mind rest and her emotions recuperate from the morning's upset, and so, in preparation for the afternoon interview, she did what she could to give herself downtime.

Right up until there was a knock at the door and Sandra, Evergreen's only detective, popped her head in. "Sheriff's got a guy in the interview room. Alonzo Gillum. He agreed to come in with a deputy who was in Halston talking to people who were known to take part in Randall Burley's gambling games back in the day. They all happened in the back of a bar that Burley used to own. Anyway, this guy says he knew your father, that they were friends for a bit. Sheriff said I can bring you to the observation room if you'd like to listen in."

Heart pounding she was up so fast, she tipped backward the chair she'd been sitting in. "He really knew my dad?" she asked the fortyish woman who, in her navy suit with a gun at her waist, still just seemed kind.

Strong. Capable. And yet... Sandra Philpot didn't appear to have lost the ability to exude compassion.

The dichotomy made Aimee itch for her workroom. A new project board. Sunflowers, to start with...

The thought took her to the hallway, and a door Sandra was showing her through. And then, as she looked in the one way mirror, her heart was pounding again.

The man sitting with his back to her was Jackson—there was just no doubting that one. She felt like she'd know him with her eyes closed, as irrational as that seemed seeing she'd only known him going on four days. And the man seated facing her...

He was sixtyish, gray hair, but still a lot of it, a weathered tan face and...kind eyes. His cheeks were broad, lips full, healthy looking. Big broad shoulders. Strong shoulders.

Miners' shoulders. The words came to mind without forethought. No one had said the man worked with her father.

And how would she know what a miner's shoulders looked like?

And yet, if she was to trust her impressions, she did know. Miners had big strong shoulders in Aimee's world.

The men's lips were moving, but she couldn't hear a thing. She took the chair Sandra pointed to, center, front row of two. The detective tapped on the glass, and she heard Jackson say, "Mason's daughter is there now, listening in."

The man glanced straight toward her, and even though she knew that he couldn't see her, she felt connected to him in an odd, comforting kind of way.

Ridiculous. He could have been a bookie. Could be the one after her...

"I'd like to tell her that I knew her dad, that I was friends with him, can I do that?"

"You just did," Jackson's voice was loud and clear—bringing an entirely different kind of comfort, and discomfort, too. She wanted to be naked with Jackson.

Apparently, any time of the day or night. No matter whatever else might be going on.

Or anytime she needed him to pull her back from the brink of feeling like a lost girl who'd never have a real life.

Panic started to spread in fingers across her stomach, and she looked at the stranger again. Let herself open up to whatever he had to say.

Jackson asked where Alonzo met her father. She wasn't the least bit surprised to hear that it had been at Oracle. That they'd worked together every day for more than four years. He talked about how he and her father, both single at the time, had hit the bar every night, and eventually started playing cards.

Aimee could feel Sandra's gaze on her, assessing? Aimee could hardly breathe, but she made herself sit there. Made herself listen. Even while it felt like the skin on her face was going to crack, and the muscles in her jaw were going to bust.

"Mason was a bit of a genius," Alonzo said. "Didn't like to hear that, but, there wasn't any denying it. The man could count cards like...what was the movie... something about rain?"

"Rain Man." Aimee said the words. Jackson did, too. His voice merging with hers in the little space she shared with Sandra.

"So he won a lot."

"I'll say."

"Piss some guys off?"

"Yeah."

"Enough to want to kill him?"

Clutching her hands together between her knees, Aimee leaned forward. Jackson knew how to get down to it.

"I wouldn't know about that." Alonzo shrugged. "Even if he did, nothing came of it. He got out of it."

"Out of what?"

"The game. Gambling. The bar. All of it."

"Got out?"

"He met a woman… Adele…and that was it. The man was gaga over her. Never seen anything like it in my life."

Aimee smiled. Tears sprang to her eyes. And Jackson said, "Did that piss you off? The way he just cut out like that?" The question came at her from left field, and her gaze shot to Alonzo.

Jackson thought this man had something to do with whatever bad was going on?

"He looks at everyone," Sandra said. "Takes nothing for granted. That's what makes him such a good cop."

"So he doesn't really think Alonzo's a bad guy?"

"I wouldn't dare guess." The woman seemed a bit bemused. "Jackson's another smart one. You never know exactly what he's thinking, but he generally gets where he's headed. Not always the first time out. And maybe not in the way you'd expect. But he'll get there…"

Good to know.

And she'd already figured that out on her own.

Still, good to know.

Chin jutting, Alonzo was silent for a long pause, and then, with a bit of a shake of the head, he gave a small grin and sat forward. "Truth was, I was pissed at first. How did a guy just get all head over heels like that and cut out on his buddies? Then I saw him with Adele and all I could think about was what a lucky son of a gun he was. Truth is, he got me thinking about my own life, about making changes. If not for him, I'd probably be a homeless drunk by now. But instead, I've got a wife I still adore, two kids, three grandkids and another on the way."

Aimee teared up again. This time she had to wipe her cheeks, too. Pray God her dad would have been as happy to be sitting at a table talking about her and her mom that way.

"So things ended well between you?"

"Pretty much."

"Mind explaining that?"

"A couple of years before you're telling me he died in that accident…" He looked up at the window for the first time since he'd first known she was there. "I'm sorry for what's to come," he said, obviously addressing her.

Aimee nodded, clutched the edges of her chair.

"The little one was seven months old, sitting up, getting teeth, rolling over, starting to crawl and Adele had a bad bout, missing her sister and home. She wanted Mason to go with her to New Orleans, but he wouldn't go. She went without him. And he called me to meet him at the bar…"

No. The story could end now.

They could all go home.

Except that she couldn't. The world outside protection wasn't safe for her now and she had to know why.

"I'd already met my Mary Elise, but he was my best bud—I had to go. I was moving to Globe, got a job in the Miami Mine up there. Even though I'd still be in Arizona, I knew we wouldn't be seeing each other again any time soon. We sat and drank a beer. Then two. He kept asking what if she didn't come back? I told him he should call her. Offer to fly out. I reminded him that he'd do anything for that baby girl of theirs, but he just kept saying he'd never make them happy in New Orleans. He got tense in the city. Was in a bad mood all the time. Drank too much. The talk went around and around, just like that. Eventually he got drunk enough that when I said I had to get home—Mary Elise had called the bar to say she'd come get me if I'd had too much to drink, which I hadn't—I offered to take him home. He said no—he was going to hang around, maybe get in on a game of cards. We'd been away from the game a couple of years by then. Didn't even know if any of the old guys were still playing. I tried to talk him out of it, but he wouldn't leave with me."

"He got back into cards, then?"

Alonzo shook his head. "He played that night. But he called late the next afternoon, from the Flagstaff airport, to thank me for being a good friend. Said he'd won big, but left the game right after. Just took his winnings and left. Was home way before dawn, which we'd never been when we played in the past, and said he wasn't ever going back. He also told me that he'd stopped at a pay phone and called Adele on the way home, it would've been six or seven in the morning her time, and I thought it was pretty ballsy of him to wake up the household that way, but Adele had been relieved to hear from him. She'd realized that she belonged with him in Arizona

and had already bought a ticket home and needed him
to get her from the airport that next night. He was waiting for her plane when he called me."

Aimee didn't even bother to wipe at the tears stream-
ing down her cheeks. She just let them fall. Caught in
a maelstrom of conflicting emotions, all she could do
was feel.

She'd been in that story. Had seen pictures of herself and her mom taken that weekend at Aunt Bonnie's.
Had heard how the visit had only been for a night. How
badly that had hurt Aunt Bonnie. How much her aunt
had missed her mom.

And now she knew the other side of the story, too.

It mattered just as much.

Maybe even more.

Jackson had given her this. It felt right that it was
him, opening her world to her. Right that he was the
one helping her.

It felt right to open her heart to him.

Maybe, even, to love him.

Jackson purposely avoided Aimee as he left the interrogation room, leaving Sandra to introduce Alonzo
to his friend's grown daughter. He had too much to do
in too little time and headed straight back to his office.

He was growing more deeply concerned about who
could be after her. The world of illegal gambling was
one of the most dangerous because of the huge sums of
money involved. Had Mason won a huge sum that night,
and then left the table before the game was done, before giving the other players a chance to win back their
losses? Did whoever had lost that money think Aimee
knew where it was and had come looking for it? Was

Alonzo Gillum telling the truth? Or had he been one of the players that night who'd been bilked?

And he was becoming too emotionally attached to the subject needing his protection. Subject. Who was he kidding? The woman was inside him. Deeper than anyone ever had been. In four days. Made no sense. Wasn't logical. Had no provable basis.

Boded no future. Adele and his mother, Celeste, had both struggled to live with their men in remote little Evergreen. As would Aimee. Yes, Adele had returned, but there'd been a marked difference in her situation in that she'd already been living in Evergreen before she'd met Mason. Maybe she hadn't expected to stay permanently, but she'd chosen the way of life. Celeste and Aimee had not. They were both city women through and through.

And… Aimee thought he was going to prove that her parents hadn't died as perpetrator and victim of a murder-suicide, when he was finding more proof they had. She wanted him to believe her inner sense that it wasn't them, and his investigation was leading him to believe it was. He could very well lose her trust and regard over that. He'd seen it happen in the past. People blaming the messenger.

The father she was "meeting," and falling in love with, was not who she wanted him to be, and Jackson had to prove it. And use her to do it.

Dr. Chase had warned him that Aimee's memories would be more likely to come, and be less tainted, if he didn't feed her information in hopes of triggering something, but rather, waited for it to come out of her on its own. So he didn't share with her that he'd found the accident report regarding the mobile home Landing had moved. Having the actual date made it a given. The fact that it had been a mobile home, not a motor vehicle, and not resulting in fatalities, narrowed his search down to one pretty quickly.

The owner of the home, dead for fifteen years with no known survivors, had proved nothing. Except that he'd been from Halston, too. Everything seemed to be leading back to that town where Burley had run his illegal games of poker.

His father's notes had been the clincher. Because they'd been Shephard Redmond through and through. A handwritten note, taped to the inside of the file, stated that he'd told the family of the little girl that her parents had been killed in an accident. They'd been dead before the accident. He'd wanted to spare her the news of the murder-suicide. Hadn't wanted her growing up with that on her. Had stated that since there was only one surviving adult and the child, telling her what he had had been merciful. Old Shep's vigilante justice. And just like the old man to make a record of what he'd done, too. He'd believed himself the quintessential lawman. The Old West Marshal Dillon variety from the TV shows his father had watched, depicting the West in the 1800s.

And to preserve the memory of her parents, he'd sent cremated remains—no account of whether or not the bodies had been formally cremated at a mortuary—and listed them as Jane and John Doe. He'd lifted them right out of the picture. Neat and clean. They'd lived in a mobile home they didn't own out in nature somewhere in the area—a very common practice of those who liked rugged small mountain town living. There'd been no mention of the murder weapon, but Jackson figured his dad had let that burn up in the fire. And though there were no notes about anyone asking questions, Jackson was certain that if anyone *had* asked about the young couple, Shephard would have said they were killed in an accident. His father always kept his story straight. And who was hurt by the tweaking his father had done? The couple was dead. Apparently the old man had seen to their things being sold, since Aimee got a college fund out of monies sent to her aunt. And no one was the wiser.

Justice had been served.

Except…it hadn't been. Didn't Adele Cooper deserve to have her story told?

And what about their daughter? Jackson's dread intensified with every piece of evidence that was added to the stack he was compiling. Those memories that Aimee had quashed…she'd seen the murder. He'd bet his life on it. She'd seen her father kill her mother. And maybe had seen him kill himself, too.

No wonder she'd buried the memories so deeply inside.

If there was a way to convince her to leave them there, Jackson would be all over it at that point. There was no good going to be served by the nightmare that she was trying to unleash. He was convinced they knew what they needed to know regarding her parents. Except that she was in danger.

And the only way to protect her was to keep pushing forward.

In spite of the fact that doing so was likely going to leave her emotionally scarred for life.

Chapter 18

Aimee wanted to accept Alonzo Gillum's invitation to get coffee with him, but Jackson immediately and adamantly vetoed the idea, through Sandra. Aimee had to settle for exchanging contact information with the man, and she promised to try to travel over to Globe and visit him and his wife before she left for home. Mary Elise had never met Mason Cooper, but she credited him with giving her her husband as Mason had shown Alonzo what he wanted out of life.

Funny how things worked. Mason had given Alonzo his family and now Alonzo was returning a piece of her father to her.

She'd only been back in the conference room, back to her emails, for about twenty minutes before a text came through on her phone, the number showing as unknown.

I knew your parents and have information. I can't come forward without severe risk to me and my family. Come out the back door that's down the little hall from the file room across from the restroom. It's exit only. I'll find you. This might be our only chance to meet unde-tected. If you don't come alone, I won't show myself. I'll wait half an hour.

She read. Reread. Stood. Read again. Looked around. She wasn't a prisoner. She could go to the restroom un-attached. Had already done so. Twice.

How did anyone in Evergreen know her? Before she'd even completed the mental question, she knew how anyone in town who wanted her phone number could have it. She'd left it at more than half a dozen shops, along with business cards, inviting owners to pass it on to anyone who might be interested in speak-ing with her about her shop, or art in general.

Stomach roiling, she told herself to relax, to act nat-urally, as she made the trek to the bathroom for a third time. The station wasn't large, and everyone was ei-ther out or busy—a lot of them because of her—and she'd had that particular hallway to herself each time. She knew the little hallway beyond, it, too, though she hadn't actually been down there.

Turning the corner she saw the commercial utility door at the end, clearly marked Exit Only. And since no one could enter through it, there was no one man-ning it. All she had to do was push the bar on the door and she'd be...

Breaking Jackson's trust. Such a stupid thing to think about at that moment, but walking out that door didn't feel right. Not without him aware. She had half an hour to get herself free and outside undetected. Easily enough time for Jackson to arrange for someone to be outside, watching her back.

Unless he refused to let her go at all.

She'd go anyway.

He'd follow behind her and her contact would quietly slip away. She'd never know who it was or what they knew about her parents.

She had to go.

Jackson could trace the phone. Unless it was a burner. Chances were, it was. The clandestine meeting. A family at risk.

She'd gotten so much from Alonzo that morning. A piece of her past that felt vital to her. Something she'd never have had if he hadn't come forward. And now a second person wanted to share with her. How could she not go?

Why was she hesitating?

A headache was coming on and Aimee knew that she had to get out that door or risk someone coming looking for her.

She had to go.

But not without telling Jackson, first. Time was ticking. Five of her minutes were gone. Turning, she made her way quickly to the sheriff's private office, one hallway over. His door open, he was sitting at his desk, focused on a monitor in front of him. She gave a light rap, stepped in and shut the door behind her. Put her phone, text message on the screen, in front of him.

He read. Stood. Picked up his office phone. Demanded an immediate trace on the number. Dropped the phone back in its cradle and came around the desk.

"You did the right thing, coming to me. I'll get people out there, combing the area…"

"Wait, no." She stood in front of him. "I'm going, Jackson. I can't not go. And I have to go alone. I just… maybe you'd want people in the area, is all…"

"I can't stop you from going outside," he said, his tone different than anything she'd heard before. Implacable. "But there's no way in hell I'm sending you out there alone."

She felt frustrated, mostly with herself for letting her feelings for him get in the way of what she'd known she should do—like she couldn't think on her own anymore. "You read the message! You or anyone else goes out there with me, we're never going to know who this is or what they know…"

"Assuming this is anyone who knows anything." His tone didn't change. He wasn't getting all het up like she was. If anything, he was the most calm she'd ever seen him.

"I'm guessing you gave Alonzo your number." His next statement brought her up short.

"Yeah."

"And he's in the area."

"Yeah."

"He wanted you to leave alone with him."

So he thought Alonzo had more to tell her. All the more reason for her to get out there and find out what it was.

"Did it occur to you that he could have been lying in there, Aimee? That maybe he *was* at that game the night he described? That he was the one who lost and was robbed of a chance to get his winnings back?"

No. It hadn't. She didn't believe it. But she wasn't

sure he was wrong, either. In the space of time it took her to have the thought, he was one the phone, ordering a sweep of the area around the back door of the station, paying close attention to the dumpster and anywhere else something could be hidden.

Something? As in…a detonation device?

Blood draining from her face, she stood straight, facing him, wondering if he'd gone off the deep end. Or if she had.

They were in a remote, relatively crime-free mountain town, not some adrenaline-pumping crime show. She might have said as much to Jackson, but he was too busy running an emergency sweep of the station, handing out orders more quickly than she could keep up with them. She started to leave the room, to give him his privacy and space to work, but he glanced at her and shook his head.

Because she respected him, because she'd agreed to allow him to protect her, because she didn't think it wise to disobey a direct order from the sheriff, she remained standing a couple of feet from the door.

And was still standing there when an officer, wearing protective gear, came to the door ten minutes later. "We got it, Sheriff. Simple explosive. Wouldn't have done much damage, except to the person walking out that door…"

Her knees went weak. Her mind numb.

Had she opened the door…

But she hadn't.

Something had told her to come to Jackson.

She was fine.

And someone absolutely wanted her dead.

Aimee didn't know how she remained standing,

seemingly calm and capable, while Jackson finished talking with his officer. Wasn't even sure what he'd last said as he closed the door behind the man. What she did know was that when he walked toward her, she needed to feel him up against her. Needed him to be real.

Needed to feel something good. Something that made sense. Something that could blot the horror her life had become. Putting her arms around his neck, she pressed her shaking body to his and held on.

Everything else be damned.

From the second she'd thrown her arms around him, Jackson had had one goal—to get Aimee Barker out of Evergreen as soon as possible. First and foremost, to keep her alive. And a close second after that, so he wouldn't beg her to stay.

Even in the midst of all that was going on—the explosive to send to Forensics in Flagstaff, the investigation branching out in various fingers, the fact that they were in his office—as soon as he'd felt her body touch his, his penis had sprung to full and complete attention.

He wanted the woman like none other. With more than just passion.

In a way he neither recognized nor understood.

He didn't like what he couldn't understand. And he most certainly didn't like the idea of being outdoors with her that afternoon.

It wasn't smart. Wasn't safe. And Kelly felt, after a talk with Aimee over lunch, that taking her out to a property like Boyd Evergreen's, deserted, but open with desert grass and some trees, was, at that point, their best hope for encouraging Aimee's psyche to let go of whatever it was holding on to. Kelly's plan included throwing a rope over a branch, making a swing like the one in Aimee's vision, for Aimee to sit in for a cognitive interview. There were likely other things that would be familiar to her—like the smell of cooking shrimp—but they didn't know what they were. She had a longing to be outside. Had had it since before coming to town. Kelly felt strongly that they had to honor that.

To listen to Aimee's instincts.

He and Kelly didn't speak about the fact that Aimee didn't believe her parents were murder-suicide victims, in spite of his evidence—except to acknowledge that his evidence was strong enough to convince him they were on the right path. And a brief mention that Aimee felt strongly that he was wrong.

Tense as hell, he stood just off to the right of the tree they'd chosen on some property owned by one of his officers. The perimeter of which was as easily managed and guarded as any that had been at their disposal on quick notice and with as little need for explanation as possible.

Though it was just him, Kelly and Aimee in sight, six armed men and women were hidden and keeping them and their areas under surveillance, while Leon, on radio, was watching from the air—as high up as he could get in the tallest tree he could find to climb.

Perhaps it was overkill. Jackson didn't much care. He wasn't going to lose a summer visitor that day.

Aimee had been gently swinging for ten minutes or so, while Kelly tried to take her back to the first day she'd come to town, to the tree she'd seen, the memory she'd had. As far as Jackson could tell, to no avail. While each second they were out there was another tick on his nerves.

It was almost a relief when Kelly motioned to him. He'd rather get the rope down and get out of there with nothing, than hang around out in the open with a killer on the loose.

Aimee was still sitting on the rope, swinging gently. As he got closer he noticed that, not only were her eyes closed, but her fingers were white where they were gripping the rope.

"Get behind her," Kelly said softly, leaning in to speak at his shoulder. "Start pushing her, gently at first, but when I give the sign, push her as high as you safely can."

He wanted them out of there, but touching Aimee… that calmed him, some. Being close enough to grab her off the rope and shield her with his body if need be helped, too. He'd only pushed her twice when Kelly gave the signal and with a full step into the movement, he sent her sailing up until her face was even with the branches that were holding her. Even with the sky.

"Open your eyes," Kelly said, just before Aimee peaked the second time. Watching Kelly for direction, he continued to push, watching Aimee's sassy short hair standing upright in the wind, settling down, then standing up again.

Maybe, once they got through this, she'd have an extra day before she left and they could drive out to the state park. He'd love to push her on a swing for real. And then, moving in front of it, slow it down, and lean in to kiss her with the air that moved her hair still touching her skin…

Movement to the left caught his peripheral vision. His focus, instant and 100 percent, caught the hummingbird hovering several yards away, feeding at a wild honeysuckle. And a reminder to keep his mind fully on his surroundings.

"Stop." It was the first word Aimee had said since he'd approached. And she was brooking no argument. Taking hold of both sides of the rope, slightly above her hands, ready to catch her if she lost balance, he brought the makeshift swing to a complete stop. Stood there a moment longer in case she needed to rest back against him.

He'd been far enough away not to overhear the conversation between Aimee and Kelly for the majority of their time out there. In light of their differing opinions on the cause of her parents' deaths, he hadn't wanted his presence to make Aimee defensive, or to shut her down in any way.

He had no idea what had transpired. What kind of state she might be in.

What she had or had not remembered.

She sat a minute, but didn't lean on him. Still, he held the rope until she vacated the swing and Kelly nodded toward the car. And then, with an arm up waving Officer Michaels in to retrieve the rope off his tree, he quickly ushered Kelly and Aimee back to his SUV.

He was turning around in the hard desert dirt, ready to gun it out of there and to the road when Aimee said, "I saw his face." She and Kelly were both in the back, and he glanced in the rearview mirror, catching both of their expressions. Kelly intent, and Aimee clearly agitated.

"Whose face?" He had to ask.

"The boy man in my dreams."

"We've been going over and over that memory she

had the first day she got here, and trying to tie it to the nightmares," Kelly said, a doctor discussing a patient.

"You think you could describe it to a sketch artist?" he asked Aimee. They'd have to head to Flagstaff for that, but then he'd be there to hear about the explosive device that was already being delivered to the lab there.

And he could get Aimee out of town, too.

"Yeah," she said. "But I'd rather do what we kind of talked about earlier, and look at high school yearbook pictures while it's still fresh in my mind. With a sketch artist, I don't know…"

"I agree with her," Kelly said. "She should look at the yearbooks."

And so she would. One quick call and he had four years of the *Evergreen Chronicle*—the name of his high school yearbook—being delivered to his house.

What this boy, her nightmare, had to do with her being in danger, he didn't know. Had pretty much figured the nameless boy was a stand-in for a part of her father she wanted to remember—that the harsh voice was the father she'd seen in the end. The violent man. But if she'd remembered a face…he had to know whose face it was. The son of a gambler?

Or the babysitter she'd been left with that final day?

Jackson was a man who made decisions based on facts. Following protocol. And a good cop followed every lead, whether his instincts told him it was necessary or not.

He was also a guy who needed a woman to find the peace she was seeking, even if it took her away from him.

Chapter 19

"That's him." The second Aimee saw the photo, she knew. Without doubt. "He looked different to me," she said. "In my memory his expression was different, his face maybe a little heavier, but that's definitely him. I remember him less...serious looking. More...innocent, maybe. I don't know, but that's him."

She was talking to Kelly who was sitting next to her on the couch in Jackson's living room. But as she spoke, he came in from the downstairs office via a small hall off the kitchen.

"Who is it?"

Kelly Chase was looking up at him. Aimee intercepted a look she didn't understand.

A warning from Kelly to him?

What kind of warning? That she was off her rocker and had to be humored?

Or something more serious...

Looking back at the book, she read the name in line off to the side of the row of photos. Second photo, second name in the list to the left.

Grayson Evergreen.

It meant nothing to her three-year-old self. The adult her sat up straight. Rigid.

Evergreen. The property she'd been trespassing on her first day in town.

She didn't want to say the name. Jackson wasn't going to like it.

He came up beside the arm of the couch, leaned over to see where she was pointing. "Gray?" he asked, frowning as he shook his head.

And while she'd meant to worry about his reaction, her mind took another route. "Gay Gay," she said. Checked herself. And said it again. "Gay Gay."

Looking at Kelly, and then up at Jackson, she told them, "That's what I used to call him. Gay Gay. He'd play with me." And like a curtain being lifted to show a full stage behind it, she sat there, watching snippets of memories play across her mind's eye. "He used to play with me," she repeated.

She remembered a ball. It was soft and they'd toss it. He'd laughed really loud one time when she'd actually caught it. She remembered him running and telling her to catch him. Remembered running after him, laughing, falling and getting back up to run some more. And the swing. He'd pushed her high and her father had yelled at him.

He'd taken her across a field to see something. She'd fallen, was starting to roll and then it was straight down. He'd dived after her. Caught her. His hands were dirty.

And he was crying…

And then, just like a curtain coming down, the memories stopped. Just stopped with those dirty hands.

She was looking at Kelly. Didn't want to look at Jackson. Was only just mentally acknowledging that she'd been talking out loud as she'd watched her little internal theater production.

"He cried a lot," she said then, and made herself peek up at Jackson. His gaze sharp, he was watching her. Taking it all in. It was like she could see his mind spinning, trying to make sense of what she was telling him.

She hoped to God he could, because she sure as hell couldn't.

"What that has to do with anything..." Aimee said.

"We've known all along that what you're trying to remember might have nothing to do with the deaths of your parents." Kelly's voice was calm. Reassuring. Kind.

"But someone's after me. They think I know something..."

"That doesn't mean you do."

Jackson sat down beside her, and she scooted over to make more room for him. Wanting him there. And needing her space, too.

Elbows on his knees, he leaned forward and looked back at her. "Grayson Evergreen was in a car accident a couple of years before your parents were killed. He suffered severe head trauma, and the brain damage was permanent. He has the mind of a seven-year-old boy."

"Has?" Kelly asked. "He's still around?"

"In an institution," Jackson said. "I thought since the time of the accident, but I was just a baby when it happened. Could be he was home, around town, until he turned eighteen. That's about the time his dad died. His older brother, Boyd, is pretty much besotted with him. Visits him diligently, at least three times a week."

"So he's close by?" Kelly again. Aimee just sat there, taking it in. Trying to make sense of what she knew, coupled with what was. Trying to find herself and a world that wasn't cockeyed.

"Until recently. A place about thirty miles from here, twenty acres of mountain and desert where he could hike and fish. But the place was damaged in a brush fire recently, and he's been sent to a facility in Phoenix. That's where Boyd is now. With Gray in Phoenix. Gray's not doing well there, and Boyd's been trying like hell to find another place where he'll be happy."

"When I knew him…it was already after the accident," Aimee finally found her voice. "That's why he seemed like a boy man to me. He had the mind of a boy, but the body of an older teenager."

At least something made sense.

But the rest of it?

Could it be that she'd come to town thinking she'd find out some huge thing about her parents, something dark that had been buried, only to find Grayson Evergreen, her mom laughing over bubbles, and crying over dirty hands?

Dirty hands.

"That's what my mom was crying about," she said slowly as more realization dawned. "The dirty hands. They were Gay Gay's. I'm sorry, Grayson's. From when I fell and he saved me…" She shook her head. "But that doesn't make sense. Why would my mother be upset that he'd saved me?"

"Maybe she was upset that your father had you living

wherever you were, because it was too close to places where you could wander and get hurt," Kelly offered.

Maybe. Made sense. Didn't click. But then, she'd been three. What had she known, really?

"But how would Grayson Evergreen and Aimee have known each other?" Jackson said, glancing between the two of them.

"It's possible that they were at the same sitter's," Kelly said. "If Grayson had the mind of a young boy, chances are good he wouldn't have been left alone. You said his father was a widower, right?"

"Right."

"So maybe, after the accident, he took Grayson to a sitter, and Aimee was one of the kids there."

Aimee nodded. "That feels right," she said. "I have no memory of a babysitter, but it seems like Grayson was only around to play with me. That's the sense I have. He was a playmate."

"Maybe Adele *was* the sitter," Kelly's voice gained momentum. "There's no record of your mom's nursing career after you were born," she told Aimee. "So maybe, like some moms, she took in other kids to help pay bills. And because she was a trained medical professional, the Evergreens chose her as their sitter."

Aimee wanted that to be the case. It made sense. "It would explain the swing incident, with my dad there."

"I'll give Boyd a call." Jackson stood, pulling out his phone. And a few seconds later, left a message asking the older man to call him as soon as he could.

So that was it, then. Her memories…they'd been little more than normal childhood snippets. That she'd probably buried because of the trauma of losing her parents in the car accident.

But…

"We still don't know why someone's after me now," she reminded them all.

"You said you got money from your parents' deaths, right?" Jackson started pointing his finger—not at them, just pointing. "I knew about it, of course, but...where did it come from? There wouldn't have been any insurance settlement. Not with a murder-suicide. And what they owned would have been destroyed in that mobile home and the fire. Mason's truck was a beater. He owned it free and clear, but it wouldn't have been worth much. Adele's car was repossessed. So where did the money come from that paid for Aimee's college?"

The question seemed to be almost rhetorical as he didn't wait for an answer before he continued. "There's something about that poker game, and it's tied to Aimee. And maybe to wherever that money came from," Jackson said, his phone still in hand. "It's possible that there's a lot more of it. That someone is living off it. And doesn't want you to find that out."

"That last game you talked about, the one you found out about this morning." Kelly was looking at Aimee now. "Mason won big and then walked out." She looked up to Jackson. "Maybe someone felt cheated, lost way more than he could afford to lose, put the wager out there because even if he lost, the night was young and he'd have a chance to win it back. Maybe that someone was threatening Adele and Aimee unless Mason paid it back," Kelly said. She turned again to Aimee. "You remember dirty hands, and your mom crying about them, but it could be that your parents were fighting because of the gambling, because of the jeopardy it put you all in. She could have said she was taking you and moving back to New Orleans."

"And that could be what drove your father to violence, and then suicide."

"No!" She spoke far too loudly. Stood, too. Ready to go head to head with him. Until Kelly's gentle touch at her wrist pulled her back down to the couch.

"I know he didn't kill my mother, or himself," she said directly to the psychiatrist.

"It's possible you do," the woman acknowledged. "And it's also possible that your mind refuses to accept something it can't process. You were three. You might have seen it. As hard as this is, it's something we need to consider…"

She didn't want to consider it. Didn't want to be the daughter of a murderer. Didn't want to know that the man her mother had left Aunt Bonnie to come back to had killed her.

She didn't want to. Didn't want to.

Didn't want to.

Like a three year old didn't want to eat her peas. Or go to bed.

Didn't matter the reasons why she should.

She didn't want to.

But when she looked back in her psyche for any memories that would disprove the theory, her mind went blank.

If she couldn't give Jackson an alternative truth, she couldn't blame him for believing what the facts seemed to be telling him.

Except she did.

She also knew, he could be right.

The text to Aimee that morning had indeed come from a burner phone. The lab in Flagstaff had a fingerprint from the explosive at the back door of the sheriff's office. Unfortunately, there were no matches in the databases Jackson had access to. Randall Burley's prints were in the database, though. Which meant he wasn't the one who'd touched the incendiary device.

Calling Leon out to guard the house after Kelly left, Jackson went straight to visit Burley. Boyd Evergreen would get back to him when he could, but other than confirming the babysitter theory, or filling in some other blank as to how Gray and Aimee would have played together, he was at peace with that part of the investigation. Adele and Mason had somehow known Gray and through that had given Bonnie the Evergreen address that Aimee had found among her aunt's things.

Why they'd done that, why Bonnie had kept it, was anybody's guess. And unless Boyd knew, would probably always remain a mystery.

Aimee was getting most of the answers she'd come for. The last piece was to find out what Pandora's box she'd opened by coming to town and finding out what she'd released. His instincts were telling him that Randall Burley was the key. He had to get the man to come clean. They'd never found the truck that had tried to run Aimee off the road. Could have been stolen for all they knew. It'd probably been pushed off a mountain someplace.

He planned to use the bomb to squeeze Burley. He knew Randall hadn't planted it, but Burley didn't know he knew that. And going down for attempting to blow up a sheriff department could put him away for life.

He walked into the man's small office at Blooming Bridges, hearing him in the residence behind the small room, and rang the bell. Chewing and wiping his hands on a napkin, Burley came out almost at once.

"Sheriff Redmond. I told Leon, I don't know anything about…"

"Can it, Burley. We know that you ran an illegal poker game in the back of the bar in Halston for years."

He gave the guy a smidgeon of credit for not immediately denying the assertion. Instead, Burley gave one more slow wipe on the napkin, dropped it on the counter that separated him from the small space just inside the door and remained silent as he looked at Jackson.

Jackson was fine with a moment or two to size each other up. He needed the older man to know that he'd met his match. Stood firm on that ground.

"So I ran a game," the man finally said, and Jackson figured he had him. "It was years ago. I got out of that racket and have no part in anything to do with gambling. Don't even let the casino bus stop here to pick up or drop off guests."

Something Jackson already knew.

Leaning an arm on the counter, Jackson said, "You know, the snake, the spider, even the sprinkler system… all that is minor stuff…pranks, really." The man's expression didn't change, but Jackson wasn't discouraged. He continued with, "and driving bad…well that could be argued in court with some success as a mere traffic violation, but when you plant an incendiary device outside the door of a sheriff's offices and then lure someone to walk out on top of it…now we're talking premeditated murder." Burley's face turned red. "With aggravators because you've attempted to blow up a sheriff's office…" Jackson added.

"Now wait just a minute!" Burley's spit hit Jackson's hand as the man raised his voice. "I ran a poker game. I got nothing to do with no murder and the only thing I know about that explosion at the sheriff's office is what people are saying…that it looks like someone lured that woman, Aimee Barker, out there."

"Yeah, but, you see, it's not going to look that way to a judge." Jackson went in for the kill without a smidgeon of guilt. Or compassion, either. Not for a man who was hiding information that could very well get Aimee killed. In Jackson's book, that was attempted murder, right there. "You're the one who answered her request for lodging. You suddenly have a cancellation and can accommodate her. As soon as she arrives, strange things start happening at her cabin only. Oh, and here's a clincher…her dead father played in that poker game of yours…see how it's all coming together, now? And that explosive…we got a print off it." He delivered the kill point as Burley's face turned white.

"Now wait just a minute here," the older man came from behind the counter, his eyes wide, his head shiny with sweat in front of his receding hairline. "I ran a poker game. And maybe her dad played sometimes. But I know nothing about any harm to that girl, intended or otherwise. I have nothing to do with any of that."

Jackson didn't want to believe the man. He knew Burley had to be lying to him. But if so, he was the best actor Jackson had ever come across.

"You expect me to believe, with you being the only connection between Ms. Barker and her dad, that you're clear here?"

"I swear to you, Sheriff. I ran a poker game back in the day. That's all. I didn't even play. Seems to me someone who might have a problem would have been someone who actually lost to the guy."

"So you remember Mason Cooper now?" Burley had denied knowing the man when Leon had asked.

"I'm not saying I do or I don't. But if I did, there's a chance he was a smart one. Counted cards, if I'm remembering correctly. My guess is, if there's any connection to that woman and my game, it's something to do with that."

Yeah, that was Jackson's guess, too. But he didn't believe Burley was as innocent as he claimed. Most definitely not after he'd stopped at actually admitting he knew Aimee's dad.

"Look, Sheriff, I'll do anything I can to help you out. I don't need any trouble here. I like Evergreen. Blooming Bridges is my life." Jackson almost bought the plea. "I've got a list of everyone who played in the game I ran," he said. "It's in the back, in my safe. I'll turn it over to you if that'll help…"

"You kept track of every player of every game?"

"I kept track of everyone who got access to the room," Burley said. "Checked the name they entered by against a valid driver's license. No license, no play."

So, Burley surprised him after all. "Get me the list."

Chapter 20

Aimee wanted to see Gay Gay. She remembered him. A piece of her past who was still living. She should want to be getting home, too, though she'd taken two weeks off from the shop for her sojourn out West. She'd checked in that afternoon with Beth, the woman whom she'd left in charge of Seeds for the Soul while she was gone. They'd discussed some of the shops Aimee had visited in Evergreen and details from the deal she'd managed to secure with the gourd artist. Aimee had also mentioned a potential Native American artist she'd discovered in one of the shops. And all the while she was curiously content not to rush back.

She loved the shop. Loved her own art, even more. Definitely loved having the chance to discover and sell one-of-a-kind pieces all over the country. It was all part of who she was. But it was a solid part. Already

grounded and healthy. She was discovering that she had
other parts, missing pieces, and she couldn't settle for
living without them anymore.

She'd discovered Jackson Redmond. A man who
raised all kind of passions in her. Sexual, for sure, but
others as well. Disagreeing with him, for instance. Instead of taking a step back, seeing the other side and
letting go, as was generally her way, she was ready to
go toe to toe with him. Just because. He didn't have to
agree with her. But she wanted it all hashed out, anyway. Wanted him to know how strongly she felt what
she felt.

Wanted to know those things herself.

She didn't want to step back anymore. At least not
where he was concerned.

She didn't want to be calm and cool or keep things
neat and tidy. She wanted it messy. Because real life
got that way.

Shrugging off her thoughts as she paced the bedroom
upstairs, telling herself she was being fanciful and ridiculous and would probably feel differently in a day
or two, she heard Jackson's SUV pull in and her heart
leaped. Grabbing her purse, and in the same black Lycra
skirt and peasant tank blouse she'd had on since that
morning, she headed straight for the stairs.

He'd said he was going to try and arrange for her to
see Grayson Evergreen yet that evening. It was only
three in the afternoon. They could be in Phoenix by an
early dinnertime. Visit with Grayson, grab a bite in the
city and be back in time for a beer with Hoot before bed.

Bed. She was going to try again not to go there alone.
As soon as Jackson figured out who wanted her dead,
there'd be no more reason for her to stay with him.

She didn't want to leave without knowing what it felt like to have him on top of her. Underneath her. Inside her.

The thought didn't even make her blush. She wanted him that bad.

And pondered different ways to get him to agree to sleep with her as they drove the lonely stretch of uninhabited highway carved into the mountain. A road that took them down to the Phoenix valley. Mostly the thoughts were incomplete, interrupted with conversation a time or two as he told her about Burley. About Leon and Sandra checking out the list of gamblers.

About the fact that her father's name had been on that list.

And sometimes her thoughts of sex with him were interrupted by such incredibly beautiful sights they took her breath away. The vastness, the drop-offs, the views as they rounded curves, the vistas…she could hardly absorb it all.

Jackson seemed to take it all in stride. The conversation, the views. He'd been all business since he'd walked in the door, told her he wanted to take a minute to change, and even when he'd come out looking like a cowboy who could fit any women's fantasy in his jeans, short-sleeved pullover, boots and his gun at his waist, he hadn't given any indication of noticing her openmouthed stare.

She was more relieved than she'd realized to get out of town. To be away from whatever danger lurked there. Away from whoever didn't want her there. If fate was good to her, Leon and Sandra would find the missing piece of that particular puzzle while she and Jackson were in Phoenix. They had a fingerprint. They just had to get poker players who were willing to give their fingerprints, as well as look them up in the fingerprint database they'd already checked, and rule them out, to be able to narrow down the pool of suspects and then investigate those who were left. Jackson had explained it all to her as soon as they'd buckled themselves into the front seat of his SUV.

Whatever her father had gotten into that was rolling over to her for some reason, should be known to them soon.

The Phoenix traffic was intense compared to New Orleans, but then, as Jackson pointed out to her, the valley's population was eight times as large. Highways branched off highways, circling in every which way, five and six lanes a side, and she was more nervous than she'd been on the edge of the mountain cliff on the way down. He didn't seem the least bit fazed. Could have been riding a horse alone in the desert based on his one hand on the wheel and his relaxed posture.

Grayson's temporary home, a facility in the middle of Phoenix, had lovely landscaping, garage parking for visitors and a luxurious entryway. Clearly no money had been spared, but she could see why someone who loved the rugged north could be uncomfortable there.

The heat kind of put a damper on things, too. She was sweating just walking from the car in the garage to the elevator bank that took them down to a breezeway leading inside. At one hundred and ten, there was no way Grayson could hike for long, even if the facilities had grounds to do so. Which it clearly did not.

"Boyd said he'd meet us in the lobby," Jackson told her, walking just behind her right elbow, as though guarding her even now that they were out of Evergreen.

She didn't feel like she needed the protection, but she was glad to have him there, just the same.

Jackson's body close to hers…she liked it. A lot.

Having him at her back when she was getting ready to meet someone she remembered knowing so long ago…was pretty much priceless. She didn't want to do it without him.

She would if she had to. But she didn't want to.

"There he is." She heard Jackson's voice just as she noticed a distinguished-looking man in light gray pants, a dress shirt and shiny black shoes coming toward them. Boyd Evergreen was easily as tall as Jackson, and straight shouldered. And wore his wealth with class, rather than obnoxiousness. His full head of hair was heavily peppered with gray.

Jackson made the introductions and Boyd smiled as he took her hand. "You're nothing like I remember, of course," he said, and then he sobered. Led them to a small private room off from what looked to be a large general visiting area with multiple seating sections set off by half walls and furnished with expensive-looking couches, chairs and even televisions.

The room they were in was furnished identically to the multiple seating areas they'd just passed. Boyd Evergreen sat on the edge of a leather armchair, his arms resting on his thighs. Jackson saw the two of them onto the matching couch. She hadn't known they were going to have a meeting before the meeting…but she supposed it made sense that they would. She'd need to learn how to speak to a man she remembered as a boy—a man whose mind hadn't aged since he'd known her as a three year old.

Her stomach in knots, she wasn't sure if she was excited, or just plain nervous. She just knew she wanted so badly to see Grayson. To know him. And hoped he remembered her. But she wanted it done, a memory she could look back on. And hopefully savor.

"I need to tell you both something before you see Gray," Boyd started, his fingertips steepled together, his gaze trained on that steeple, not them. "Because he's likely going to tell you himself."

Aimee nodded, eager to be ready, to do all she could to make the reunion a good one.

Boyd's brow raised as he looked up at Jackson, and the pain in the older man's gaze, the moisture in the blue eyes, the way his lips came together, puffed out and then tightened, made Aimee's stomach sink. He was preparing them for something bad.

Maybe even horrible.

She felt like she was going to cry and she hardly even remembered Grayson. Hadn't recognized Boyd at all. Not even a vague memory.

"Jackson's told me what you remember," Boyd said. "And asked how you came to know Grayson…"

She nodded again, her hands pressed between her knees.

"Your mother watched out for him sometimes during the day, when my father and I had to attend meetings, that kind of thing."

So it was as Kelly had suggested. The knowledge still brought a measure of peace.

"He's had the same psychiatrist all these years, Dr. James Harris. He was the head of the facility where Grayson's been living and now he's retiring. He's the only person alive, besides me, who knows Gray's full history."

Boyd's gaze was back on Jackson, then. As though

assessing him for something. His reaction to what was to come?

But why would Jackson have any stake in it?

"Mason and Adele Cooper didn't die in a murder-suicide." The words fell like bullets into the room. Staccato. Loud. One at a time. Painful beyond measure.

She heard her own gasp. Felt the sharpness of the intake in her chest. And put her hand on Jackson's knee, palm up.

When he covered it with his own, she licked her lips, meaning to speak, but couldn't get any words out.

"What's going on?" Jackson's question came softly. His skin warm against hers.

Boyd looked straight at Jackson. "Your father came up with the murder-suicide scenario to satisfy the coroner. And then told the mortuary that they'd died in an accident. That story was to spare the family. He handled everything like the pro he was. Said that, with only the little girl…" Boyd's voice trailed off as he glanced at her, bowed his head in her direction and then peered at Jackson again. "There was no justice to be served, other than to clean up the mess and move on. With one caveat. Grayson had to be institutionalized for the rest of his life."

She was shaking her head, frowning. "I don't understand."

"You're going to tell me that Grayson killed them, aren't you?" Jackson asked, no inflection in his tone, but there was definite pressure against her hand on his leg.

His lips sucked inward, tears in his eyes now, Boyd nodded.

And Aimee had to excuse herself to the ladies' room where she lost her lunch. And probably her breakfast, too.

Nothing made sense. None of it. How could she feel such affection for someone who'd obliterated her family?

How could her brain not remember? Even if she hadn't been there…she'd have known they were gone. Why couldn't she remember anyone telling her they were gone?

How did she trust anything anymore?

How could… Gay Gay had been such a child…so innocent…so sensitive.

I'd never… I wouldn't hurt her. She heard the words in her mind, as she had before.

Believed them.

But…he hadn't said he wouldn't hurt anyone else. He'd been a boy, but in a strong, nearly adult body.

He'd pushed her too high.

He hadn't known his own strength.

She had to go. Couldn't see him.

Rinsed her mouth. Washed her face and hands. Dried them. Repeated the process. And pulled open the door to the hallway.

Grayson stood there, so much older, wrinkled, and yet…astonishingly the same, too. The eyes, the way he smiled. "Aimee," he said in his slightly thick tone. "Boyd told me you were here and I couldn't believe him, and here you are."

Yep. There she was. "Gay Gay." She didn't want to call him by the childish name. Didn't want to see him at all. He'd murdered her parents! But another part of her remembered how much she'd loved him. How he'd made himself her protector. Her keeper.

I'd never… I wouldn't hurt her.

He never would have hurt her parents if he'd known how much that had devastated her entire life. The understanding came. Not with forgiveness. Maybe that would come, later. Maybe not.

"You got old." The man child said to her, his body still as athletic looking as she remembered.

"You did, too."

His nod took up half of his body. Back and forth, back and forth, several times. And then he stood upright, his shoulders completely straight. "I told Boyd, and Dr. Harris, over and over and over and over and over that it's my fault and I did it, and I'm sorry, and you weren't here, Dr. Harris said, so I couldn't tell you, but I wanted to tell you that. That I'm sorry." Tears filled his eyes. "They took you away and I couldn't tell you I'm sorry." He started to cry in earnest then, and it was like she was three again, with someone so much older than her, but feeling like the older one.

"Don't cry, Gay Gay." As soon as the words escaped, she knew she'd said them to him so many times. Because her childish heart had somehow understood what her adult heart couldn't grasp. The things he did, he couldn't help.

"I have to go now," the man said, and turning, strode down the hallway and through a door to another hallway.

Somehow, she made it back through the lobby, down the breezeway, up the elevator and to Jackson's car. She'd heard him and Boyd speaking most of the way, as the older man walked with them to the elevator before turning to go back to his brother.

She heard about Grayson taking her too close to a cliff, about her near-fatal accident and about her father insisting that the Evergreens were going to have to put Grayson in an institution. Telling Grayson that he couldn't come to their house anymore. Couldn't see Aimee. And how Grayson started to cry, to try to get to Aimee, and when they wouldn't let him, how he picked up her father's souvenir bat out of the corner and hit him with it. And then, when her mom rushed over, hit her, too.

She was crying as Boyd told Jackson that as a favor to Boyd's father, to the Evergreen family, Jackson's father had taken care of the bodies, the report, even naming the deaths as John and Jane Doe so there'd be nothing to find if anyone ever came looking. If charges had been made, and the case went to court, it would have been a huge, painful scandal for the family who had been supporting Evergreen since the town's inception.

And the only justice that would have come out of it would have been Grayson institutionalized for life. Clearly he wasn't competent to stand trial. As far as records went, Mason and Adele Cooper just disappeared off the grid, as adults were allowed to do. Boyd's father knew someone with a rig big enough to move a mobile home, paying the guy a hefty sum to do it under the table, but the guy had done a shady job and crashed the thing, and Shephard Redmond had stepped up again, arranging for Landing to come get the home. Her parents were renting to own, she'd heard. And Boyd wasn't exactly sure where the mobile home had been parked. On some land a friend let Mason use. Boyd knew the area, but he'd never been there. He did know that Mason had built the front porch himself.

The last piece of information was a crowning touch. Or the feather that broke Aimee's heart.

The answers were all there. All of them.

Except one.

Why couldn't she remember any of it?

Humiliated, in despair for his father's gargantuan wrongdoing, and for Aimee's loss, as well, Jackson maneuvered traffic until they were out of Phoenix, and then pulled off into one of the many sightseeing overlooks on the way back up the mountain, and put the SUV in Park.

Aimee hadn't said a word since Grayson had walked away. She'd cried a bit. He'd seen her wipe her face a time or two. He couldn't even imagine what she was thinking. Feeling.

Figured he'd be one of the last people she'd want to talk to.

But some things had to be said. "I'm sorry," first and foremost.

"For what?" Her gaze seemed truly perplexed as she glanced at him. "You didn't know, clearly. You walked into that just like I did."

"No, but my father…"

"Did what he did, Jackson. You were three. Same as me." She shrugged.

"If you'd never come looking…"

"No one would ever have been the wiser." She almost sounded as though she'd wished it had been that way.

"I don't know if you heard there at the end…you were already in the elevator… Boyd said he'd like to meet with you, tomorrow even, as he knows you'll want to get back. He wants to compensate you…"

"I don't want anything from him."

"I told him I didn't figure you would. But he's happy to answer any questions you have about your folks. It sounds like he knew them well enough. He'd just been following my father's mandate, to deny knowing you when I asked if he remembered you all."

She nodded. "I'm fine to talk to him," she said. "It's the right thing to do. Being polite to him. Because he's being so kind." She sounded as though she was talking to herself, more than to him. "And because I'm starving for more," she said then, looking straight at Jackson. Her gaze cutting into him with the pain it bore. "More answers. More information about my parents' lives. About my life with them." She glanced out at the landscape in front of them, dotted by hundreds of saguaro cacti. "It's nice of him to offer, seeing that I could be running to the papers right now about what his family had done."

"He's prepared for that, too. Says it should have happened thirty years ago."

Boyd would have said it all directly to Aimee, but she'd walked ahead of them, leading the way virtually without pause, out of the building and back to the vehicle, stopping only to hold the elevator button when Jackson had stopped to finish his conversation.

"He can rest easy. I don't intend to tell anyone. Grayson is already paying for what he did. And I don't want any publicity over it."

Jackson glanced over at her almost dry tone. Needing to do something for her. Anything. To take some of the anguish onto himself. Remind her that there was still good in the world.

He needed her to know she wasn't all alone.

So, when they got home—the deputy watching the house signaling that all was well—and she went straight for a beer, two of them, bringing one for him, he took it. He shouldn't have. Not with all of the emotions surging, overloading their circuits. And her potential killer still on the loose. But he did. And gulped down a fourth of it, first sip.

And when she took his hand, looked up at him with those big brown eyes, kissed him lightly and whispered that she didn't want to sleep alone that night, he didn't send her upstairs as he should have done.

He took her to bed with him.

And loved her for hours. Hard. Soft. Quick. Slow. It was like they couldn't stop. Couldn't satiate the hunger, or use up all of the energy coursing through them. Couldn't do it fast enough to outrun the bad they couldn't change. Or slow enough for the tenderness to ease their burdens. Couldn't relax. Or close their eyes to sleep.

And so they just kept touching, exploring, tasting, entering, pumping, until, finally, Aimee laid her head on Jackson's chest and dozed off.

He slept, intermittently. Exhausted beyond measure. And awakened, too. He loved her. He knew that now. Suspected that she was the first person he ever really had loved. Shephard hadn't been open to the tender emotion. His mother had abandoned him. His family had been a town, not people.

And it still was.

Aimee might be his first love, but he wasn't going to ask her to stay with him. To the contrary, as soon as he knew she was safe out on her own, as soon as he had her want-to-be-killer in custody, he was going to push her out of his life.

She was a city girl. Like Celeste. And he was an Evergreen boy.

Just like his father.

But he didn't suffer from the god complex his father

had had. And he damn sure wasn't going to repeat the old man's mistakes.

He'd rather die alone than trap Aimee in a love, and a town, that would suffocate her.

Or maybe, man that he was, who'd grown up without love, he'd rather die alone than risk living in love.

He was his father's son.

Chapter 21

Jackson was gone when Aimee got up the next morning. She'd woken, very briefly, as he'd carried her upstairs just as dawn was breaking. Remembered being cradled against him, her arms around his neck, her head tucked under his chin.

Remembered not letting go of his neck when he first laid her down. Remembered the soft taste of his lips against hers. And then she'd been out again.

They were going to have to talk about it—the incredible night they'd shared. But until she saw him again, she could savor it. Relish it.

Making love with Jackson Redmond had been far more powerful than anything she'd imagined or ever fantasized about. They hadn't spoken, other than to ask *You want it like this?* or *Do you like that?* punctuated with animalistic moans that said far more than she could ever have articulated.

He'd given her exactly what she'd asked for, when she hadn't even really known what she was asking. He'd known what she'd needed.

And, based on his reactions, she knew that, in bed with him, she'd given him something great, too. The man hadn't been shy about his pleasure.

But day had come. The first day of living her real truth. She wasn't just the beloved adopted daughter/niece of a successful, loving artist who saw the beauty in everything. She was the biological daughter of loving parents, one with a gambling addiction that he'd had the strength to beat, who'd been murdered by a boy they'd been trying to help.

She'd come for her missing pieces and she'd found them.

All that was left was finding who was after her for something she didn't have, and she'd be free to go back to the life that was waiting for her.

The life she and Aunt Bonnie had built together.

The business she adored.

For all she knew, the person who wanted her dead had already been caught. Jackson had told her when he left to call him when she woke up.

She vaguely remembered those words vibrating softly against her lips.

She wanted so badly to be free from the fear.

She didn't want to go. To leave Jackson.

And it hit her...if Grayson was responsible for her parents deaths, had Boyd known and been trying to get rid of her to hide that secret?

Jackson had known the man his whole life. Trusted him.

And she trusted Jackson.

In a floral, pink-and-white tank dress that she chose strictly for comfort and white flip-flops with rhinestones, she stood at the refrigerator, staring in, trying to talk herself into something sounding good for breakfast. She'd eat, then call Jackson.

She wanted those last few minutes to completely savor and shiver with thoughts of the night they'd shared before the day's sense of reality coated it all in cement.

Disappointment crashed through her as she heard an engine outside. A vehicle, larger than Jackson's, pulling into the circular drive. Savoring wasn't meant to be.

And neither, apparently, was her privacy. She had an uncharitable sense of resentment as her phone rang, and saw that it wasn't Jackson's number.

It was Leon, who'd apparently been stationed outside since Jackson had left a couple of hours before to follow up on a lead.

Catching the person who'd tried to kill her?

Nervous for his safety, wanting to grill Leon about it, but not doing so, she told him that yes, she was up, dressed and downstairs.

Leon said there was a visitor outside, but wouldn't let him in unless she gave him the go-ahead.

Boyd Evergreen.

The deputy sheriff was holding Boyd Evergreen outside for her okay? The man could finance the Evergreen sherrif's office ten times over.

"It's fine," she said. "Jackson told me last night Boyd wanted to speak with me this morning."

Didn't seem like that conversation, or meeting Grayson, had been only the previous evening. Seemed like days ago, not hours.

Figuring it was just as well she hadn't had any breakfast yet, she went to the door, smiled at Leon, first, and then held her hand out to the older brother of the man who'd been her friend and killed her parents, inviting him inside.

"He's got beginning stage dementia, Jackson, so take that for what it is, but you need to hear what he's saying." In beige pants and a matching jacket, Sandra led Jackson down the hall of a nursing home just outside Evergreen. "We've talked to two dozen men since last night, all on that list Burley gave you, and not one of them knew anything. It's like they're stonewalling…"

Not liking the sound of that one bit, Jackson sped up his step. If Sandra thought the old man who couldn't remember his family members had something useful to say, he needed to hear what it was. But he didn't have time to waste.

The lack of any answers, talking to so many people… either they were all in something together and covering for each other, someone had something over them, someone they feared, or someone was buying them off.

Someone knew some damn thing.

"Mike Chambers was a regular in Burley's games," Sandra was saying. "He was around fifty the night we now know Mason Cooper played for the last time. I think he was there, Jackson. When we mentioned poker, I'd actually asked if he'd liked to play a hand or two, he lit right up. But…he's in horrible cognitive health so I didn't want to be the one to make a call on whether or not to follow up on what he says. And I know anything he says won't end up in court. But, neither could I ignore what he told me. I don't want to be the only one who heard it. You'll understand—just humor me here…"

Tension and impatience made Jackson's nod terse. He kept his mouth shut.

Aimee would be up soon. He'd expected to have already had her call. If it didn't come by the time he was done there, he was calling Leon. He trusted his deputy 100 percent. Trusted him with his own life. Wasn't in the habit of checking up on him. Or expecting him to call in with reports on a protective witness duty, but fate had to cut him a break on this one.

He needed to hear from the woman who'd spent the night in this bed.

And Sandra was expecting him to follow her into the room she'd just entered, a space resembling a hospital room, if not for the brown wood dresser, the love seat and coffee table, the family photos all over the walls and the quilt on the neatly made hospital bed sporting a camouflage design.

"Mr. Chambers? This is Jackson Redmond—I told you about him."

The old man in the wheelchair by the window, what hair he had slicked back behind his ears, made suckling noises, as though he had a piece of candy in his mouth, and said, "Nope. I don't know neither one of you."

Sandra's flash look at Jackson warned him to hold on a second.

"You play poker, don't you?" Sandra asked.

"I do. But I'd beat the pants off you, little lady, and you don't want that."

"No, but Jackson here, he's a darn good player."

Admiring the way his detective took the chauvinistic comment without losing her stride, Jackson still wanted to inform that man that Sandra Philpot had beaten Jackson at blackjack the previous year during their casino night fundraiser.

But the meeting was Sandra's. She had the lead.

"You play cards, young man?"

"I do." In his uniform with his striped credentials on his chest and his gun at his hip, Jackson wasn't used to being called anything as irreverent as *young man*. And let that slide, too.

Sandra had him there for a reason.

"Tell Jackson about that game you used to play in Halston," Sandra said. "The one behind the bar."

Mike cocked his head, clearly assessing her. "You know about that game?"

"Of course I do. You told me about it."

Seeming to think on that one a moment, the old man must have decided that since he'd already spoken about the game, it was okay to do so. He started in about different nights, different hands, different players, going on for a good five minutes—during which Jackson about lost what little bit of patience he had left. Ordinarily, he'd be fine to sit with Mike Chambers for however long it took, but he was anxious to get back to Aimee.

They were no closer to finding whoever was after her and with every hour that passed without the guy in custody, she was at more risk.

"What about the game with the deed on the table?" Sandra asked when the old man fell silent. "You remember that one?"

"Course I do!" Mike said, sounding affronted. "No one in that room that night's likely to forget that one."

Sandra sent Jackson another pointed look, and he tuned in. Listening intently now, for whatever it was he was supposed to pick up on.

"Weirdest damn thing," Mike was saying, his face almost aglow. "The Evergreen kid, you know the one... the older of the two, a bit of a pompous ass if you ask me, anyways it's his twenty-first birthday. He's all het up. Just came from dinner with his dad, where, for his birthday present, the old man gave him a deed to a couple of acres of land on the estate—no road to it, out back of the property. Damndest thing, the old man had the address registered, did the paperwork, but it wouldn't be recorded until road infrastructure's in. Tells the kid the land is there for him to get married and build a house. Road goes in when he gets married. Kid went on and on about it. An address for a house that didn't exist. And about the fact that he didn't intend to live under his old man's oversight for the rest of his life. And he'd get married when he was damned well ready to do so..."

Jackson heard roaring in his ears. An address that wasn't registered. For a house that didn't exist. A poker game. A deed.

Mason Cooper won huge, called his wife and they moved out of the garage apartment.

He looked at Sandra. She nodded.

And, heart in his throat, Jackson was out of there.

Boyd Evergreen was pleasant, talking to her about her parents, sharing priceless tidbits with her, like the style that her mom preferred for her hair, the way she used to can tomatoes and make spaghetti sauce, the time her father had saved a guy's life at the mine. He offered, several times, to set her up for life. He could afford it. And wanted to make up to her, in any way he could, the life his brother had taken from her.

She didn't want his money. And the longer he sat

there, the longer she listened to him talk about her parents, the more agitated she became. She wanted the information, but she didn't want him giving it to her. It made no sense, and as the tension grew in her, so did her emotional unease. She felt like she was going to cry. Kept looking at her phone over on the kitchen counter, where she'd left it. Was upset that she hadn't called Jackson to let him know she was up.

Had Leon told him?

There'd been no reason to let Jackson know that Boyd Evergreen had come to visit. Jackson had practically arranged the meeting himself.

After getting up from the couch, she moved over to the front window, just to reassure herself that Leon was still out there, that she could motion him to come in in case she needed him.

Why she would, she had no idea. But she wasn't herself.

Didn't feel right.

Should have had breakfast.

Saw Leon outside, standing by his car. Looked like he was reaching for his phone. Jackson calling to check up on her? Since she hadn't called him?

And as she turned back to the room, telling herself that she was fine, that all was well, she caught a glimpse of the license plate of the car Boyd had parked in the driveway. Not the plate itself, but the frame of it.

The way it glinted in the sun, with nuances of blue and red...

Because of the Evergreen emblem, she saw now...

Evergreen as in family crest, not the town.

Her heart dropped. Felt like it was literally in her stomach. She couldn't breathe. Was strangling. Her head hurt, pounded, with lightning bursts of pain.

"It was you," she cried, turning completely to face the man who was slowly rising from the couch. Her gaze went to his right hand.

And the ring he wore there.

A memory pricked at her... The ring with the colors on it. On her dad's stick in the corner. Swinging it even though you weren't allowed to touch it. Hitting her father in the head.

She saw her Dad's face—instead of laughing, his eyes were wide, filled with something awful, his mouth open. He was yelling and her mother rushed over and...

The big splat of blood was like rain, flying everywhere. Hitting her leg. And...

She was hiding under the house. Gay Gay had done that once. When he'd been in trouble for pushing her too high on the swing. No one could find him for a long time.

Until they'd heard him from inside the house...

A mixture of adult interpretation and childhood memories assaulted her. But the feelings...they were all innocent. Horrifying. Beyond anything she could... darkness. She couldn't...

But she had to.

She couldn't let him get away with it...

Blinking, Aimee focused. Heard her phone ring at the same time there was a knock on the door and an arm clenched her around the neck.

She felt the hard metal pressing up against the side of her head at the same time the door burst open.

Heard the shot.

Figured, since she felt nothing, she must be dead.

And called out for Mama and Daddy.

They were finally all going to be together again.

Chapter 22

Jackson knew, the split second before he got the door open, that when his deputy had called him, he shouldn't have ordered Leon to wait for him to get there. Going in alone was not only against protocol—could get two people killed instead of one—but Jackson knew Boyd Evergreen. He'd have the best shot at diffusing the situation if there even was one.

Unless he was too late.

He'd had Leon keeping watch through the window. He'd known that Aimee and Boyd were still sitting as they'd been since the man had arrived, him on the couch, her on the chair, talking.

Until seconds before he'd pulled into his drive. Leon had seen her come to the window. Jackson had run as fast as he could, burst open the door, gun in front of him.

And got his shot off just in time.

One second later and Aimee would have been dead.

As it was, Boyd's bullet, off mark as he'd jerked at Jackson's entrance, had grazed the skin on the side of her head.

And left her right ear ringing *not too bad*, she'd told him, while sitting on the end of the exam table in the emergency room.

Boyd Evergreen had killed Mason and Adele Cooper, in front of their three-year-old daughter. Jackson had never seen it coming.

There were so many unanswered questions—many that might remain that way since Boyd's body was on its way to the morgue.

Jackson had killed a man in his own living room.

Someone he'd looked up to, respected his entire life.

The head of his family, so to speak.

And he wasn't sorry.

The sight of Evergreen standing there with a gun to Aimee's head was a vision that was never going to leave him. He knew that as surely as he knew he had to breathe to stay alive.

He was finding the latter difficult, breathing, as he stood outside the exam cubicle waiting for Aimee to change out of the gown they'd put on her and into the clothes Kelly had brought. Her bloodstained dress had been bagged as evidence.

Leon and Sandra would be handling the rest of the case. He had to be off active duty until the shooting had been investigated and cleared. With Leon as a witness, and the fact that Evergreen had died with his gun still in his hand, the inquiry would be brief. He'd been told to expect to be back on full duty by nightfall.

When news of Boyd Evergreen's fall hit, his town was going to need him.

He needed to see, first, if Aimee needed him. The town mattered. She mattered more.

Maybe the realization should be huge. It settled on him with a naturalness that just made it seem normal.

The only thing in the past hour and a half that hadn't been shocking.

Kelly had suggested that he get looked over, too. He'd shrugged her off. He'd shot his gun at a person before. Had aimed it for a man's hand once, to knock his own gun out of it, and succeeded.

Leon had already brought Randall Burley in, who, once he heard that Boyd Evergreen was out of the picture, admitted that Evergreen had been a regular at his poker games, paying off everyone who came to the games to keep quiet about his involvement. He wasn't there for the money. He was there to get good at cards.

And piss off his father.

He'd started playing after Mason Cooper had quit. The only time the two men had ever been at the table together had been the night Mason won the deed Boyd's father had just given him as his twenty-first birthday present.

And then, to cover up his blunder, he'd told his father that he was letting a good guy down on his luck live on the property just until he found a woman he wanted to marry. He'd told his dad how Mason had saved a guy's life at the mine—one in which the Evergreen family was a silent partner. Silent because they were in direct competition with themselves as they owned the rivaling operation.

So many secrets and cover-ups.

Was anything as it seemed?

Leon had told him in their fairly brief phone conversation minutes earlier that Burley had been truly shocked to hear that Evergreen was a murderer. He'd thought, as everyone else had, that the Coopers had died in an accident. But he'd known the kid's name and when he'd seen it show up on the reservations panel, he'd grabbed up the reservation before anyone else had a chance to look at it. Just in case. He'd told Boyd and he'd wanted Aimee to come town, to find out what she knew, why she was there. After she showed up Evergreen had admitted to him that he'd been bilking Aimee out of her inheritance because it had been in the middle of Evergreen land, and with everything that had happened, some bad investments, Grayson's care, he didn't have the money to buy her out. He also admitted that Evergreen had given him the money to buy Blooming Bridges, and that for his generosity, he was buying a lifetime of Burley's loyalty. Boyd had searched for the deed Cooper had won, but never found it. Over the years Evergreen got more and more paranoid about the little girl growing up and coming to town to try to get back her father's land. He'd been keeping tabs on her for years.

Burley hadn't known any of that until he'd mentioned to Boyd that a girl with the same name as Cooper's wife, with the same odd spelling of Aimee had just booked a cabin. That's when Boyd had reminded Burley that he owed him. Burley had agreed to question her at check-in about her reason for visiting, and he'd planned to do that, but when she'd checked in online after landing in Flagstaff, he'd just chatted with her online before she'd arrived. He'd ascertained that she didn't remember her past, and so Burley, at Evergreen's bidding, had tried to get her to leave town once and for all. He didn't want her renting someplace else local. Or coming back.

Little had Burley known that Boyd Evergreen's paranoia had grown because Aimee had grown and he worried about that three-year-old girl who'd witnessed her parents' murders remembering what she'd seen.

Burley swore, though, that all he'd done was sabotage Aimee's stay at the cabin. He'd had nothing to do with the road rage, nor the explosive device outside the sheriff's office.

Evergreen had been the one to shoot the bullet on his land the day Aimee had arrived in town. A move which he'd later regretted as it got Jackson involved in her search for her truths. And a move that had made Randall Burley very nervous.

So, they still had at least one criminal at large, since Boyd was out of town after the shooting. Someone on Evergreen's payroll, obviously. Someone who Sandra and Leon were tracking like dogs after a steak bone. Starting with Evergreen's bank accounts. People didn't kill for free.

And in the meantime, Jackson was sticking to Aimee. Period.

Whether she wanted him there or not.

He'd failed her. Let her killer walk right into his living room. And he'd made the wrong call at the end, too, having Leon wait for him to get there.

The one thing he'd always been was a great cop, and when it mattered most, he'd been so engrained with protocol, he'd nearly gotten the love of his life killed.

The old man wouldn't have done that.

But his father was responsible for other mistakes.

Ones just as great. He'd destroyed evidence when he'd destroyed that mobile home. He'd failed to investigate. He'd locked up an innocent, handicapped man, and let a killer go free.

It was all going to come out. The city council could vote to let him go as sheriff. A new sheriff might not even choose to hire him as an officer.

As he stood there in the deserted back area of the tri-age unit where they'd rushed Aimee—their only current patient—smelling antiseptic, listening to beeps and voices in the distance, he knew what he faced, and didn't even care.

All he cared about was on the other side of the curtain, taking an inordinately long time to get some clothes on.

Or so it seemed to him.

His watch told him it had been less than three minutes.

He yanked at the curtain, ducking his head in, anyway. He'd seen her naked. And wasn't content to have her anywhere he couldn't see her.

Aimee, still sitting on the end of the examining table in the hospital gown, looked at him, tears dripping down her cheeks.

"What?" he asked, immediately filled with concern as he slipped inside, pulling the curtain closed behind him. Looking for the call button.

"I can't get the gown untied," she said. "The tie between my shoulder blades is knotted and I can't reach..."

Weak with relief, he went to work immediately, telling himself not to look at her back, or remember his hands all over that soft skin—to remember his body pressed up against it, or that skin on top of him, making him wild...

"I've been waiting right outside," he said as his big fingers fumbled with the knot. "Why didn't you just call out to me?"

She sniffed. Grabbed a tissue off the box on the tray next to her. And then said, "I've ruined everything for you, Jackson. If I'd just stayed home, instead of being so full of my need to... I don't even know what...look at the mess I've caused...and for what? To know how my parents died? It doesn't bring them back."

"You brought the truth out of the darkness, Aimee. Boyd Evergreen is a killer. Who knows who else he might have hurt over the years, whatever other crimes he might have committed and gotten away with. And Grayson...he's let that poor man believe, all these years, that he killed your parents? I don't even know how he pulled that off. He had us all fooled..." Jackson stopped, midsentence.

"Wait...you said in the ambulance on the way over that Grayson wasn't there when Boyd killed your parents..."

He'd untied the gown, come around to the front of her. She stared up at him, mouth open, but didn't seem to be focused.

"What?" he asked, not wanting her to leave him yet, not even for seconds.

"Grayson. He was there. I didn't run. He grabbed me up. Ran outside with me and hid us under the house. He just kept saying, *It's all my fault. It's all my fault. I did it.*"

Frowning...she looked up at him. "But he didn't do it. So why would he say that?"

Jackson didn't know, didn't know if they'd ever find out, but he knew that he'd die happy if he could go with Aimee looking at him just as she was doing right then.

* * *

Kelly spent most of that afternoon with them at Jackson's place, sitting in the kitchen, talking. Debriefing. Interspersed with casual conversation. The crime scene had taken less than an hour to process, and then another hour to clean—a feat made more expedient by the fact that Jackson ordered all furniture to be disposed of. By the time they'd left the hospital, he'd been cleared to be back inside and his house was the only place Aimee wanted to be at the moment—even if she just stayed upstairs in her room. His personal effects were along the far wall, by the staircase, and the rest of the room was bare and pristine. If there'd been any blood on the hardwood floor, it had been cleaned. The wool throw rug that had covered most of the room had caught most all of it.

And Jackson didn't want her out in public until they found whoever had been working for Boyd Evergreen. There was no guarantee the person or persons didn't know Boyd was dead, and was, then, still "on the job" so to speak.

Jackson had been on the phone on and off, not part of the investigation, but being kept apprised by his people, who were still looking to him for his thoughts and suggestions.

And a couple of county deputies were stationed in the front and two more in the back of his property. Protecting them, not keeping them in.

Aimee was free to go. Jackson just didn't deem it safe for her to do so.

Other than him not being able to participate in the investigation, he was under no restrictions at all. He didn't have his police-issued gun on him, though. That had been taken in as evidence. He'd strapped his own nine millimeter to his waist before they'd ever left home after the shooting.

Shortly before Kelly left, Aimee announced that she wanted to call Alonzo Gillum, her father's old friend. "I'd just like him to know the truth about how my dad died," she told them.

And maybe she wanted to connect with the man who'd been a good friend to a man she was only just beginning to remember.

More and more memories had been coming back to her all afternoon. Nothing big, or specific. Little snippets. Ice cream on her nose and her dad licking it off. Her licking ice cream off from his nose. Holding her mom's hand walking into a grocery store.

Innocuous things—and priceless to her.

Alonzo answered on the first ring. "I was hoping I'd hear from you," the man said. "My wife and I have been talking nonstop about all of this since I met you. She wants to meet you."

While she wanted to connect, Aimee didn't feel at all ready to socialize and, instead, gave Alonzo a brief rundown of what had happened that morning and the things she'd remembered.

A long pause followed her words. Dead silence, more like. To the point that she glanced at her phone to see if the call was still connected.

Alonzo's cough alerted her to the fact that, while yes, the lines were connected, he was still there as well.

"My wife is sitting here with me, Aimee," he finally said. "Is the sheriff there with you?"

"Yes."

"Can you put me on Speaker phone, please?"

Frowning, she glanced at Jackson, who'd been watching her, eavesdropping unabashedly at her end of the conversation. Kelly had gone in to use the restroom and put a call in to her friend. The two of them were going to be staying around for a few more days and had been talking about heading downtown for dinner that night.

Such normal everyday activity seemed so far-fetched to Aimee. So out of reach…

She touched an icon on her phone. "You're on speaker," she said.

Jackson, sitting directly across from her at the island counter, nodded.

"Sheriff?"

"Yeah, I'm here."

"I told my wife something when I got back from there, something I haven't told anyone since the day it was told to me. She's been after me ever since to tell you…"

"Tell me what?" Jackson didn't sound at all congenial then. "You realize that withholding evidence in a crime is obstructing an investigation…"

Eyebrows raised, Aimee stared at him. Definitely not what she'd come to recognize as normal Jackson behavior.

The man wasn't as calm and contained as he'd seemed all day. And that tidbit made her feel better. Odd, but it did.

"I know, sir. I told you what I felt safe saying. I led you to the poker game."

"You knew about the deed."

"No, sir. I wish I had known. I honestly didn't see Mason after that night, and we rarely spoke. There weren't cell phones in those days and Mase didn't have a phone at the trailer."

Mase. A regular guy. With regular friends. And her parents didn't have a phone at their trailer. Which would explain why her mom hadn't called Aunt Bonnie more often than once a month—something that had hurt her aunt. Pay phone long distance would have been expensive.

As far as Aimee knew, her mother hadn't written, either.

Just those monthly calls. And no more visits. For two years…

"But he called me once, not long before he died. Said he was going to come clean about something we'd both witnessed, and then figured out…"

"Lonzo, just tell him." The female voice coming over the line had to belong to Mary Elise, Alonzo's wife.

"Not long before Mase quit coming to the bar, him and I were out in the parking lot one night, having a smoke. Two guys came out. An older guy and a kid. We'd seen them inside. From behind. They were sitting a few booths up from us, and all we could see was their backs. No way the kid was old enough to drink, but the older guy was buying him shots. Outside, we were in the shadows. They were, too. No idea who they were, but we could hear them arguing plain as day. The older guy had met a woman and thought he was going to get lucky. He wanted the kid to get lost. Take their vehicle and go home. Kid said, no way. He wasn't driving drunk. Didn't even have a license. The older guy tells him if he didn't get in the truck and get his ass home, he was going to tell their old man the kid had been drinking. Kid gets in the truck and bounces it out of the parking lot."

A pause came over the line and Jackson's tone was urgent as he said, "And?"

If the day didn't hurry up and end, she might forget what good felt like.

Might never be able to call it up again.

"Neither of us thought much of it," Alonzo said. "Stuff like that happens all the time."

"Yeah, go on." Jackson wasn't sparing the guy any compassion.

"When Mase called, he said he'd figured out who that kid was. That there'd been an accident that night. And that he was going to tell what we'd seen. He was just giving me a heads-up in case someone came asking me about it. He wanted me to have a chance to have my story ready—whether I was going to back him or not. Didn't seem to matter to him much whether I did or not. He just didn't want me blindsided. Because that's the kind of guy he was."

"He never told you who the kid was?"

"No, but after you all came asking about everything, I started asking around about accidents that could have happened in surrounding towns that fall and found only one involving a teenaged boy. In Evergreen, not Halston where we were both staying at the time. Mase used to bunk with me on weeks when we were working the north portion of the mine. The drive was shorter than going all the way back to Evergreen…"

Another tidbit…another piece of a life that meant the world to her. Her father, as a bachelor, bunking with a friend during the week…

That's what she wanted to think about. Friends. Good things involving her parents.

Not the thing that got them killed.

Please don't let her dad doing the right thing be what got him killed.

Jackson's hand came across the counter. Covered hers.

"It was Grayson Evergreen."

Gay Gay's accident had been Boyd's fault. And her dad had confronted him about it. That's what Grayson had been talking about when he said he did it. That it was his fault.

She remembered the argument. Something she hadn't understood at the time. There'd been yelling about an accident. Grayson's car accident. Her father had figured it out. Confronted Boyd. Told him either he told his father, or Mason was going to. Grayson deserved to know it wasn't his fault.

Aimee hadn't thought she had any tears left.

She'd been wrong.

Chapter 23

Jackson's department had a lead on a guy who they believed was responsible for both trying to run Aimee off the road and the sheriff's office bombing. Leon called him just after Kelly left.

"Boyd had a charter jet gassed and ready to go at a private airstrip five miles from here," Jackson told Aimee as he got off the phone.

How could he so have misjudged the man? All his life he'd served the Evergreen family. Holding them in high esteem. Kissing Boyd's ass a time or two because of the funding the family provided to the city, even more than sixty decades after her founding. Evergreen money helped fund the sheriff's department.

And Boyd Evergreen's support hadn't hurt when Shephard Redmond had retired and Jackson's name had been put to the city council as his replacement.

"I look like I was bought," he said, laying his guts

right on the counter where he and Aimee still sat, across from each other, with beers in front of them. He'd ordered pizza. It would be delivered to the station and Leon was going to drop it off himself on his way home to get some sleep.

"Who sees you that way?" Aimee's question flew at him with little sympathy. "Life is too short to take on things that don't exist," she continued. "Believe me, I know."

She did know. The woman had lived the majority of her life without her full reality and when it had started to come back to her, risked her life to find it. To live it. Even with the probability that it was going to be painful.

Looking over at her he grinned. Not a happy expression, but an honest one. "I'm suffering from a bit of disillusionment here," he told her. "Give a guy a second or two of slack."

Her gaze changed immediately. Softened. Those brown eyes filled an emotion that drew him. Made him want to drown in it. "You're the one not cutting yourself any slack, Jackson. You stayed down deep in this all the way through, even when the rules started to change on you. You never faltered. Never lost course."

"I took a wrong road or two."

"Because the evidence led you there, and even then, every road you were on led to the intersection that brought out the truth."

Was she trying to kill him with kindness?

Not a bad way to go.

And yet, strangely, he was feeling better.

But had more to tell her. Things that should have come before self-doubt. Way before.

"They've got a BOLO out statewide, city police, state and county, for the guy Boyd hired to pilot his plane.

They'd been heading to Mexico. Would have been in the air within minutes of him killing you. Been in Mexico before we figured out where he'd gone, and who knows what country before we got to him. But you can bet it would have been one that doesn't extradite. The pilot has no record, but he owns a beat-up blue pickup truck and recently purchased the exact explosive that blew up outside the back door of the station."

"They think the guy is still in the area."

Trust her to hit on the worst piece of what he had to tell her.

"Yeah."

"But he has no reason to want me dead, now. Even if he doesn't know yet that Boyd's dead, he knows he didn't show for the flight. He won't get paid with Boyd in the wind."

"Unless he thinks you can ID him from the road incident." He had to be honest with her. "And…so far we've managed to keep Boyd's death under wraps while we try to lure this guy out. Sometimes it helps to live in a really small town. Only the mortician and sheriff department know who the dead man was who was pulled from my house. Identities being held contingent upon notification of next of kin."

She sat back, her eyes widening. "Grayson. Who's going to tell him?"

Jackson shook his head. "That's yet to be determined. I suggested that we wait until tomorrow, get with the Evergreens' lawyer—he's a good guy, I know him—and see what provisions were made for Grayson's care on the event of Boyd's death. Seems probable that whoever is named as executor and or guardian of Evergreen funds on Grayson's behalf should be the one to tell him. Or maybe Dr. Harris. He's retired, but Grayson knows and trusts him. I'd think there's a good chance he'd be willing to step in given the circumstances."

Aimee looked sad as she nodded. And then, she reached for his hand. "So, I'm still under protective custody for the night?" she asked. The sadness didn't leave her gaze, but something else entered. A light that made him feel things he most definitely had no business feeling in that moment. Under the circumstances he'd just referred to.

"Yes." He had to tell her the truth. He was who he was. He had to take accountability to stay right with himself, and that's what mattered.

Same as his old man, he supposed. Jackson didn't agree with some of Shephard's ways, but his father had had a brand of internal integrity that had never wavered.

Apparently, he'd passed it on to his son.

If Jackson could be that lucky.

"My dad...he died saving a woman and two kids from a drunk abuser," he said, the words totally killing the moment. But there they were, for some reason. Out in the open for the first time in his life. One of the many things he never spoke about.

"Oh my God, Jackson! I knew he earned a commendation, but...why didn't you say something?"

"When?" It wasn't like they were dating. Or even friends. They'd known each other five days.

"What happened?" She didn't seem to grasp the magnitude of his question. The facts it was meant to bring out.

"We got a call...guy beating up his wife...had a gun...protocol says we go out in bulk, surround the place...someone gets the kids out first and foremost, then go for the woman...but my dad, he knows the guy, perp was the son of a friend of dad's who'd died in the mine. Dad had helped him out a time or two. Had been certain that if we surrounded the place, we'd lose him, send him over the edge. Maybe killing his whole family. But if Shephard Redmond went in alone, he was equally certain that he could talk him down. Get him to give up the gun and no one would be hurt. We all disagreed, as a department, en masse, but old Shep was the sheriff. He made the call. He went alone.

"Perp didn't give him a chance to get a word out. Soon as my dad exited his personal vehicle, in jeans, but with his gun up, guy shot him. Dad shot, too, taking the guy with him. No one else got hurt—other than the beating the wife had already taken."

"Sounds like your dad knew someone was going to die. Why else would he have gotten out with his gun up? Or been able to get a shot off so quickly? Sounds like he knew whoever he sent in was going to get shot."

Her words stunned him. As in sitting there, open-mouthed, staring and seeing nothing.

It was so obvious? Why hadn't seen it? Why hadn't anyone else figured that out? They were cops. And... they all knew.

They all knew.

Probably assumed Jackson had figured it out, too. Maybe that's why no one asked him to talk about it. Because the Redmond way was to do the job, serve the town, with no glory.

Glory blinded a guy.

Allowed him to be open to being bought.

And Redmonds weren't that.

Jackson wasn't that.

He'd trusted Boyd Evergreen because he'd taken him at face value. Because he'd grown up being taught to respect him. Because all he'd ever seen, in all his life of knowing him, were Boyd Evergreen's good actions. The bad had been hidden—even from his own flesh and blood.

Turned out he really was his father's son.

And he was damned thankful for that.

And thankful to Aimee Barker for giving him pieces of himself he'd been missing.

She went to bed with him. There was no conversation about it. Or during it, either. They made love as passionately, and for as long, as they had the night before. Her on top. Him on top. Side by side. Upside, downside, with their hands, their mouths, their bodies. And other than talking about the pleasure in the moment, there were no words spoken between them.

No breaching the wall between real life and making the darkness bearable.

And morning came far too soon. Before dawn.

Jackson's phone rang just after five. Leon, back on the job, telling him that the perp had been caught. A guy who'd worked at Grayson's long time mental facility had been on Boyd's payroll for years. Mostly keeping a close eye in case Grayson started to regain any facilities and start talking. After the place burned, the perp was out of work, and willing to do what Boyd needed. His fingerprints matched that found on the explosives, and his phone's GPS showed that he'd been by the nursery on the day Aimee had been run off the road.

She was free to go.

It was over.

Jackson had left the bed to take the call, pulling on a robe as he did so. Wrapping herself in a sheet, she'd followed him out to the kitchen. Sat on the stool she'd occupied for most of the day before as he put coffee on. A full pot, not the single cup she'd seen him make before.

There'd been no specific explanation for that note with the Evergreen address in her aunt's thing. Obviously, her mother had given it to her. Probably when Mason won the deed.

Maybe Aunt Bonnie had suspected wrongdoing, maybe she'd even looked into things and had gotten nowhere. Maybe Aimee had said some things when she'd first moved to New Orleans.

Maybe Bonnie had chosen to just let it all go and keep Aimee safe.

And maybe her aunt hadn't had a clue about any of it. Had taken everything she'd been told at face value.

Maybe she'd just forgotten she even had the address.

"I'll call and get a flight back to New Orleans," Aimee said, because she had to go. Her life was there. And he'd given her no indication that he wanted her to stay.

Not that she would if he asked, necessarily, but he hadn't even given her the choice.

He nodded, which irked her.

Okay, hurt her.

But she couldn't blame him. She'd known the ropes going in. Hell, she'd set the bar—saying it was just sex.

Note to self, next time set the bar high enough to leave a door open for possibility.

"I'd like to stay long enough to hear what Grayson's lawyer has to say," she blurted, as the lifeline occurred to her—the one thing that wasn't yet resolved.

All other questions had been answered.

"His office opens at eight," Jackson came back, his tone commonplace. Unemotional. Looking so so so good to her in that light cotton robe, with the belt only haphazardly tied around his waist. "I'll call him then."

Aimee used the time in between to call the airlines, book herself a flight that afternoon. Call Beth and let her know she'd be arriving, though she had her own car at the airport and wouldn't need a ride. Still, it was good to have someone know she'd be landing, be home. She showered. She packed.

She didn't cry. There'd be no more tears.

She'd found her missing pieces and had a whole life ahead of her.

She was standing beside Jackson when he made the call to the attorney, and was surprised to hear that the man wanted to see the two of them. Not just Jackson, but her, too.

That compensation that Boyd had talked about? Had he actually gone so far as to contact his lawyer about it? Had gifting her been part of his plan before leaving the country? Not killing her? As long as she didn't remember…

In a short-sleeved plain black cotton dress that hung to just above her knees, and her black-studded sandals, she rode with Jackson to the lawyer's office. It wasn't like she had her own car to drive.

"Will you take me to the airport this morning?" she asked. If not, she could get a rideshare. Or…wait…did rideshares come out to small remote mountain towns? If not, Kelly had offered to take her.

"Of course."

Okay, good. She'd have two whole hours with him before she left. Maybe they could talk. Maybe decide to stay in touch. Maybe he'd even come to New Orleans for a visit some time.

Half an hour later she walked out of the lawyer's

office completely stunned. Not in tears, but shocked to her core.

"Boyd knew all along that his father had left all the Evergreen personal assets to Grayson, with Boyd as the executor and trustee of the funds, but with *me* as the heir upon Grayson's death, and as trustee in the event of Boyd's death." She'd repeated the statement twice since leaving the office.

Someday, she was coming into a fortune. And she didn't want it.

Starting from that moment, she was in charge of Grayson Evergreen's financial care. Something that could be easily tended to from New Orleans. The attorney had made that clear. Offering to act as fiduciary on her behalf. She'd left, promising to call him to arrange just that. She'd just needed a minute or two to process and he'd already had another appointment scheduled first thing that morning.

"The business assets are all going to Boyd's son," she said aloud, though Jackson had been sitting in the room with her. Had heard everything she'd heard. "He's going to get a heck of a phone call today."

"He hasn't seen or spoken to Boyd since he was a kid," Jackson offered, but, otherwise, had been strangely silent.

As he'd been all morning.

If she hadn't known better, she'd think she'd spent the night with his twin. Another man entirely.

It was like the tenderness, the passion, the intimacy they'd shared had never been.

And so, when she got back to his house, she went straight upstairs, put the last things in her suitcase, zipped it up. Loaded her laptop into the carry-on and

closed that up, too. Ready for Jackson to take everything downstairs.

He'd said he'd be right up.

She heard his step on the stairs.

And sat on the side of the bed. Arms crossed.

One leg flung over the top of her suitcase.

He stood in the doorway, looking at the bag he was
supposed to take down to his car.

She didn't remove her leg.

"What's up?" he asked. Attentive as usual.

"I don't want to go, Jackson." She hadn't planned
the words. They'd just flown right out. But she wasn't
sorry. She liked them.

"What do you mean, you don't want to go?"

"I don't want to go." She'd said what she meant. But,
for his sake, added, "I want to stay."

"Stay where?"

The man was not that dense. But he also wasn't mean.
If he didn't want her, he'd tiptoe around telling her so.

She didn't want tiptoeing. She wanted messy.

"Here. In this house. With you." She'd only known
him going on her sixth day. Didn't care. Had never been
more sure of anything in her life. "And I want us to be
Gay Gay's family. I want us to be his fiduciary, to get
him in a facility closer to Evergreen, and maybe even
have him home for weekends if his doctors think that
would work."

"I was born in this town," she continued, and when
started, words just came pouring out of her. "If Boyd
hadn't killed my parents I'd have grown up here. With
you. We'd have gone to kindergarten together, and grade
school. And high school."

Tears clogged her throat at what might have been.
She blinked, and, when she could said, "Think about it,

Jackson. No way you and I would have been in a small class together and not hooked up. Look at us—five days and we're all over each other all night long."

He still wasn't talking. But his expression was intense as he looked at her.

"So…stuff happened," she said. "Boyd Evergreen happened, and our future together was interrupted, but it called me back here. I couldn't move forward…thirty years and no significant relationship. Pieces of me were here all along, Jackson. The biggest pieces. I've found them now."

He swallowed. Blinked a couple of times.

And she took the greatest risk of her life. "And the biggest one…it's standing right in front of me looking like he's feeling a bit green. You can stop me anytime. Load up my bags and I promise I'll be silent all the way to Flagstaff…"

He didn't load up her bags. He didn't even take a step toward her bag. He looked shell-shocked, like too much had hit him.

Maybe not green, though. Maybe more red. She'd call Beth. The woman had managed the shop for Bonnie long before Aimee became a partner. Aimee mostly handled the online side of things. They could work something out.

"Family is what matters most, Jackson," she said softly. "And my family is here. It always has been."

He leaned a bit in her direction. Didn't take a step. So, standing, she took one. "Family isn't rules and laws and protocol," she said softly. "It's ice cream on your nose. Tears. The deepest pains. Incredible passion. And the greatest joys. It means never being alone, even after death. Because family is in the heart. You got what it takes to handle that, Sheriff?"

She knew he did. Just needed him to know he did.

She wasn't going it alone anymore. Not even to be with him.

She'd wait. Another thirty years if that was what it took for him to figure it out.

She saw the well of moisture in his eyes, and had her answer. She couldn't see him clearly anymore, not through her own blurred vision, but she met him halfway. Fell against him, into his arms, wrapping her own so tightly around him, she hurt. And didn't care.

"I know it's soon, but I love you, Jackson Redmond," she whispered against his neck.

"I love you, too, Aimee. You are my first love. And my last." The words were said shakily, right into her ear. "Wherever you go, I will follow."

The lyrics of a song she used to love. She didn't question how he'd known that.

Her heart knew. And sighed. Filling with happiness.

Because, finally, after thirty long years, it was open, again.

* * * * *

Don't miss these other Sierra's Webb titles:

His Lost and Found Family, *Special Edition.*
Reluctant Roommates, *Special Edition.*
Tracking His Secret Child, *Romantic Suspense.*
Her Best Friend's Baby, *Special Edition.*

COMING NEXT MONTH FROM

(H) HARLEQUIN

ROMANTIC SUSPENSE

#2227 COLTON'S UNDERCOVER SEDUCTION
The Coltons of New York • by Beth Cornelison

To investigate the Westmore family, rookie cop Eva Colton goes undercover as ladies' man detective Carmine DiRico's wife on a marriage-retreat cruise. As the "marriage" starts feeling alarmingly real, Eva becomes the lone witness to a shipboard murder and the target of a killer determined to silence her...permanently.

#2228 SAVED BY THE TEXAS COWBOY
by Karen Whiddon

When Marissa Noll's former high school sweetheart and now-injured rodeo star Jared Miller returns to Anniversary, Texas, and needs her help with physical therapy, she vows to be professional. After all, she's moved on with her life. But when she starts receiving threats, the coincidental timing makes her wonder if Jared might have something to do with it.

#2229 THE BOUNTY HUNTER'S BABY SEARCH
Sierra's Web • by Tara Taylor Quinn

Haley Carmichael discovers her recently deceased sister had a baby—a baby who's currently missing—and she knows her ex-husband, Paul Wright, is the only one who can help. Reuniting with his ex is the last thing the expert bounty hunter wants, but he isn't willing to risk a child's life, either—and a second chance might help both of them put past demons to rest.

#2230 HUNTED ON THE BAY
by Amber Leigh Williams

Desiree Gardet will change her address, her name, her hair—anything—to leave her past behind, but when fate brings her to sweet and sexy barkeep William Leighton and the small town he calls home, she longs for somewhere to belong more than ever before. Unfortunately, her past has a way of catching up with her no matter what she does, only this time Desiree finds that she isn't alone in the crosshairs.

YOU CAN FIND MORE INFORMATION ON UPCOMING HARLEQUIN TITLES, FREE EXCERPTS AND MORE AT HARLEQUIN.COM.

HRSCNM0323

HARLEQUIN
PLUS

Try the best multimedia subscription service for romance readers like you!

Read, Watch and Play.

Experience the easiest way to get the romance content you crave.

Start your **FREE TRIAL** at
<u>www.harlequinplus.com/freetrial</u>.